AN IMPERFECT ENGAGEMENT

WILTSHIRE CHRONICLES

BOOK TWO

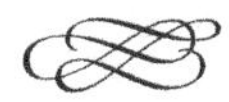

USA TODAY BESTSELLING AUTHOR ALYSSA DRAKE

For more information on Alyssa, please visit her website Alyssa Drake Novels or sign up for her newsletter, Love Notes, delivered directly to your inbox.

Summary: Planning her wedding takes a dangerous turn, when a woman realizes a member of her engagement party would rather kill her than walk down the aisle.

Cover design by Tina Adams
Editing by Personal Touch Editing
www.alyssadrakenovels.com

For Nico, who believes

CHAPTER 1

She am anguished.

Not the normal kind of worry that plagues young ladies of the time, but stomach-churning, soul-wrenching agony.

She deliberately disobeyed the wishes of not only her brother, Edward but those of her future husband, Benjamin, Lord Westwood—the two men she loved deeply. Worse, she abandoned Wilhelmina, her brother's wife, to host a luncheon without the guest of honor—her, the future Lady Westwood. Those transgressions were horrendous enough, but she also neglected to leave a note regarding her whereabouts, or better, her destination, the townhouse. *Or whatever was left of it after last night's horrific fire.*

Her mind replayed the prior evening—the moment of panic when she realized the significance of the fire burning in the distance, the worry etched across Edward's face, and Benjamin wrapping her in his arms, a protective gesture. His scent overwhelmed her senses, drifting through the carriage as though he was seated next to her. She closed her eyes and inhaled deeply. The air tasted like his skin. Her mouth curved into a smile, and unconsciously, she arched her neck, leaning into his invisible embrace.

Tingles danced across Sam's arms as she felt Benjamin's sinful lips nibble a delectable path across her collarbone. The ghostly sensation elicited a tremble, which originated in her shoulder blades and shot down her spine. Sam blushed deeply, her eyes jumping to her cousin, Mr. Franklin Morris, who stared out the window, absentmindedly rubbing the edge of the curtain between his thumb and forefinger. Pulling aside her curtain, Sam peered out the window, endeavoring to hide the telltale color of her wayward thoughts.

There was no need to upset Franklin further with intimate details of her inability to remain a proper lady in the presence of her fiancé. She shuddered at the title. Never in her life did she expect to hear the word *fiancé* attached to gossip surrounding her name. *Miss Hastings engaged to Lord Westwood*—the sentence would be the main headline in the society pages for weeks. Franklin only just learned of her engagement the prior evening. He appeared devastated by the announcement.

Poor Franklin. He was such a dear man. Sam's eyes raked over his oblivious visage. Why had he been unable to find himself a suitable match? Surely, a man with Franklin's humor would have no trouble attracting the fairer sex. A few thinning hairs would hardly stop a woman's interest. Perhaps Sam could enlist Wilhelmina's help. Her sister-in-law had introduced Samantha to Lord Westwood. Although that particular introduction was not intended to encourage a permanent attachment to her temporary guardian, Sam allowed it. She bit her lip and swallowed a smile, fighting the blush creeping back into her cheeks. Benjamin's visit last night was definitely not on Wilhelmina's list of acceptable activities. Sam sank her teeth into her lower lip.

Franklin chose to look over at that moment. His dark eyes

flicked over her face, an unreadable expression passing through his features. He tilted his head as he studied her, and a shiver ran the length of Sam's spine. She wasn't certain if the sensation was caused by a sudden draft under the carriage door or the odd way Franklin wordlessly continued to watch her.

Rubbing her arms for warmth, Sam regretted her hasty departure—no gloves, no shawl, hair unbound. Traveling in mixed company in such a state didn't add to her colorful reputation. *Who would kill her first upon returning to the Westwood estate? No doubt, both men and Wilhelmina would volunteer for the opportunity.* Sam grimaced. Wilhelmina would beat both Edward and Benjamin to that happy task.

How would she explain her reckless behavior? Treasure hunting hardly seemed like an acceptable justification for missing her own engagement party, even if it was to retrieve the ransom demanded by her father's faceless murderer. Although the threatening missive—currently hidden underneath an inkwell in Lord Westwood's bedchamber—did not explicitly state to recover the missing Hastings' family jewelry, Sam was certain those were the items requested.

After several minutes of silent inspection, Franklin spoke, his hollow voice barely carrying across the coach. "Are you alright, my dear? You seem preoccupied."

"I should have informed someone of our destination," Sam blurted out, unable to control her tongue a moment longer. "Edward will be extremely worried."

"I see," Franklin replied in a soft voice. He steepled his fingers over his slightly protruding belly, resting his arms for a moment. "We wouldn't want to cause Edward any undue strife. Perhaps you would like to send him a note before we begin our little adventure?"

"That is an excellent idea, Franklin." Sam nodded, gratitude seeping through her body. Her muscles relaxed, and she leaned back on the bench. A short letter would ease both

Edward and Benjamin's minds, but it would not alleviate Wilhelmina's anger, no matter how eloquent the prose. That apology would need to be done in person... *after* Sam ensured her father's killer never threatened the family again.

Her eyes swept over Franklin. His companionship during this expedition was reassuring. Even though she only intended on searching the townhouse, Sam hesitated at the idea of completing the task alone. Franklin's presence eased many of the fears dancing around in her erratic mind.

"I doubt you will be able to send a missive from the townhouse. With the extent of the fire damage, there's no way you will be able to find paper and ink, let alone a safe place to compose the letter," Franklin said, tapping his fingers on his leg in an unrecognizable rhythm. "I keep an apartment nearby. You should be able to find everything you need to allay your brother's overprotective tendencies."

Sam grinned. "You know him so well."

"While you are corresponding, I will gather supplies for our little treasure hunt." Franklin returned her smile with an exaggerated wink. "We'll need something to carry all that jewelry."

Concern scrunched Sam's forehead, deflating her excitement. Certainly, it would be prudent to pen a quick letter to Edward. However, an engaged woman shouldn't visit a man's lodgings without a chaperone. Even though Franklin was her cousin, his overly friendly attachment to her could be enough to start the societal tongues wagging. She bit her lip with indecision.

Franklin must have sensed Sam's hesitation because he leaned forward and patted her hand. "Mrs. Clark will be most delighted to converse with you again. She's currently residing in town with me and finds my lack of visitors most discouraging."

Relief washed over Sam, tension ebbing quickly from her,

disappearing under the carriage door like wisps of smoke. "I would be delighted to visit with Mrs. Clark again. It will give me the opportunity to express my gratitude for the lovely birthday cake she sent."

The coach turned on its own accord—without direction from its occupants—and headed down a nearby street. Sam's stomach grumbled, protesting the lack of food. She had rushed out without even a piece of toast.

"Perhaps Mrs. Clark has prepared breakfast?" she inquired over another loud rumble.

"It's quite possible," Franklin replied and fell silent, twitching aside the curtain and watching the cityscape move past his window.

Fifteen minutes later, the carriage stopped in front of an older building in an unfamiliar neighborhood. As Sam gaped at the shabby townhouses, one shed a piece of its roof, which clattered to the broken cobblestones below and shattered. A collection of building debris cluttered the length of the street, hiding a thin layer of grime.

Why did Franklin choose to keep his lodgings in such a dilapidated part of town? This must be the reason he had very few visitors.

Producing a key ring from his waistcoat pocket, Franklin emerged from the coach—his lips pressed into a thin line—and gestured for Sam to follow. He glanced to his left and right before marching up to a decaying door.

An ominous squeak emanated from ancient hinges as he wrenched it open, the sound echoing down the empty street, causing rats to scatter from a nearby trash pile. A scream bubbled in Sam's throat. Franklin grabbed her wrist, tugging her into the dingy darkness of the dwelling.

The door closed, aided by a strong yank from Franklin, who wrestled it shut with a muttered curse word. The door groaned as it latched. Silently, Franklin led Sam up a winding staircase to what she calculated was the third floor of the building.

He leapt lithely over the last step onto the landing. Sam glanced down at the stair and noticed the rotting wood already bowed under the weight of a tiny mouse, which scurried ahead of Sam into the hallway and disappeared under a crack in a door. Sam bit her tongue and made no mention of the staircase or the mouse.

Franklin must be having financial difficulties. Perhaps she could speak with Edward about offering some assistance to Franklin.

Turning to his right, Franklin rapped three times on the only door visible in the hallway, the same door under which the mouse had disappeared. There was no answer. He tapped again, repeating the same knock, and waited. Again, no one appeared at the door. Franklin shrugged, offering Sam a half-smile. He lifted the keyring to eye level and flipped through several keys.

"Ah!" He shoved a brass key into the lock and twisted the large piece of metal firmly, pushing the door open. Sam expected the peeling door to scrape along the floorboards, but it swung easily, the hinges noiselessly complying with his request.

"Mrs. Clark must have gone to the market," Franklin said as he led Sam into a small entranceway. Squeezing past her, he inserted the brass key again and locked the outer door. He dropped the keyring on a small ornate table near the front door and murmured, "This part of town is not quite as sheltered as where you reside."

"Franklin, if you need..."

"It was a few bad business decisions. I will recover in time." He squeezed Sam's arm, forcing an empty smile to his lips. "Thank you for your concern, dear cousin, but I shall be fine. Please, allow me to show you my apartment."

Franklin's lodgings were tastefully decorated, radically different from the depressing exterior. The parlor, bedecked in deep hues of green and gold, reminded Sam of the German forests Franklin described from his exotic travels. The entire apartment was spotless, scrubbed from the rafters to the floorboards, a tribute to Mrs. Clark's efficiency. Elephant statues of varying sizes littered the room. Sam wondered how long Franklin had been collecting them; he never mentioned an affinity for pachyderms. The statue nearest her looked to be as large as a horse. She laid a hand gently against the cold surface, marveling at the pristine ivory.

After shaking off his coat, Franklin laid it over the back of a nearby chair, then gestured to his left. The study, doubling as a guest room, was situated off the parlor. It was this room which Franklin directed Sam to, pointing out the desk featured prominently near a dirty window, which seemed out of place in Franklin's otherwise immaculate accommodations. A large spider web stretched intriguingly across the frame, leading Sam to believe the room had not been cleaned for quite a few months.

"Please make yourself comfortable," Franklin said from the doorway, a falsely bright tone forced into his words. She'd embarrassed him, pointing out his poverty. "There should be ink and paper on the desk. I will scrounge up some breakfast for us. It may not be as delicious as Mrs. Clark's cooking, but I daresay I do have some culinary talents." He patted his belly and wandered toward the back of the apartment, his footsteps fading.

Sam glided to the desk and sank down with a sigh. She had already written the note countless times in her mind, but putting a quill to paper made the task more difficult. *How does one explain why they intentionally broke a promise?* There was nothing she could say that would excuse her thoughtless behavior. Sighing again, she extracted a heavy sheet of creamy paper from the stack on the far corner of the desk.

The scent of roses hit her nostrils sharply. Sam glanced up, perplexed, expecting to find a bouquet of fresh flowers in the room. There was not one visible rose. She peeked out the door into the parlor but found the smell lessened as she moved away from the study. Curiously, Sam returned to the desk and lifted the sheet of paper to her face, inhaling deeply.

Rose-scented paper. Sam's hand began to tremble, the page clasped in her fingers vibrating wildly. Sam's mind flashed to the threatening note she hid in Benjamin's chamber at the Westwood estate. It had the same smell. It was the same paper. The paper slipped from her fingers and floated featherlike to the floor.

It was Franklin.

Franklin sent the threatening letter to her brother. Franklin set fire to the townhouse. Franklin murdered her father and attempted to kill Edward. Franklin was the sinister face behind the mysterious terror gripping her family. Sam's mind sifted through the past, quickly analyzing her interactions with Franklin. It did not seem possible. *How did he fool her so easily?* Her childhood memories of her parents' last ball bubbled in her brain—Franklin whirling her in dizzy circles, her father laughing merrily, the beautiful necklace adorning her mother's slim neck. *At that moment, did Franklin know he would commit murder later that evening?*

"My dear," Franklin said as he entered the room with a plate of fruit and cheese. "You look as though you have seen a specter."

Sam glared at him with rounded eyes. "How could you, Franklin? He was your cousin!"

"My dearest Samantha,"—Franklin laughed, the hollow, mechanical sound ringing in Sam's ears—"I fear you may have deduced my little secret."

Sam nodded mutely. Her eyes searched the room, darting from the tiny, filthy window, over the wooden floorboards to the open door, yawning widely behind Franklin, his wide frame blocking the only exit.

"How did you figure it out?" he asked, popping a grape in his mouth as if they were discussing the weather.

"The paper," Sam whispered and gestured to the innocent stack in the corner of the desk. "It smells like roses."

"Damn. I've always loathed scented paper." Franklin shook his head with a disgusted grimace. "However, I'm surprised Edward shared my little note with you. He's usually quite secretive when it comes to questionable affairs."

"He's unaware I read the note," Sam replied and rolled her shoulders back, elongating her frame—her feeble attempt to appear intimidating.

Franklin's lips stretched across his face, forming a thin, grotesque smirk. "You are an intelligent little thing. I repeatedly warned Uncle Ephraim it was a terrible decision to educate a girl, more trouble than it's worth. I see now, I was correct in that assumption."

How would she escape? Sam's eyes skipped about the room again, focusing on the door leading into the parlor. *If she charged Franklin, would she have enough strength to knock him over? Where was Mrs. Clark? Surely, she would not permit Franklin to slaughter Sam.* Sam took a deep breath to calm the macabre thoughts dancing through her imagination.

Franklin tilted his head, baring his teeth. "There is no one to hear your scream."

"M-M-Mrs. Clark?" Panic bubbled in her throat.

"Mrs. Clark is happily working at my country estate. She refuses to visit town for any reason. She has never been to this apartment, nor does she know of its existence."

"Why, Franklin?" Sam asked, her eyes flashing back to the grimy window. She needed a distraction. Conceivably, she could squeeze through it and climb down the roof to safety. She could also slip on the loose slate and fall to her death.

"I think you are going to be more of a nuisance than I originally anticipated." Without warning, Franklin lunged forward and struck Sam with the plate. It split in two as it crashed down on Sam's head, sending the fruit and cheese flying in various directions as she crumbled to the floor, unconscious.

Humming, Franklin stepped over her immobile form and extracted a rope hidden under the bed. He dumped Samantha's body on the mattress and lashed her arms together at the wrists. His eyes fell on the rose-scented paper. Plucking it from the floorboard, he laid it on the desk and sat down, staring at the blank page. With a nod, he lifted the quill from the inkwell and penned a quick message. Leaning out the window, he called over a boy passing underneath, tossing the letter and a coin to him with strict instructions to deliver the message to the Westwood estate.

WILHELMINA SCOURED the house for Samantha, stomping through empty rooms and snarling at the staff. As she crossed the entranceway, a knock sounded at the front door. Scowling, she jerked open the door, her eyes falling on a small boy who held out a missive with a trembling hand. Once his soiled fingers released the note to Wilhelmina, he spun and dashed off, running until his legs became a blur of gray.

Ripping open the letter, Wilhelmina pursed her lips, expecting to read the far-fetched excuse Sam invented to forgo her own engagement party. Instead, Wilhelmina fainted, the missive clutched in her fingers.

. . .

Good afternoon Mr. Hastings,

I want to thank you for the generous donation of your sister's life to my worthy cause. Interestingly, Miss Hastings seemed more than willing to assist me with my current endeavor. If she proves most helpful, I shall return her body to you for a proper funeral. However, if she becomes willful, as she has proven to be in the past, I regret I will only be able to return pieces of her to you.

Rest assured, once I have found my inheritance, I will no longer haunt your family. I appreciate your patience in this matter.

Please give my regrets to Lord Westwood for stealing his fiancée so young. However, I do believe he will be happier without her.

CHAPTER 2

Benjamin bolted from the kitchen, barreling through the swinging door. Catching the toe of his boot on the carpet runner, he tripped and crashed into the back of a dining room chair. Its current occupant, Miss Daphne Clemens, screamed and knocked her plate to the floor, shattering the dish. Pieces shot across the floor, ricocheting off the walls.

Get to Samantha.

The thought echoed in Benjamin's mind, desperation racing through his veins. He needed to get back to Westwood Estate and warn Edward before Franklin Morris had a chance to attack.

They'd never expect Morris. He was family, and a close companion of Miss Hastings'. They would let him into the house without question—a wolf in the henhouse.

Benjamin shoved off the back of the chair with a grunt, spun toward the exit, and stumbled across the room, smashing into the door with his shoulder.

"Nephew!" Aunt Abigail slammed her hands on the table, rising to her feet. "Apologize to Miss Clemens."

Benjamin froze, his hand flat against the half-open door. *Aunt Abigail was his elder...* He deflated under decorum and turned, his somber gaze locking on his aunt. Benjamin swallowed, his eyes flicking to Miss Clemens, who trembled, winding her napkin around her fingers.

"Miss Clemens, please forgive my brutish manner." He bowed slowly so as not to startle her further and flashed a dazzling smile. Every nerve in his body railed at the delay.

Samantha was in danger...

Miss Clemens blushed, clearly embarrassed to be singled out. She managed the barest of nods, dropping her eyes to the tablecloth, and murmured, "Thank you."

Aunt Abigail sat, replacing the napkin on her lap, and picked up her fork. She eyed Benjamin and cleared her throat.

"Tell me, what has you in such a hurry all of a sudden?"

"Mr. Morris is responsible for the death of his cousin, Mr. Matthew Hastings and the attempted murder of his son, Edward." The words burst from Benjamin. Miss Clemens gasped, paling.

Arching an eyebrow, Aunt Abigail placed her fork on the plate, her face blank. "How did you come by this accusation?"

Benjamin stepped forward and clasped his hands together as though he were reciting a lesson in school. "Mrs. Grace's brother worked for the Hastings' family at the time of the deaths of Mr. and Mrs. Hastings."

"I recall the man." Aunt Abigail nodded in agreement. "Such a shame he died so suddenly."

"The physician attending Mr. Hastings' death made an error," Benjamin ground out the word. *Error* was the wrong word, but he wasn't sure how much he could trust Aunt Abigail's young charge.

"What kind of error?" Aunt Abigail asked, skepticism in her voice.

"Edward's father was poisoned."

Her jaw dropped. "Was Mr. Grace murdered, too?"

"It is quite possible," Benjamin replied, his gaze sliding toward the window.

He was wasting time.

Aunt Abigail pursed her lips, her gaze landing on Miss Clemens. Whatever questions flew through her mind, she kept to herself. She flicked her wrist toward the door, dismissing Benjamin from the room.

"You're forgiven. However, you must relate the details to me at some other time."

He bowed—a sharp jerk of his upper body—to both his aunt and Miss Clemens, then disappeared into the entry hall and burst through the front door. He leaped from the porch, bypassing the four steps which led to the footpath. An empty street greeted him, compounding his frantic despair.

Where was his carriage?

Neither Mr. Davis, his manservant, nor the coach waited at the curb. Panic lodged in Benjamin's throat. In all his years of service, Mr. Davis had never abandoned his post.

Had Morris attacked Mr. Davis?

Turning to his left, Benjamin raced to the corner. Eddies of mist danced down the street, dampening everything they brushed. His eyes searched for his coach, a coach, any coach... nothing, not even the whiny of a horse. Benjamin growled.

A familiar sound, wheels on the cobblestone, pricked his ears. He spun around, squinting. One lone carriage traveled along the far side of the park. Benjamin rushed back down the road toward Aunt Abigail's house. The coach approached at a rapid pace, rounding the second corner of the commons, and rapidly heading in his direction.

Perchance he could convince the occupant to provide him with emergency transportation.

Waving his arms, Benjamin stepped into the street. The carriage veered off its current path and drove straight toward him. However, as the carriage continued to bear down on Benjamin, it failed to slow.

Realizing the danger too late, Benjamin didn't jump out of the path of the coach in time. The wheel struck him in the torso, knocking the breath from his lungs. He flew backward, crashing into the stairs, and cracked his head on the top step. He groaned, his mind fuzzy, and tumbled down the steps, then rolled toward the street. His body came to rest on the edge of the curb, his long limbs dangling in the street.

The coach evaporated around another corner, leaving no trace of its transgression. Benjamin laid bleeding, alone and indiscernible in the early morning fog. His eyes closed, his last conscious thought of Miss Hastings.

"There are more comfortable places to sleep." Thomas' voice broke through the blackness.

Benjamin's eyes snapped open. He was staring at a ceiling, more precisely, Aunt Abigail's parlor ceiling. With a grunt, Benjamin attempted to sit up but found his movement restricted by a heavy weight. Rolling his head to the right, tiny lights danced in front of his face. He squeezed his eyes shut, rubbing them, then reopened them, focusing on the mirror image of himself.

"Nice to see you again, dear brother." Thomas grinned, lifting his hand from Benjamin's chest and saluting.

"Samantha," Benjamin said, shoving his twin brother off the settee and struggling into a sitting position.

"Aunt Abigail sent word to Mother, warning her not to allow Morris on the property," Thomas replied, climbing to his feet. He feigned fear of injury, checking all his limbs in a state of mock distress, then, pretending to be relieved to discover no harm had occurred, claimed the chair beside

Benjamin. Leaning forward, Thomas snatched the last cookie from a crumb-covered plate.

Benjamin exhaled. The tension melted out of his body, allowing pain to ebb into his muscles. He leaned back against the settee, agony rolling through his limbs.

"How did I find my way back into the house?" he asked, swallowing a grimace.

Thomas chewed slowly. "The housekeeper, Mrs. Grace, found you sprawled—unconscious—and alerted Aunt Abigail. She, Miss Clemens, and Mrs. Grace managed to carry you up the stairs and into the parlor. Although considering your size, I am surprised they were able to lift you without assistance. It must have been a sight. What happened?"

"I was struck by a carriage." Benjamin rubbed his forehead. His muscles throbbed, protesting the movement.

"Who did you anger this time?" Thomas wiggled his eyebrows.

Benjamin ignored his brother's teasing. "I don't know. I couldn't see the driver."

Thomas' playful demeanor evaporated. "Do you think it was Morris?"

"I wish I knew."

"I *am* curious to learn how you were hit." Thomas glanced at the window. "Did the carriage travel off the road?"

"I was standing in the middle of the street."

"Why?" Thomas asked, his head whipping back to his brother.

"My coach vanished," Benjamin snapped and shifted, pain radiating through his leg. He sucked in a sharp breath, clamping his teeth together.

Mr. Davis was due a severe reprimand for abandoning his post.

Thomas glanced upward, and a frown tugged at his mouth. "That may have been my fault."

"May?" Benjamin's eyes narrowed.

"Mr. Davis returned to collect me from the estate. He was with me when the attack on you occurred."

"It would have been much more convenient to travel together," Benjamin grumbled, his teeth grinding in irritation.

"Ideally, yes." Thomas offered him a small grin. "However, only you and the chickens are awake at such an early hour."

"Then, how did you learn of my injury? I doubt Aunt Abigail's house was your original destination."

"In accordance with our discussion last evening, I went to the club to glean information from the male gossips in town." Thomas smiled a lopsided grin. "Apparently, I'm a rather predictable man as I was summoned to the main lobby not five minutes after I arrived."

"Aunt Abigail went to a gentlemen's club?" *Of course, she would know exactly where to find Thomas.* He could actually imagine her marching into the club, swinging her cane, dragging Thomas out by his ear.

"Certainly not." Thomas scoffed and crossed his arms. "She sent Miss Clemens."

Benjamin choked. "I would love to hear that story."

Thomas glared at him. "Like a proper lady, Miss Clemens waited outside the building after giving the message to the concierge."

"I hope you did not keep her waiting too long."

"Of course not," Thomas replied, his eyes flashing with indignation.

"And?"

"I escorted Miss Clemens back here so I could attend to you."

"I see." Benjamin pursed his lips to hide a smile. "I wonder why Aunt Abigail sent Miss Clemens to fetch you instead of Mr. Davis or even Mrs. Grace."

"Mr. Davis had not yet returned to Aunt Abigail's house,

having just delivered me to the club. As the matter was of some urgency, Aunt Abigail sent the first able person she found."

"Surely Mrs. Grace would be more adept at fetching men from gentlemen's clubs than naïve Miss Clemens," Benjamin pressed, catching the faint pink tinge crawling into his brother's face. Thomas must have realized the same thing.

"Miss Clemens did seem very much out of her element when I discovered her loitering outside," Thomas said, his voice tight. "A gentleman—if you use the word loosely—was unsuccessful, attempting to gain her favor."

Benjamin's gaze dropped to Thomas' hands, where fresh cuts decorated his knuckles. "Am I to understand you were forced to intervene on Miss Clemens' behalf due to this *gentleman's* inappropriate advances?"

"Yes," Thomas growled, an intriguing luminescence blazing from his brown eyes. "I needed to educate him on proper behavior in the presence of a lady."

Benjamin raised an eyebrow at the protective tone in Thomas' voice.

"What happened?"

"The man offered a rather disgusting proposal, endeavoring to shepherd Miss Clemens into the nearby alley in order to allow him the opportunity to take liberties. She was effectively trapped between his body and the side of the building." Thomas' hand clenched at the memory.

"What was Miss Clemens' reaction?" Benjamin leaned forward despite the objection from his bruised body.

"She stated 'No,' and the man refused to release her. Consequently, she slapped him."

Benjamin burst out laughing. "It appears as though Miss Clemens may have received some etiquette lessons from Miss Hastings."

"The man did not find her response as amusing," Thomas

replied grimly, his face holding a dark, almost fierce snarl. "He raised his hand to strike Miss Clemens. I intervened before he had the opportunity to hit her."

"As you should have." Benjamin banged his fist on the settee cushion. "The gentleman lacked the very manners the moniker would indicate he possessed."

Even with Thomas' sordid reputation, he would never allow a lady to come to any harm, including sweet, naïve Miss Clemens. Benjamin smirked, thinking there may be a wedding in Thomas' future as well. Especially if Thomas continued rescuing Miss Clemens...

"I suppose we must add one more person to the growing list of society members who are not our supporters." Thomas didn't seem the least bit concerned.

"Who was the man?" Benjamin asked, falling back onto the settee. He prayed the scoundrel was not the son of a business partner.

"Mr. Robert Shirely," Thomas spat, as if the words themselves tasted repulsive.

"Miss Shirely's brother? I thought he was away at university."

"Apparently, he is no longer welcome at the school," Thomas replied and lowered his voice, knowing the staff would love to overhear any rumor about members of the ton. "The story surrounding his expulsion is murky. However, the rumors circling the club claim Mr. Shirley nearly beat another student to death."

Benjamin adjusted his leg and groaned. "Was there a reason for the use of excessive violence?"

"Mr. Shirely accused the boy of theft."

"Was the student guilty?"

"No, he wasn't. Mr. Shirely had hidden the object himself as an excuse to attack the other man." Thomas flashed a cheeky grin. "Thankfully, you came to your senses and chose not to unite that family with ours."

Benjamin rolled his eyes. "Did Miss Clemens discuss the incident with you on the walk back to Aunt Abigail's house?"

"We returned in your carriage." Thomas flashed a sheepish grin. "Aunt Abigail dispatched Mr. Davis the moment he arrived at her townhouse. He pulled up just as I had completed expressing my displeasure to Mr. Shirely."

"How did Miss Clemens react to your chivalrous deed?" Benjamin asked in what he hoped was a nonchalant tone. *He was becoming as meddlesome as his mother.*

"Miss Clemens barely spoke four words during the journey. I think the experience severely upset her. I hoped Aunt Abigail would be a confidant in this delicate matter." Thomas' gaze slid ruefully toward the empty cookie plate. He pressed his finger to the dish, collecting the crumbs, then sucked them from his fingertip.

"You are quite sure it was four words?" Benjamin grinned, unable to forgo an occasion to tease his brother.

"Thank you, Mr. Reid." Thomas counted each word with his fingers. "The rest of the time, we rode in complete silence."

"Where are Aunt Abigail and Miss Clemens at this present time?" Benjamin pushed up and glanced over his shoulder at the empty corridor.

"Both ladies left for the engagement luncheon at Mother's estate, not ten minutes ago. Mr. Davis drove them in your carriage."

"You decided not to attend?" Benjamin laughed.

"I sacrificed my stomach and stayed behind to care for the invalid." Thomas folded his arms across his chest. "You may express your gratitude for this sacrificial gesture."

"Thank you for stealing my carriage." Benjamin leaned back, closing his eyes.

"Borrowing."

"Am I to assume you didn't learn any information during your brief visit to the club?" asked Benjamin, his body throbbing.

"I did not."

Opening his eyes, Benjamin touched a bruise on the right side of his face, grimacing.

"We should return to the estate as well. With Morris exposed as the murderer, we will need to plan our next move before he realizes we've discovered his name."

A light tapping came on the parlor door, then Mrs. Grace opened it and peered around the room. "Lord Westwood, I am pleased to see you are conscious again. I apologize for the interruption. This missive just arrived from your mother's house."

Thomas rose and accepted the letter from Mrs. Grace. "It is Edward's writing," he said as he tore open the seal. His jaw dropped. Wordlessly, Thomas passed the note to Benjamin. Only three words were scrawled on the paper—three little words—and Benjamin's world shattered.

Franklin took Sammie.

Both men bolted for the door. Benjamin tripped unsteadily on his feet and leaned on Thomas as they burst through the entryway. Thomas flagged down a hackney, pausing at the top of the steps as he assessed his brother's health.

"Normally, I wouldn't recommend you stay behind—"

"Then don't," Benjamin growled, glaring at Thomas.

Thomas clamped his mouth shut with a curt nod. Allowing Benjamin to awkwardly scramble down the steps, Thomas ignored the painful wheeze which escaped Benjamin as they climbed into the waiting carriage. Benjamin collapsed on the bench, his pale skin beaded with sweat.

"How has Morris been able to remain so close to the Hastings' family without suspicion?" Thomas asked, averting his eyes and pretending to be blind to Benjamin's physical struggle.

"He had no motive," Benjamin replied, struck with an overwhelming wave of guilt. *I should have realized the danger. It was my duty to protect Samantha... I gave my word.* His labored breathing eased as the coachman whipped the reins, the carriage rocking forward.

"If Morris harms Miss Hastings, I will rip him apart with my bare hands," Benjamin snarled, his eyes glittering black.

"Why would Miss Hastings leave with Mr. Morris?" Thomas asked, his tentative voice cutting through the anger settling in the coach. "She is aware of the danger we face."

"The engagement luncheon is this afternoon. She would have accepted any excuse to avoid attending." Benjamin frowned and shifted his gaze to the scenery dragging past them. They'd underestimated Morris. He shook his head. "Her cousin must have provided her with an irresistible offer."

"I thought Miss Hastings promised both you and her brother that she would stay on Mother's estate," Thomas said, drawing Benjamin's attention.

"I don't believe the words *I promise* crossed her lips on either occasion." With a heavy sigh, Benjamin returned his eyes to the window.

"We will find her," Thomas vowed, his voice hard, but Benjamin didn't respond, his mind churning with worry.

Would she still be alive when they did?

CHAPTER 3

"You hit her too hard."

The words floated through Sam's subconscious, hollow and tinny. Her eyelids fluttered, and dim light assaulted her eyes. The dull headache at the base of her neck flared, exploding through her head. Her arms refused to budge, disobeying her silent commands to raise. Dread churned her stomach.

Where was Franklin?

He wheezed next to her ear. Sam's fingers twitched, and rough bed sheets scratched against her fingertips with each convulsion. Franklin's humid breath painted chills over her skin as he inspected Sam's face callously, his fingers biting into her chin.

"I did not." He hissed, his cold hand pressing roughly against Sam's parched lips. "She is still breathing."

"Barely," the cold voice replied.

Franklin had an accomplice! Sam's breath caught, her brain flashing through the myriad of faces she'd met over the past few weeks. *The voice sounded familiar...*

"Does it honestly matter?" Franklin said as he traced an icy finger down Sam's cheek, making her fingers jump. "She won't live to see her wedding day."

"Franklin." A note of caution hung in the air. "Only she knows the location of the jewelry."

Sam imagined Franklin's shoulders slumped under the chastisement. However, the image quickly replaced itself with a sneer; the new face of this crueler, calculating Franklin.

Without warning, he struck the side of her face with his palm. The hard slap caused Sam to cry out, stars exploding behind her eyelids. The throbbing in her head increased tenfold, agony vibrated through her body. She gritted her teeth, and her left hand closed in a fist.

"She is fine," Franklin bit off, a smirk in his tone. "Now, you must take your leave before she fully regains consciousness. We cannot allow anyone to learn of your involvement."

Franklin and his anonymous visitor moved to the front of the apartment, leaving the door to the small bedchamber slightly ajar. Sam held her breath, listening and hoping to discern the identity of Franklin's mysterious guest. Snippets of garbled conversation drifted from the foyer. *Man or woman?* She couldn't decide, the pain in her head distorting the words. A small groan escaped her lips.

Silence. She gulped. *Had they heard her?*

A reverberating slam indicated the visitor's departure, followed by the click of the front door lock and a muffled thump when Franklin redeposited the brass key ring on the hallway table. His weight eased across decrepit floorboards. He paused in the parlor, then turned in the direction of the rear of the apartment, lumbering toward—Sam assumed—his bedchamber.

How much time did she have before he returned to check on her?

She forced her eyelids open and cried out when sunlight burned her eyes. Smashing her lips together, she smothered the scream hovering in her throat and screwed her eyes shut as tears streamed down her cheeks. Slowly, she dragged in a ragged breath.

"You can do this," Sam said, her doughy lips mangling the words.

Gradually, she peeled one eye open, then the second. After three rapid blinks, her eyes focused, sharpening the bleary shadows into recognizable shapes. The room remained unchanged—fruit and cheese slices lay forgotten, scattered among broken pieces of the plate.

How much time had passed?

Sunlight streamed through the tiny window, an indication of late morning. One or two hours, she surmised, long enough for Edward to discover her disappearance. Although with no clue to her whereabouts, how would he find her? How would anyone?

She sucked in a deep breath, slowly raising her heavy arms, and gasped. Her wrists were lashed together! Lifting her hands in front of her face, she inspected the thick rope wrapped twice around her arms. Her head throbbed, the pain radiating into her jaw. Touching her fingers to her scalp, Sam pressed against the spot where Franklin struck her with the plate, her fingers brushing over a wet area. She yanked them away—blood. Terror clogged her throat.

Franklin intended to kill her, perhaps in this very room, and he would take pleasure in the violent action. Sam shuddered. She needed an escape plan. *Where was an ivy-covered balcony when she needed one?*

Her eyes, now accustomed to the light, scanned the room for a weapon; there was none. Her only chance would be to take him by surprise. She could strike Franklin with her bound arms, stun him long enough to snatch the key from the tiny table where Franklin deposited it, and scurry for safety. *That sounded just crazy enough to work.* As long as his faceless visitor didn't linger in the hallway, she should be able to reach the street and draw the attention of a passing carriage. If there were none, she would run. Eventually, the road would lead to someone who could help her.

Suddenly, the room spun, and her stomach flipped, churning violently. She tumbled to the side, flipping her body over the edge of the bed, balancing precariously on her restrained hands as she vomited. Her throat and stomach burned from the acidic taste, and the hammering in her head worsened. She retched again, pain radiating through her body.

"I see you are awake, my dear." Franklin pushed open the door with a macabre grin. His eyes swept the room, landing on Sam, who sprawled gracelessly across the bed and the growing puddle of bile on the floor beneath her. He wrinkled his nose, disgust flickering across his face. "A horrible side effect of the medication I administered while you were unconscious."

Franklin had poisoned her! He grinned as horror crossed Sam's face.

"Don't worry, my dear, you will be long dead before the effects of the drug subside. Think of it as my last gift to you—a painless demise and freedom from the shackles of society."

Sam glared at him, her entire body ablaze as she seethed with anger, hatred overwhelming the agony. With a snarl, she flew off the mattress and lunged at Franklin, her restrained hands clawing at his face, but he easily slid away from her fingernails.

The room tilted, and Sam collapsed on the floor at Franklin's feet, a lump of immobile limbs and ire. She convulsed violently as another wave of nausea overtook her, curling into a tight ball as the bile gathered in her mouth.

Franklin chuckled and shook his head. He watched her contort on the floor with mild interest, patiently waiting until Sam's writhing body stopped twitching. She glowered up at him from her twisted position, panting as she gasped for oxygen. Swiping the strands of hair clinging to her sweaty face, she curled her lip and spat at him.

"Such behavior from a lady. A shame Rebecca was not able to raise you properly," Franklin chided, still grinning.

"She never had the opportunity. She was stolen from me," Sam replied as the dizziness ebbed. She pushed herself to her knees and wiped her mouth on the sleeve of her dress. *Another garment ruined.*

"Not by my hand," Franklin said, snatching Sam from the floor by her hair. He yanked her to her unsteady feet, grasping her elbow to prevent her from falling into him.

"Not directly." Sam exploded, twisting to face Franklin, his painful grip the only reason she remained upright. The wooziness surged again, blackness rimming her vision. She swallowed several times, her mouth watering under a new bout of queasiness.

Franklin raised his eyebrows, his blue eyes—the same blue eyes as her father, as Edward, as herself—filling with curiosity. "I'm not one to deny my crimes; however, I had no part in Rebecca's death."

"She died of a broken heart!" Sam latched onto her anger, fighting to retain consciousness. "You shattered it when you murdered my father."

Laughter echoed around the room, pressing against Sam with an edge of hysteria.

"Rebecca belonged to me first. She loved me. Matthew was a distraction, akin to your Lord Westwood. Her death could hardly be attributed to something as minor as Matthew's execution."

"He was her husband." Sam seethed, struggling against Franklin's iron grip, his strength surprising her. She had underestimated Franklin's physical capabilities. Overpowering him was not an option, especially in her incapacitated state. She needed a new plan, a distraction.

Franklin ignored her outburst, his eyes clouding with a yellowed memory.

"I remember the first day I met Rebecca. I was visiting Uncle Ephraim for the summer. Matthew was away at school and due home in several days. We were close at the time, despite our age difference. He was the only family I felt comfortable around, and I was looking forward to spending the next few weeks with him, two mischievous boys."

Sam pursed her lips, remaining mute and watching for an opportunity to flee. Franklin tightened his grasp on her arm as if able to read the mind of his unwilling prisoner, bruises forming under his merciless fingers. Ripping her eyes away from her arm, Sam gave the barest of nods, and Franklin continued his story.

"One beautiful Tuesday morning, I saw her." Franklin's voice took a reverent tone. "Rebecca glided next to the stream, elegant and completely unaware I observed her. The sunlight glinted off her auburn hair, sparking like fire." Franklin turned, assessing Sam, his eyes traveling the length of her. "That is something you have in common with your mother. She loved to walk barefoot."

A ghost of a smile crossed Sam's lips in spite of her dangerous situation. As Franklin described the scene, Sam imagined her mother strolling along the riverbank, swinging her shoes to inaudible music, laughing as she kicked her feet in the water. A tiny tear trickled down Sam's cheek. She hastily swatted it away.

"I watched her for three days before I plucked up the courage to speak with such an alluring water nymph. I startled her, a gangly boy leaping out from behind a rotting tree trunk, and she dropped her shoes in the stream. The current was strong enough to carry the shoes far out of her reach. Without a thought, I leapt into the water after her wayward shoes, and she chased after me with a splash. I caught them a quarter-mile downstream. By then, the two of us were completely soaked. Our sopping garments clung to our bodies as we climbed back onto the riverbank, laughing until we gasped for air. I brought her to Hastings Manor to dry her clothes. Uncle Ephraim took an instant liking to her. From that day forward, she was a welcome and constant guest." Franklin's voice trailed off, distracted by the memory. He shook himself and began speaking again.

"We had grand adventures together, exploring the riverbank for pirate treasure. She was convinced there was gold buried in the stream." He paused. Once more, he was overcome. "She was exquisite. Her smile, her laugh—it's as though she is still with me." Franklin's countenance cleared. He tilted his head and stared at her. "I wonder if you would still bear the same resemblance to your mother if I had been your father."

Sam's jaw dropped, but she held her tongue.

"I professed my love to her, bearing my soul. However, Rebecca rejected my proposal. The previous evening, Matthew had convinced her to accept his hand in marriage. She tried to pacify me, but our friendship was strained from that moment on.

"Frankie, you will always be my favorite cousin," Franklin mimicked with a growl. "How could she believe that would satisfy me? It wasn't until years later, I learned Uncle Ephraim had encouraged the attachment between Matthew and Rebecca—meddlesome old man."

"She loved my father," Sam said, yanking her arm and wrenching it sideways. Franklin's grip tightened, pinching her skin.

"No!" he shrieked, his face twisted in anger. "She loved me. Matthew stole her away with false promises, just like he stole my inheritance. He betrayed me, but I made him accountable for his crimes." Franklin released his hold on

Sam's arm and paced the room, a caged animal, snapping at ghosts. Foam gathered in the right corner of his mouth.

Sam rocked back on her heels, eyeing the open door to the parlor. Flashes of green and gold beckoned. Waiting until Franklin stalked toward the grimy window, Sam bolted for the open door, her eyes locked on the entrance hall.

Threading through the furniture dotting the parlor, Sam dashed around the ornate obstacle course. As she skirted the ottoman, a heavy weight struck her from behind. She stumbled and crashed to the floor, grunting as her chin smacked against the floorboards, her jaw snapping. Twisting to her side, Sam balanced on her hip and blindly kicked her right leg out behind her, connecting with Franklin's head. A sickening crunch echoed in the apartment. He howled with anger as blood spurted from his nose.

Sam inched along the floor, using her bound hands to drag herself forward while Franklin moaned behind her. Just as she neared the edge of the parlor, a wave of medication rolled over her. The walls tilted, hampering Sam's attempt to crawl further. She heaved uncontrollably, fighting against the overwhelming dizziness. Her body stopped cooperating, and she mentally screamed at her useless limbs.

Franklin leapt onto her numb legs, trapping Sam against the wood floorboards. He flipped her easily onto her back and slammed her arms to the floor, pinning them above her head. Struggling to move, Sam attempted to kick her legs, but Franklin's weight was too great. With his free hand, he slapped her across the face, rattling her teeth. The barrage of pain did not stop, more blows following as Franklin rained down his ire.

"You will not deny me what is rightfully due. Do you understand, Samantha?" Franklin snarled, his wild eyes dancing.

Sucking in a breath to scream, Sam choked, tasting blood.

Moisture trickled from her mouth, dribbling down her chin. Franklin reached back to slap her again. Sam screwed her eyes shut and twisted her head to the side, waiting for the excruciating explosion of pain.

"I will take you to the jewelry." She whimpered.

One minute passed.

She opened one eye, then the second, rotating her head hesitantly back toward Franklin. He remained stationary, hand still poised to strike, staring skeptically at Sam, streaks of dried blood decorating his jaw in a ghoulish design.

"Where is it?" he asked, his eyes searching hers.

"It is hidden in the study at the townhouse." Sam took a shuddering breath as she revealed her secret.

The pale face of her captor split into a wide grin. He slowly rolled off Samantha's legs and stood with a grunt.

"Now, why did you make that revelation so difficult?"

Sam forced herself to a sitting position, glaring at Franklin, who hummed happily as he circled her, his demeanor frighteningly calm. Grabbing the rope still binding Sam's wrists, Franklin yanked her to her feet. She nearly toppled into Franklin, who quickly sidestepped and allowed her to crash into the sofa. She rebounded onto the unforgiving floorboards, crying out in pain.

"Shall we, my dear?" Franklin smirked and grasped her restraints again, half-dragging Sam through the apartment with a sneer. "We are wasting valuable time."

CHAPTER 4

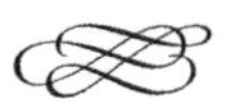

Gruesome pictures of Samantha's broken body haunted Benjamin, the images growing more horrific with each new suggestion. How could he have missed Morris? Unobtrusive, amiable, and polite, he didn't possess the characteristics of a cold-blooded murderer. Mr. Franklin Morris was a gentleman… and a killer.

The carriage lurched, rolling into a rut carved into the waterlogged road. Benjamin twitched and inhaled sharply, then exhaled a soft curse. With a hiss, he rearranged his left leg, which was stretched across the cushion. His eyes slid over to Thomas, who stared out the window, clenching and unclenching his hand. Benjamin wasn't certain if his brother was imagining striking Morris, Shirely, or both… The carriage jolted again, and a second curse echoed in the cabin.

"Don't suggest we slow the coach," Benjamin growled, earning a brief grin from Thomas, but he didn't acknowledge it. His pain didn't matter, only Samantha's life. He'd failed in his assignment as a guardian and as a fiancé. He would never forgive himself.

"Your fiancée would be appalled by your language,"

Thomas replied, dropping the curtain and turning his body fully toward Benjamin in a transparent attempt to distract his brother from his despondent thoughts.

"Miss Hastings is well acquainted with blasphemies as she frequently employs them herself." Benjamin grimaced, bracing his body against the corner of the coach as the wheels hit another section of rough road.

"Would that delightful characteristic be due to Edward's irresponsible instruction?" Thomas struggled to match his face to the severity of the situation. He was, no doubt, already plotting how to draw those inappropriate words from Samantha after they found her.

If they found her.

"It would," he replied, biting his tongue when the coach jerked again.

Benjamin slammed his fist against the carriage wall, and the entire vehicle shuddered. One of the horses whinnied in protest and shied away, pulling the coach to the left before the driver intervened with a quick snap of the reins.

"I should have realized Morris' true nature," Benjamin said, voicing the guilt torturing his mind.

"How?" Thomas asked.

The quiet question echoed unanswered in the tiny compartment, bouncing from bench to bench until it became a constant buzz in Benjamin's mind, overpowering every other thought.

How could he have known?

As they rounded a bend in the road, the coachman halted the carriage suddenly and leapt from the bench without explanation. Thomas leaned his head out of the window and issued a loud curse, jumping from the carriage.

He couldn't handle another delay. He would walk—hobble—the rest of the way if necessary. Flying off the bench, Benjamin slid from the carriage and landed awkwardly in a mud puddle, wrenching his leg. With a curse, his gaze rose to Thomas, and all feeling drained from his body.

Several meters away, Thomas and the driver knelt beside the immobile form of a woman with dark hair. Benjamin felt his heart splinter into tiny pieces as he hastened to the woman's side, then Thomas shifted, revealing the striking visage of Miss Randall, her pale skin glowing white against the deep brown of the muck where she was lying unconscious.

Benjamin collapsed on the ground next to Thomas, pain radiating through his injured left leg, causing him to gasp aloud. Thomas ignored Benjamin's complaint, continuing his efforts to revive Miss Randall. Her breath came weakly, but she remained immobile.

Glancing up at Benjamin, Thomas indicated the direction of the country estate with a wrench of his head. "Take the shortcut through Flannery's property," he said, not allowing Benjamin an opportunity to argue. "I will stay with Miss Randall and make sure she is given any medical treatment she requires."

"Thank you, brother." Benjamin placed his hand on Thomas' shoulder and climbed to his feet, swallowing a groan.

Miss Randall moaned softly, and Thomas' head whipped around. Lifting her wrist, his thumb caressed the back of her hand. Her eyelashes fluttered open.

"Mr. Reid." She sighed, her mouth curving into a small smile as her violet eyes focused on his face. "I'm pleased to see you." Her eyes rolled backward, and her body went limp, her slight hand sliding from Thomas' fingers, splashing into the mud. Benjamin hovered nearby, conflicted.

"I told you to leave," Thomas said, without taking his eyes from Miss Randall. "We need to be in two places at the same time. Get moving."

Benjamin turned and limped toward the low wooden fence which ran the length of the road. Swinging one leg over the beam marking the perimeter of Mr. Flannery's estate, he set off at a half-run, half-stumble toward the estate. His feet found a familiar trail—one he and his father walked many times in his youth.

"Father, I thought this land belonged to Mr. Flannery?" Benjamin asked on one such hike as they climbed over the fence.

"It does," his father replied, patting Benjamin on the head. "Mr. Flannery and I have a mutual accord. We watch each other's land; it is a neighborly agreement. You must always know your allies, in business and in life."

"Stop where you are!" The issued command—in thick Irish brogue—accompanied the unmistakable sound of a cocked rifle.

"Mr. Flannery." Benjamin greeted the old man wearily as the image of his father faded from his mind. This was not the first time Mr. Flannery had threatened him with a rifle, although Benjamin was much younger the last time.

"Raise your hands." Mr. Flattery gestured with the rifle. "Turn around slowly."

Benjamin complied with a groan, lifting his arms. "I was just passing through," he said as he rotated in a half-circle. Putting his back to a man with a gun, even if that man was Mr. Flannery, was never a good decision. Benjamin peeked over his shoulder at the barrel of the gun poking him in the back.

"My coach was waylaid."

"Where are you headed?" Mr. Flannery raised a skeptical eyebrow. His wispy white beard held only a few stray red hairs, survivors from his youth.

"Home," Benjamin replied, indicating the direction with a flick of his wrists, his hands still raised.

"Humph. I know the boys who live there." Mr. Flannery growled, scratching his chin. "You, I don't recognize."

"I spent my childhood here. I'm Benjamin, Lord Westwood's eldest son."

"Prove it." The muzzle ground into Benjamin's spine.

"When I was ten, your son, Aidan and I stole two of your horses. The mare threw both her shoe and Aidan before we cleared this precise rise. You were not two minutes behind us, charging up the hill, waving your rifle—the very gun you are currently aiming at my back."

"Benjamin." Mr. Flannery lowered the rifle and spun Benjamin around, grasping him to his chest. "You are a bit larger than I last recall."

Stifling a moan, Benjamin hastily returned the embrace, then detangled himself from Mr. Flannery. "It has been many years. How is your lovely wife?"

Mr. Flannery's head dropped. He turned away, staring down the hill. His morose answer pained Benjamin. "We lost Noreen last fall."

"I am sorry, I hadn't heard." Benjamin placed his hand on Mr. Flannery's shoulder.

The older man raised an arm and shook off the condolences, keeping his back to Benjamin. "I still can hear her melodic voice echoing through the fields whenever a breeze blows softly over this ridge. She calls to me, whispering, *Aengus*."

Mr. Flannery collapsed on the grass, his body shaking from his sobs. Benjamin dropped to the ground next to him, ignoring the throbbing pain in his leg. Wrapping a comforting arm around the old man's shoulders, Benjamin's eyes roved over Mr. Flannery, his second father, thinner than he recalled. Retrieving the fallen rifle, Benjamin laid the gun over his legs.

"Da, what are you doing all the way out here?"

Benjamin recognized the drawl immediately and called out to the approaching man, who'd appeared as if conjured from his memories. "It's been many years, Aidan."

"Lord Westwood," he replied, adding a belated bow, then snorted upon spying the rifle resting across Benjamin's lap. "Bring back any memories?"

"A few." Benjamin grimaced as he rose, passing the weapon over to Aidan.

Aidan sighed and looked down at the man resting on the hilltop. "Da, you cannot keep trying to shoot visitors."

"Trespassers!" Mr. Flannery shouted. He leapt to his feet and lunged for the gun, ripping it from Aidan's grasp. "Your mother told me to protect our land."

"Not against our neighbors," Aidan groaned. He reached for the gun, but his father danced out of reach and dashed down the hill, swinging the rifle over his head. Turning to Benjamin, Aidan fished several bullets from his waist pocket and winked.

"The rifle isn't loaded."

Benjamin stared down the hill after Mr. Flannery's retreating form.

"How is he faring?"

"Not well." Aidan sighed, dropping the bullets back into his pocket. "After Ma passed... he thinks she still talks to him, claims she plays the pianoforte in the middle of the night. He sits for hours in the same chair, staring at the piano bench, listening to soundless music. I stayed on after the funeral, hoping his temperament would improve. Instead, I spend most of my time chasing the old man around." He paused, glancing at Benjamin, his eyes filled with misery. "I've asked Alana to return. I cannot handle this situation alone."

"It's been a while since she's been home. I hope she's well," Benjamin said, sidestepping Aidan's unasked question.

"Does he ever talk about it?" Aidan asked.

So much for ignoring the past.

"No," he replied, his tone curt.

"Neither does she," Aidan said, the corner of his mouth

quirked. "It was a shame what happened between the two of them."

"Many years have passed." He hoped that would end the conversation. There was no need to add to Aidan's burden by revealing the truth of Thomas' continued torment.

"It would be helpful to have a second pair of eyes on Da." Aidan's gaze flicked to the fading outline of his father. "I'm exhausted, chasing him across the meadows. He continues to disappear with that bloody rifle. Claims marauders are invading our lands."

"Perhaps you should allow your father to patrol the estate with a gun."

"Why?" Aidan turned to Benjamin, suspicion in his eyes.

"Do you mind if we continue moving toward the house while we discuss this delicate matter? Unless you have something pressing?" Benjamin jerked his head in the direction of Mr. Flannery.

Aidan patted the pocket where he'd stored the bullets. "He'll be fine for a few minutes."

"I've recently become engaged," Benjamin said as they hiked along the ridge, his leg pulsated with each step.

"Pregnant?"

"No," he growled, his tone surprising Aidan, who took a step away from Benjamin's abrupt ire and held up his hands.

"Who is the lady?"

"Miss Samantha Hastings."

"Cousin Samantha?" Aidan laughed and dropped his hands. "I was under the impression she detested the societal constraints of marriage. At least, that was her belief the last time we saw her."

Benjamin glanced heavenward and shook his head. "Of course, Miss Hastings and Alana know each other."

"Concerned?" A ghostly smirk crossed Aidan's lips.

"Mildly worried." His last encounter with Alana also involved a rifle.

"Alana taught Samantha how to shoot one summer, the year her uncle passed. Edward wanted to distract her, and I volunteered to keep her occupied," Aidan said, his face threatening to split into a large smile. "If I remember correctly, she had exceptional aim."

Stopping on the ridge, Benjamin massaged his burning leg and turned to Aidan.

"Edward needs your help again, as do I." He paused, debating his involving Aidan in their situation. "Do you know Mr. Franklin Morris?"

"He's a distant relative who I met on a handful of occasions, heard his name around the club, nothing interesting. Why do you ask?"

"Morris is responsible for the death of Edward's father."

Aidan gasped.

"He also abducted Miss Hastings this morning."

"Edward must be frantic." Aidan's face hardened into anger. "Go, find Samantha. Da and I will stand guard for as long as you require our assistance."

"Your father will be so pleased." He earned a dry smile from Aidan.

"The gun will be loaded this time, so try not to startle the old man. He gets a little jumpy." Aidan clapped his palm on Benjamin's back, flashed a quick grin—a fleeting image of the cheery companion Benjamin recalled from his boyhood—and shoved hard, propelling Benjamin down the decline.

A multitude of carriages were parked in the drive, neatly arranged in a graceful arc, indicating a house overrun by meddling engagement well-wishers. He hoped Mrs. Hastings had the good sense to sequester them to one room or better yet, kept them outside. What excuse had she invented to explain Miss Hastings' sudden absence from the luncheon?

He hobbled up the steps and wrenched open the front door, falling into the deserted entranceway. A curse flew from his lips as he corrected his gait to prevent himself from crashing into a nearby table, the sudden jerk sending pain radiating through his already aching limbs. He swore again.

"Lord Westwood?" a tentative voice called from the staircase. "It's a pleasure to see you again."

Benjamin's head whipped around. Seated mid-staircase was Miss Daphne Clemens. Behind her stood young Lucy Hastings, quietly plaiting braids of various sizes into Miss Clemens' unbound hair.

"Miss Clemens, Miss Hastings." He acknowledged them with a sheepish bow.

"Lady Westwood thought it best to continue the luncheon as planned so as not to stir up any unnecessary gossip," Miss Clemens said, either ignoring or dismissing Benjamin's disheveled appearance and foul language. "The guests are currently in the garden."

"Thank you." Benjamin nodded and limped toward the study, leaning heavily on his right leg.

"I have a message for you." Miss Clemens' soft voice rolled over his shoulder.

Stopping halfway to the study, Benjamin turned back, craning around the banister to see Miss Clemens.

"Which is?"

"Stay where you are," she repeated in a dutiful tone.

"From whom is this direction?" Benjamin took a menacing step toward Miss Clemens.

She glanced down at her hands, twisting anxiously in her lap. Apparently, she was uncomfortable issuing commands, especially to someone she considered above her social standing.

"Lucy," Miss Clemens quietly addressed the little girl plaiting braids, "will you pretend you are a pirate and pilfer some more of those delicious sandwiches from the luncheon?"

With a wink, Lucy rose and descended the staircase with an impish grin. "Would you like the same kind as last time?"

"Surprise me." Miss Clemens smiled. The tiny child nodded, scooted around her, and disappeared down the corridor. When Lucy's footsteps faded, Miss Clemens returned her eyes to Benjamin and dropped her voice. "Mr. Hastings made the request. He and Mr. Walton traveled to Mr. Morris' country residence to question the housekeeper. They don't think Miss Hastings is captive at the estate, but Mr. Hastings hoped to find a clue to her true whereabouts."

"Why would Edward request I remain here?" Benjamin asked, speaking more to himself than to Miss Clemens.

Leaning forward, she cupped her hand around her mouth and whispered, "Mr. Hastings suspects there may be a second kidnapping."

Benjamin's jaw dropped. Why would Edward involve an innocent person like Miss Clemens in this horrid ordeal? It seemed completely opposite of his overprotective tendencies.

"Mr. Hastings confessed that particular concern to you?" Benjamin asked, crossing the foyer and stopping at the foot of the staircase.

"Not aloud," she replied, weaving her fingers together.

Groaning, Benjamin lowered himself onto the stairs, sitting next to Miss Clemens. Stretching out his throbbing leg, he rubbed his thigh. His intense gaze locked on Miss Clemens' brown eyes.

"Please explain."

She gulped and quickly looked away, a faint red decorating her face. The blush reminded him of Miss Hastings, her beautiful skin tinted with that delectable glow. His heart thudded in agony.

How would he find her?

"Mrs. Hastings received a threatening missive this morning before the warning from Aunt Abigail was delivered." Miss Clemens' meek voice broke into his thoughts. "By the time we arrived, Mrs. Hastings was recovering upstairs, having fainted. Mr. Hastings met us in the courtyard, briefly explaining Mrs. Hastings was feeling ill. He said he had an errand to attend, and when I saw you and Mr. Reid, I was to ask you both to remain here."

"Then what happened?" he asked after Miss Clemens lapsed silent.

"When Mr. Hastings rushed out, he left the letter on the hallway table... and I read it. It was horrific." She paused, a visible shudder traveling the length of her spine. Raising her eyes, Miss Clemens stared at Benjamin, tears sliding down the ends of her lashes. "Is Miss Hastings still alive?"

"I hope so," he answered fervently, having no other answer to give except his own hope. He ran his hand through his hair and thought of Mr. Flannery. The poor man helplessly watched his wife die and now wandered his land in a permanent state of fantasy. Would he plunge into the same madness? Could he endure life without Miss Hastings? How could Edward expect him to sit here patiently doing nothing?

"What has everyone been told regarding Miss Hastings' unexpected absence?" Benjamin inclined his head in the direction of the gardens.

"Miss Hastings and Mrs. Hastings have both suddenly taken ill. They are extremely grateful to everyone who attended to celebrate the upcoming nuptials. A proper engagement ball will be held once they are fully recovered," Miss Clemens recited.

"I'm certain Miss Hastings will be pleased to hear she did not miss her own engagement celebration," he muttered, thinking she would be anything but pleased.

They glanced up as the front door burst open. Thomas

and an extremely muddy Miss Randall entered together. She was draped over him, her arm wrapped over his shoulders, and his arm wound about her waist. Miss Clemens' face crumpled at their intimacy. She turned her head, plucking at her unfinished braids. Thomas and Miss Randall approached the foot of the stairs, sluggishly gliding across the floor.

"Miss Randall, I trust you are feeling better," Benjamin said, attempting to rise. He bit his tongue as a sharp pain rewarded his sudden movement and collapsed back onto the step, his legs refusing to cooperate. He grunted in frustration.

"I am. Thank you, Lord Westwood," Miss Randall replied with a graceful wave of her arm, indicating Benjamin remain seated on the staircase. Turning her full attention to Thomas, she beamed, and he radiated under her smile. "Mr. Reid rescued me."

"Your gratitude is unnecessary," Thomas said, patting her arm. He lowered her onto the step directly below Miss Clemens.

"What happened to your dress?" Miss Clemens asked, staring at Miss Randall's ruined clothes.

"Since Westwood Estate is within walking distance of my aunt's house, I decided to travel by foot, so I could enjoy the fresh air," Miss Randall said, her melodious voice filling the foyer. "I left in the late morning to allow plenty of time to arrive at Miss Hastings' engagement party."

"A marvelous idea," Thomas replied with a quick smile.

"Indeed," Miss Clemens echoed.

Benjamin picked up a tone of jealousy in Miss Clemens' response. Perhaps Thomas ought to stop rescuing young ladies. Both Miss Randall and Miss Clemens seemed equally smitten with him. If this practice continued, Thomas would be heading down the aisle before him.

"As I rounded the bend where you discovered me unconscious, a black coach sped down the road. I assumed the driver would see me and veer to the right to avoid running me down. However, the coachman did not, and I couldn't avoid being struck. There was a deafening crash and a rush of intense pain, which coursed through my entire body like lightning. My next recollection was of you, Mr. Reid, saving me."

She offered Thomas a second luminous smile, her violet eyes sparkling like brilliant jewels. Thomas, mesmerized by their beauty, gaped silently. He shook his head briefly as if clearing his mind and glanced away.

Benjamin caught sight of Thomas' reflection in the hallway mirror and raised his eyebrows. Thomas flashed a grin.

"Coincidence?" Benjamin mouthed silently. Thomas shrugged imperceptibly.

"Did you see the inhabitants of the coach?" Benjamin's voice cracked as he shifted on his stair, wincing.

"No, I didn't." A tear rolled down the side of Miss Randall's cheek. "Why would someone want to hurt me?"

"How very brave you are." Miss Clemens offered her an intricately embroidered handkerchief in an attempt to comfort the other woman. "I would have been terrified."

Benjamin was struck by Miss Clemens' kindness. She forwent Miss Randall's obvious interest in the same gentleman in favor of sympathy. Even if Thomas never recognized Miss Clemens' gentle disposition, Benjamin felt as though she had allowed him a tiny peek into her true nature. Perhaps their mother had witnessed the same generosity. Lady Westwood seemed most taken with Miss Clemens.

"I was." Miss Randall gave Miss Clemens' hand a tight squeeze as she accepted the delicate silk. She dabbed her eyes and glanced down at her mud-covered skirt, sighing. "Apparently, I will be attending the luncheon in less than acceptable attire."

"I believe we can save your dress," Miss Clemens said,

inspecting the hem. "Would you like to accompany me upstairs?"

"I would be so grateful to you," Miss Randall replied, her face shining. She and Miss Clemens rose and ascended the staircase, Miss Randall wrapping her arm through Miss Clemens' arm in an affable gesture. "Your handkerchief is beautiful. Did you embroider it yourself?"

"Yes," Miss Clemens replied as their voices faded down the corridor.

"Edward wishes we remain on the estate until he returns." Benjamin smacked the stair on which he sat, anger punctuating his statement.

"We will find Miss Hastings," Thomas replied, placing his hand on Benjamin's shoulder.

"Aunt Samantha is missing?" A little voice, stuffed with sandwich, spoke from the left of Thomas' hip.

"Lucy!" Benjamin twisted toward the girl. How long had she been listening to the discussion?

Lucy set the plate on the stair, just within reach of Thomas' outstretched fingers, and turned her attention to Benjamin, who sat eye level to her. She chewed her lower lip, then clasped her hands behind her back, rocking back on her heels, and drew in a deep breath.

"Lord Westwood," she said, her voice filled with hesitation. "I know where Aunt Samantha went this morning."

CHAPTER 5

Franklin ripped open his apartment door, dragging Sam toward the rickety stairs, his hand wrapped tightly around the rope binding her wrists. Descending the stairs rapidly, he yanked Sam behind him. She stumbled onto the decaying top stair, unable to grab the railing for support, and her foot slipped. Twisting to avoid falling, Sam crashed into a crumbling wall, and her ankle rolled sideways, drawing an anguished cry from her lips.

Glancing backward, Franklin's face held no sympathy. "No dawdling, Miss Hastings."

He jerked the rope, and Sam flew forward, tripping down two steps, pain radiating in her swelling ankle. Franklin turned, pulling her down the second flight of stairs. She stumbled after him, her arms stretched out in front of her. Unable to hold up her skirt, she stepped on her hem, catching and tearing the material. Losing her footing, she pitched forward. Her hands were torn from Franklin's grasp as she tumbled down the last set of stairs.

Sam landed hard, smashing her knees on the floorboards, and crumpled. Her chin ricocheted off the wood, ripping the breath from her lungs. Crying out, she rolled onto her side, screaming in agony, and shrank into a tiny ball.

After leisurely descending the staircase, Franklin crossed the entranceway, stopped at her feet, and kicked her shoe. "I don't recall you being extremely clumsy. How many undesirable traits have you developed since your mother's death?"

Sam uncurled, glowering at him. Blowing a tendril of hair from her sweaty face, she lifted her head from the grimy floor, a barrage of pain catapulting down her spine. She squeezed her eyes shut, swallowing her scream. Taking several deep breaths, Sam reopened her eyes, scowling at Franklin's amused face.

"Let us see how well balanced you are when your wrists are bound, Franklin." A wave of medication overwhelmed the pain. She heaved twice, her body contorted with nausea. She vomited and collapsed, not caring about the disgusting floor or the mouse poking around her ankle.

"Give me your hands," he growled, his voice moving toward her head.

His cold instruction did nothing to relieve the terror rippling through her body. Even with her wrists unbound, she couldn't escape him, not when her stomach betrayed her at every possible instance. With a groan, Sam raised her arms, refusing to lift her face off the floor.

Snarling, Franklin grabbed the rope, and yanked sideways, jerking Sam into a sitting position, then he dragged her torso upward until she perched uncomfortably on her bruised knees. Her arms, dotted with specs of blood from tiny cuts and splinters, ached as he held them over her head.

"Try not to move," Franklin said, the corner of his mouth twitching into a sneer, "I would hate to carve up your beautiful face." He fished a penny knife from his waistcoat pocket and unfolded it. The blade glinted dangerously in the sunlight streaming in from cracks in the roof. With a flick, he sliced the sharp edge across the ropes, and they fell, hitting the floorboards with a muffled thud.

The binding had etched painful burns into Sam's delicate skin, the red marks glowing in the dim lighting of the entranceway. Massaging her wrists to ease the prickling feeling crawling through her fingers, Sam moaned with relief.

"Manners, Samantha." Franklin clucked and crouched in front of her. "Now, you must say, *Thank you, dear Cousin.*"

"Thank you, Cousin," Sam ground out through clenched teeth.

"No." Franklin shook his head, accompanying the movement with a wave of the knife. "I said *dear.* Can you not follow even the simplest instructions?"

"Thank you, *dear* Cousin." She forced a smile.

"You're quite welcome." He rose, pushed open the outer door, and bowed low, a mocking grin stretching his lips. "Your carriage awaits, my dear."

Tearing her eyes from Franklin and the sharp blade clutched in his hand, Sam stared through the open entranceway. Bright sunlight highlighted the dingy cobblestones, falling on the top of a black coach that waited just outside the building.

Sam rose unsteadily, using the doorframe to haul herself to her feet. Taking several minutes to brush real and imaginary debris from her skirt, her eyes studied the buildings along the road. She hoped someone would pass by, but the street remained empty.

In truth, not one person had crossed her path since Franklin brought her to this horrid place. Outrunning the carriage was not an option, and with her injuries and the poisonous medication coursing through her body, she would never escape without some sort of distraction. She prayed an opportunity would present itself when they reached the townhouse. Once Franklin had possession of the jewelry, he wouldn't need her alive.

How long would that be?

Her eyes flicked to the coachman. The faceless mass, bundled in rags, refused to acknowledge her presence. He sat stoically, frozen in his hunched position, a ghoulish marionette waiting for its master's commands. Resolutely, she squared her shoulders and attempted to walk elegantly through the door. A burning sensation stabbed her ankle, sucking the air from Sam's lungs. She gasped, tripping forward, and grabbed onto the carriage's wheel.

Franklin stepped forward and offered his hand, a smirk on his lips. "May I offer some assistance?"

She shied away with a shiver and shook her head. Lifting her skirt, she stepped onto the carriage rung and climbed into the darkness without a word. As she settled on the cool bench, a shudder ripped through her spine.

Sliding the knife blade closed, Franklin dropped it back into his pocket. He ambled to the front of the coach, gesturing for the driver to lean down. After whispering to the featureless coachman, Franklin returned to the cabin door, whistling a hollow tune. As he climbed into the carriage, he pulled the door closed behind him and seated himself across from Sam, knocking on the window. The coach jerked forward.

"Our adventure begins." He grinned, rubbing his hands together.

They rode in silence for several minutes. With the curtains drawn tightly, it was impossible to determine their location or the route the coachman followed. The only light that entered the cabin crawled through a crack at the bottom of the door.

How far were Franklin's lodgings from the townhouse? Had they traveled long enough to reach the edge of the park?

She debated screaming. If they were on a populated road or passing individuals strolling along the walkway, someone would hear her yell. She quietly drew in a deep breath, filling her lungs.

A flash caught her attention in the coach's semi-darkness. She glanced up and gasped. Franklin had extracted the knife from his pocket and was using the tip of the blade to draw light patterns across the palm of his hand. He seemed pensive, watching little white lines appear in his skin. Two minutes passed before he spoke.

"How did you come to learn of the location of the jewelry?" Franklin's dark eyes flicked toward Samantha's face as he etched bizarre sketches in his skin.

She gulped, unsure of the direction of the conversation, responding in what she hoped was a nonchalant tone.

"I deciphered the note from Father, the one we discovered in the back of the watch."

"I see." Franklin's eyes gleamed, his voice terrifyingly calm. "Where did the clue direct you?"

"To the study in the townhouse," Sam replied without hesitation, knowing a delay in her response would increase his mistrust, and she needed him to believe her weak and frightened.

With a skeptical look, Franklin leaned forward, stopping an inch from her face. Sam could feel his hot breath tickling her skin as he studied her eyes.

"Where in the study?"

Her mind raced. If she revealed the true location, there would be no further reason to keep her alive. However, if she lied, Franklin would know, and she wouldn't be able to fight off his fury. Faced with the possibility of her imminent demise, she opted for deception.

"They are hidden in a desk," she said, forcing her voice to crack on the last word.

"Did you inform anyone of the true location of the jewelry?" Franklin regarded her with a peculiar expression.

"No." Sam shook her head. *That part was true.*

"Rebecca's desk?" Franklin pressed, his forehead nearly touching hers.

"Yes," she squeaked, praying Franklin believed her lie.

They weren't in her mother's desk. They were beneath it, stuffed in the dollhouse... hopefully.

"I checked the desk," Franklin muttered, leaning back on his bench. He fell silent, his head tilted oddly as the knife continued its macabre dance across his hand.

Sam's breath caught as the pensive look in Franklin's eyes cleared. He shot across the tiny coach, shoving her against the wall and pressing the knife blade into her throat. She choked, trapped between the coach and Franklin's gleaming knife.

"I checked the desk." His eyes narrowed. "You're lying to me, Samantha."

Pain erupted in Sam's jaw as Franklin struck her across the face with the back of his hand, her cheek throbbing from the blow. Franklin hit her again. The force threw her against the opposite side of the coach. She slammed into the carriage wall and slumped on the bench, unable to escape Franklin's brutal rage.

He bore down on her, yanking her from the bench and wrapping his hands around her throat, then pushed her onto the coach floor, straddling her legs. His fingers tightened around her neck. As he squeezed, she struggled to shove his body off her chest, kicking her feet futilely. Her strength failed. Franklin crushed her chest with his knees, pressing the oxygen from her lungs, his black eyes glittering with venom.

Sam clawed her fingernails across his hands, raking deep scars through his skin, yet his hold didn't lessen. Her hands flailed, sliding along the floor in search of a weapon. The wasted effort drew a bark of laughter from Franklin, who, with a malicious grin, watched her struggle under his weight like a fish gasping for air. Creeping in from the sides of her vision, darkness threatened to overtake Sam's mind.

"Edward," she whispered, "please forgive me."

She refused to allow Franklin's sneering face to be her last memory. Twisting her head sideways, her eyes fell on the tiny crack under the door. Flashes of color whipped past in hues of deep green. A deafening roar rushed in her ears, then... nothing. Peace. Everything stopped.

The carriage halted.

Franklin's head whipped up. He grinned with delight, slowly releasing his fingers from her throat one by one. Oxygen saturated Sam's fevered brain, and she sucked in raspy gulps of air, her chest heaving. Benjamin's green eyes burned briefly in the darkness before fading into the shadows.

Ripping open the coach's door, Franklin bounded from the carriage. He spun around with a feral grin and offered his hand again in a dramatic gesture. Sam shook her head stubbornly and remained crouched on the floor, refusing to budge. With a shrug, Franklin leaned into the carriage and seized Sam's closest leg, his fingers digging into her skin. Dragging her forward—hand over hand—he murmured in a low tone as she slid onto the street.

"If you make one sound or draw any attention to us, I will kill all three of those wretched nieces in front of you. Do you understand?"

Sam nodded, her wide eyes focusing solely on Franklin.

"Excellent." He grasped her elbow and bobbed his head at the driver. A whip cracked, and the carriage disappeared down the street, Sam's hope vanishing with it. With a snicker, Franklin grabbed her chin and forced it toward the townhouse.

She gasped. A burned shell remained in place of the parlor. All the family memories and pictures were destroyed. Wilhelmina's favorite settee, now a pile of ashes, smoked ominously in the center of the room. Sam choked down a sob as her eyes scanned the scorched space.

Grinning, Franklin dragged her closer to the damaged abode. "Would you prefer to enter through the front door or the parlor?"

Her gaze jumped from the charred townhouse to his jeering face.

"Why, Franklin? Why would you do this horrible thing?"

"I'm not responsible for igniting the fire. I received assistance with that happy task." He gestured at the burned ruins. "The Hastings family has more than one enemy."

Shoving Sam toward the townhouse, he wrenched her arm behind her back and propelled her up the ashen steps, their shoes leaving prints in the soot. As Franklin ripped open the door, a shudder raced down Sam's spine. This was her last opportunity to escape. She glanced left and right, pushing back against Franklin's bulk, hoping someone would notice them, but no one spared them one glance. Franklin thrust her inside and slammed the door.

The motion disturbed the ash flurries floating languidly through the hazy air, whipping them around Franklin and Sam like a gray snowstorm and embedding them in Sam's hair. He pushed her forward, prodding the center of her back with the knife tip.

"Lead the way, my dear." His gleeful voice was in direct contrast to the destruction surrounding them. "I hope the jewelry is here... for your sake."

Sam inched along the hallway, avoiding unrecognizable pieces of charred furniture. Franklin dug the blade sharply into her spine, a silent reminder of his presence. She took a deep breath and pushed open the study room door, relief washing over her. The study remained mostly intact. The only damage came from the shared wall between the study and the parlor. Singe marks, from where the flames entered through the grate in the lower portion of the partition, danced their way up the wall in gruesome patterns.

Her gaze sought out her mother's desk, highlighted in the light of the fading afternoon sun, which streamed in through a wide gap in the drapes covering the window. Approaching the desk, Sam's heart hammered. *Please let the dollhouse have survived.* Her fingers trailed over scorch marks, which licked their way across the delicate surface of the desk. Sam's breath caught, her teeth sinking into her lower lip. A flash of light caught her eye—peeking out from underneath the desk was the dollhouse. She exhaled.

Franklin followed her to the desk and shoved her to the side. She stumbled, crashing into Edward's desk with a groan. Ignoring her, Franklin ripped the top of her mother's desk up, revealing the writing surface and six drawers, still organized in her mother's haphazard manner. Franklin thumbed through the paperwork on the desk, flinging loose sheets over his shoulder as he searched. He tore open the drawers, dumping their contents on the ground with a growl. In the final cubby, he discovered a stack of letters, loosely bound by a blue ribbon, which he tossed in Sam's direction. Unprepared, she dropped the stack, and the letters hit the floor, exploding into a flurry of envelopes.

"I see no jewelry." Franklin glowed at Sam, his black eyes shrinking to slits.

Spinning around, he grabbed her, slamming her body against the bookshelf, his hand closing around her throat again. She struggled, kicking her feet. Franklin pressed himself against her body, pinning her legs against the wall. He extracted the knife, placing the blade against Sam's neck.

She swung her arm, knocking books off the shelves, one volume striking Franklin in the head. Leaping backward, Franklin slashed the knife through the air, the arc barely missing Sam's face. She scrunched herself against the bookshelf, trying to avoid the blade. Without warning, Franklin reached out, grabbed her hair, and yanked her to his side, ignoring her screams.

"Where are they?" He snarled, spit flying from his lips.

"I will never reveal their location!" she yelled, fumbling behind her. Her fingers closed around the rim of a vase, situated on a small table next to the bookshelf. She swung the vase into Franklin's head, smashing it and scattering pieces across the floor.

Franklin stumbled and released his hold, a trickle of blood leaking from the cut on his forehead. He howled in frustration, blindly swiping the knife at her.

If she could get to the front door and wrench it open, someone would assist her. She limped across the floor, but as her hand touched the study doorknob, her head slammed against the wood.

Franklin spun her around and flung her across the room. Colliding with the corner of her mother's desk, she tumbled over the edge. It upended itself with the force of her body, and she crashed to the floor with a pain-filled moan. Franklin wound his fingers through her hair again, lifting her from the ground, and pitched her across the room. She rammed into several armchairs, knocking them askew, and landed in a heap, her feet twisted in a morbid dance.

After rolling onto her stomach, Sam crawled on her elbows toward Edward's desk. Franklin advanced on her and grabbed her ankle. Wrapping her fingers around the leg of Edward's desk, Sam screamed. With a snarl, Franklin kicked her in the ribs, sending agony shooting through her body and cutting off her cries for help. He dragged her back to the middle of the room with a sneering grin.

"I have all day, Samantha. How long do you think you will survive?" The knife flashed.

CHAPTER 6

"Aunt Samantha left to retrieve my dollhouse." Lucy twisted her fingers into small knots as she revealed the information.

Benjamin's gaze slid to Thomas, who shrugged, wearing the same perplexed expression, then returned to Lucy.

"Where is your dollhouse?"

Leaning forward, the little girl glanced over both shoulders, then cupped her hand around her mouth and whispered, "I hid it in Father's office the morning of the fire."

"Why did Miss Hastings travel—unchaperoned—to the townhouse to rescue your dollhouse?" Thomas asked, popping one of the pilfered sandwiches into his mouth.

"She didn't go alone." Lucy punctuated the statement with an eye roll, twisting toward Thomas, clearly irritated he would hint at Miss Hastings' lacked proper manners.

"With whom did she travel?" Benjamin asked, the patience in his voice directly opposite to the turmoil raging in his mind.

Lucy turned her plump face toward him and grinned. "Cousin Franklin took her in his coach."

"Lucy!" Nancy's voice echoed from the top stair. Lucy's head whipped toward the sound.

Benjamin grasped Lucy's upper arms, recapturing her attention.

"Why did your aunt believe the recovery of your dollhouse was urgent enough to leave without your father or me?"

"I don't know, Lord Westwood." Lucy sank her teeth into her lower lip, her eyes flicking toward the top of the staircase as her name echoed through the upstairs again. "Aunt Samantha said it was a house that was not a home. I didn't understand what she meant."

"Lucy! Where have you been hiding?" Nancy chided as she rushed down the staircase.

Lucy paled, squishing herself closer to Benjamin.

"I wanted to see the luncheon."

"Please accept my apologies for Miss Hastings's intrusion, my Lord," Nancy said to Benjamin with a curtsy.

"Actually, she has proven quite helpful," Benjamin replied, winking at Lucy.

"Thank you, Lord Westwood." The little girl curtsied, then Nancy scooped her up, along with the plate of leftover sandwiches, and carried her upstairs into the nursery.

"Why would Miss Hastings risk her life to retrieve a dollhouse?" Thomas asked, turning to Benjamin once they were alone. "What did she mean when she told young Miss Hastings *a house that is not a home*?"

"I don't understand either." Benjamin stood with a grimace, shaking off Thomas' offered arm. "However, it doesn't matter what it means. I'm leaving for the townhouse immediately."

"Edward—"

"Has no right to order a lord to do anything," Benjamin cut off his brother, a hard edge in his retort. "Remain here until he returns and inform him of my destination." Instead of heading down the staircase, Benjamin turned and stumped slowly upward, climbing one step at a time and swallowing the hiss that accompanied each movement.

"The townhouse is in the opposite direction," Thomas said, his confusion evident.

"I'm aware of its location," Benjamin ground out as he climbed. He winced, pain radiating through his body and setting his teeth on edge. "I need to retrieve something from my bedchamber."

"If you turn right at the bottom of the staircase, the corridor will lead you to the informal parlor. You can access the gardens from that room." Miss Clemens' voice drifted toward them. Miss Randall appeared a moment later, her dress fully restored. She curtsied to Benjamin as she descended the staircase, greeting Thomas with a wide smile.

A lopsided grin froze on Thomas' face. Benjamin groaned. Now was not the best time for Thomas to fall in love. However, he could do worse than Miss Charlotte Randall. Benjamin held no qualms regarding her, apart from her relation to the abhorrent Shirely family, whose esteem continued to plummet in his mind.

Thomas tracked Miss Randall as she turned the corner toward the rear of the house, watching until she disappeared into the parlor. He glanced up at Benjamin, a sheepish expression crawling across his face when he realized Benjamin had caught him staring at Miss Randall. He shrugged, a silent admission, and added a jaunty grin. "Are you certain you want to go alone?"

"Edward specifically requested someone must remain here until he returned from Morris' country estate," Benjamin replied, sucking in a sharp breath. Agony accompanied each step.

"He shouldn't be absent much longer," Miss Clemens

interjected morosely from above them, her attention solely on Thomas. "If you would prefer to escort Lord Westwood, I can inform Mr. Hastings of your destination."

"That's very kind of you, Miss Clemens," Thomas replied, lifting his gaze to her. "However, I don't wish to impose any further on you. Besides, my stubborn brother would never willingly accept my help. Therefore, I must decline your offer and remain here, avoiding the luncheon."

"Whenever I don't wish to be disturbed by societal pariahs, I hide in the gazebo."

Benjamin scowled as he bumped his foot against the top step of the second-floor landing, causing Miss Clemens to scurry away from the muttered blasphemy that escaped from his lips.

"An excellent idea." Thomas flashed a smile at her. "Would you care to join me in avoiding an unnecessary public function?"

"I would be pleased to accompany you in your endeavor," she replied after a moment's hesitation. Avoiding Benjamin, she descended the staircase and accepted Thomas' offered arm.

As they strolled toward the front door, Thomas mumbled a comment which earned a soft giggle from Miss Clemens, but Benjamin could no longer discern the words of their conversation. *Rescuing another female...*

Benjamin entered his chamber, shaking his head clear of Thomas' problems. The aroma of honeysuckle hung in the air. Miss Hastings' scent surrounded him, lightly kissing his face. He limped to the fireplace, counting down the bricks until he came to the loose stone. Extricating the brick, he removed a pistol hidden behind it, sliding it into his coat pocket, then replacing the brick. Turning on his heel, Benjamin spied the corner of a missive peeking out from underneath the inkwell on his desk.

Hobbling over, he removed and unfolded the note,

reading it quickly. He cursed. Of course, Miss Hastings had found the threatening letter. How could he be so neglectful? He didn't even realize it was missing. She must have determined what Morris sought. However, not knowing the author of the missive, it made sense she would employ her cousin in one of her adventures. Morris was always game for an expedition, even encouraging a young Miss Hastings to join him in India.

Edward nearly murdered Morris when he discovered his sister at the shipping yard, dragging her trunk up the gangplank, her cousin's letter clutched in her little fist. Thankfully, the sailors found the image of a slight eleven-year-old girl with braids amusing and allowed Edward to collect her from the ship without incident.

Miss Hastings was livid, screaming and pummeling Edward as he flung her over his shoulder and carted her off the ship toward a waiting carriage. It was her Uncle Ephraim who calmed her, explaining she would have plenty of time for adventures after she completed her education. Miss Hastings accepted his rationalization without argument. Now, it seemed as though Morris managed to entice her again.

Crumpling the note in his fist, Benjamin stumbled from the room.

"I am coming, Samantha."

THE SMELL of burnt wood singed Benjamin's nose. Clouds of smoke clogged the hallway of the Hastings' townhouse, casting eerie shadows on the walls. He heard a scuffle, the sound amplified by the scorched skeleton of the parlor. Benjamin crept down the hallway, his shoes leaving footprints in the ashes. He noticed two other sets of fresh prints leading into the darkness. Cautiously, he felt his way down the corridor, following the faint light stemming from behind the ajar study door.

Peeking around the corner, Benjamin peered into the room, his shoe creaking one of the distressed floorboards. Cursing under his breath, Benjamin froze, his muscles tensing. The noises coming from the study stopped. Fearing the worst, Benjamin pulled the gun from his pocket and rushed into the room.

"That is far enough, Westwood. Any closer and I'll slit her throat." Franklin Morris tightened his grasp around Miss Hastings' waist, his voice a menacing growl.

Benjamin's eyes drank in the scene in front of him—chairs flipped over, one with a broken leg, Mrs. Hastings' desk upended, its soft surface marred with scorch marks, papers and books scattered across the floor, Edward's desk stripped bare, its items strewn throughout the room, ink dripping down the far wall.

Morris wheezed as beads of sweat dripped from his red face, frustration etching deep lines across his brow.

Reluctantly, Benjamin allowed his gaze to travel over to Miss Hastings' face, the sight igniting an inferno of ire blazing through his veins. A bruise blossomed on one cheek, its morbid shade of purple discoloring her pale skin, and blood leaked from the corner of her mouth. Wiggling against Franklin's iron grip, her face shone with fear as the knife pressed harder against her neck. Benjamin slid his foot forward, the subtle movement noticed by Morris, who shook his head slowly, gripping the knife handle tightly.

"Perhaps you didn't understand my warning the first time." Morris pressed the blade deeper into Miss Hastings' neck. She choked, her delicate skin whitening under the pressure of the knife blade. A strangled sob forced Benjamin to freeze, his heart hammering loudly.

How would he save her?

"That's much better. I'm pleased to see you can follow directions," Morris said in a disarmingly calm manner. "Now, if you would be so kind as to place your pistol on the floor."

Leaning over with a grunt, Benjamin laid the gun on the ground, then stepped back, raising his arms in a friendly gesture, and awaited further instruction.

"Lock the study door. I would prefer no further interruptions until our business is concluded." Morris gestured with his free hand.

Benjamin complied. He needed a plan, a distraction until Edward arrived, except he didn't know how long he would need. Benjamin spun around with a half-smile, spreading his arms wide.

"Mr. Morris, there is no need for such violence."

"Of course, there's no need. I happen to enjoy it." He chuckled, adjusting his grip on the knife. "At first, I was a little squeamish. However, over time, one can become immune to anything."

Where was Edward?

"Why did you resort to murder?" Benjamin asked, taking a minute step forward.

"They stole from me," Morris snarled, pressing the knife deeper into Miss Hastings' throat. She crushed herself against his chest, unable to escape the blade.

"What did they steal?" He inched closer, scraping the sole of his shoe on the floor. Morris shook his head, swiping the knife toward Benjamin, a silent warning.

"My inheritance," he bit off when Benjamin froze.

"The jewelry was a wedding gift from Uncle Ephraim. You were not the oldest. You were not next in line to receive them," Miss Hastings yelled and clawed her fingernails down Franklin's arm. He slapped her. Her anguished scream cut off as Morris pressed the knife against her neck again, a thin line of blood trickling from the blade.

"Manners," Morris murmured against her ear, then gave her cheek a loud kiss. "The adults are conversing, Samantha."

Benjamin clenched his fists, forcing himself to remain immobile. He feared any sudden movement would give Morris reason to slide the knife quickly across Miss Hastings' throat.

"Ephraim should have given the jewelry to me. Your father didn't need the collection. He received both estates." The arm encircling her waist jerked upward, squeezing until she cried out.

"You would have sold every piece," she choked out.

Morris slid his arm up her body, trailing his fingers intimately over her torso, wrapped his hand through her hair, and wrenched her head back until she was forced to stare into his eyes. A tear slid down one of her cheeks.

"It was my right." His lips brushed against her mouth, and a shudder raced through Miss Hastings.

"You must have felt betrayed," Benjamin said, forcing a soothing tone. He was struggling against the burgeoning desire to beat Morris into an unrecognizable mass of skin and bones.

"I was robbed," Morris replied, releasing Miss Hastings' hair. He locked his sinister gaze on Benjamin, tilting his head. "That necklace is worth thousands."

"Surely, your uncle would not deny you an inheritance."

How long could he keep Morris distracted? If Edward didn't arrive soon, Morris would kill Samantha in front of him.

"My uncle bestowed everything upon his favorite nephew." Turning his macabre grin toward Miss Hastings again, Morris inhaled deeply, rubbing his nose against her curls. He glowered at Benjamin over her head, daring him to protest, then stroked a hand over her tresses as if petting her, causing Benjamin to unconsciously advance. When Morris finally spoke, his voice came from the past.

"I would have traded every bit of jewelry to marry Rebecca, but Matthew stole her, too. I couldn't swallow his betrayal. I left town immediately following their engagement announcement. The convenient death of my father provided a moderate living, so I chose to disappear. Eventually, my funds dwindled, and I found myself in significant debt. The need to return overpowered my broken heart."

"You have no heart," Miss Hastings whispered, and Morris ignored her.

"Uncle Ephraim refused my request, stating the sum was too large. I decided to ask Matthew for a loan. Rebecca opened the door when I called on the household, and I was immediately transported back to my youth. She glowed like an angel in the afternoon light."

"She must have been overjoyed to see you after such a long absence," Benjamin said, sliding slid closer to Miss Hastings. He could almost touch her.

Morris nodded, still lost in his memories.

"Rebecca invited me to their ball that very evening, and I was overjoyed to attend. At a late hour, she retired upstairs to put little Samantha back into the nursery—even as a little child, you were a brat." Snagging his fingers in her hair, he closed his fist and yanked again. Miss Hastings yelped with pain, her hands flying to her head. Grinning, he relaxed his grip, raising his gaze to Benjamin.

"I followed Rebecca stealthily. As she exited the nursery, I emerged from the shadows, startling her. I presented my case, falling to my knees and professing my love. She paled and fled. Seconds later, Matthew slammed me against the windows, his hand wrapped around my throat. I still remember his face as he tried to choke the life from me. He radiated anger, commanding I leave and never return. Seizing the opportunity, I explained my current financial situation and requested compensation."

"What did Mr. Hastings offer?" Benjamin asked quietly.

"A modest sum, to which I countered, adding I wanted immediate possession of the Hastings' ancestral jewels. He adamantly refused. We did eventually arrive at an agreeable figure. I returned late that evening, after the party dispersed, to collect my portion."

Benjamin remained silent for a moment.

"Then you killed him?"

"With poison."

"And your father," Benjamin pressed, knowing the answer, and yet needing to hear the words. "Was his death a result of your greed as well?"

"Undeniably." Morris grinned, seemingly pleased Benjamin had discovered his crimes. "No one suspected his demise was unnatural. I can still picture his face—bewildered as he realized my deceit. By then, the poison already coursed through his body."

Benjamin stared in revulsion, his thoughts whirling. "How many people have you murdered?" he asked with horror.

"I've lost count." Morris shrugged, broadening his evil grin.

"Franklin." Miss Hastings' hoarse voice barely reached Benjamin's ears. "Please. I will help you. Please, Franklin, let us go."

Maniacal laughter echoed around the study as Morris studied the girl in his arms.

"My dear Samantha, you had an opportunity to comply with my wishes, but you denied me. I have no intention of allowing you to live. Your whole family must be punished."

"Franklin, please," Miss Hastings begged, widening her blue eyes and cupping his face with her free hand. "I thought we were friends, family."

"An act. You are easily misled," he replied, shaking off her hand.

"Once you kill her, how will you escape?" Benjamin asked, his ears straining for sounds in the entranceway. Edward should have arrived by now. "I'm not going to step aside and allow you to leave."

"That is a valid point." Morris scrunched his mouth, considering the question for a moment. "I suppose I will have to kill you, too."

"You could." Benjamin took a miniscule step toward him. "However, you would spend the rest of your life in hiding. Edward knows you're responsible for the death of his father, and he wants revenge."

Morris raised his eyebrows, digesting Benjamin's words.

"I'm not afraid."

"There's no reason you need to die."

"You have a different suggestion?"

"I do." Benjamin took another step.

Morris tightened his grip on Miss Hastings.

"I'm a reasonable man, Lord Westwood. What is your proposition?"

Benjamin stared at Miss Hastings for a moment, praying she would understand his intention or at least forgive him. He took a deep breath and refocused his attention on Morris—then opened his mouth and lied.

"The Westwood Estate is insolvent, a situation to which I am sure you can relate. There are so many debts, I can hardly fathom them all. I have been borrowing money from Edward for years to keep the creditors at bay. When he disappeared two years ago, all my old debts were forgiven." He inclined his head toward Morris. "Thank you for your assistance with that matter. Although it became apparent of late, I needed to marry a wealthy woman to preserve my extravagant lifestyle.

As you are aware, appearances must be maintained. The truth is, I was only marrying Miss Hastings for her money."

The shock on both Miss Hastings' and Morris' faces was evidence they believed his deception. Miss Hastings' stood frozen, her mouth opened in a tiny "o." The color drained from her face, further accentuating the purple bruise on her cheek. The audible shattering of her heart was as if an icicle was plunged deep into Benjamin's stomach.

"Imagine my surprise when I discovered Mr. Hastings named me guardian over his ill-mannered little sister and all of her holdings. It was the answer I had been searching for. Unfortunately, I had the laborious task of discouraging every suitor who inquired about Miss Hastings, not to mention the painstaking steps I took to woo her."

Benjamin forced a grin, his eyes locked on Morris' face. The image of Samantha's raw pain floated through his mind. Even if she never forgave him for his deception, he would spend every moment of his life fighting to convince her how much he truly loved her.

"Mr. Lockhearst's proposed bribe for her hand tempted me. However, he was unwilling to match the sum I requested."

"A true businessman," Morris said, nodding in approval.

"When Mr. Hastings shockingly reappeared, so did my entire monetary obligation. I realized he would never force Miss Hastings to repay my loans and increased my efforts to pursue her hand. Mr. Hastings did consider me an inappropriate match at first. However, I was able to convince him otherwise."

Morris studied him with curiosity. "How did you manage that feat?"

Benjamin shook his head with a wink. "Trade secret, Mr. Morris. I can't reveal all my tricks."

"Oh ho," laughed Morris, joyful tears streaming down his face. "Samantha, you really are a terrible judge of character. You never should have involved yourself with such a notorious rake. I only hope you didn't fall prey to his charms." Morris spun her around in his arms. Grasping her chin, he lifted her face and stared into her despondent eyes. "My, my, my, I guess you're a ruined woman after all."

Benjamin held his attention on Morris, watching the exchange silently. Miss Hastings swayed unsteadily on her feet, her pale face haunted and empty, refusing to look over at him.

"Lord Westwood, I must tip my hat to you." Morris' eyes flicked to Benjamin. "You're a kindred spirit. I, myself, attempted a similar plan. However, I had no idea I was competing against such a master in the art of seduction."

"My proposal," Benjamin said with an encouraging smile.

"Yes, what sort of arrangement did you have in mind?" Morris waved his hand, gesturing impatiently.

"It will take some time to find another wealthy bride. I will need some sort of compensation to survive until that happy event occurs."

Morris' eyes narrowed. "What sort of compensation?"

"Five thousand, no less, and I will walk away right now." Benjamin jerked his head toward the door. "I'll inform Edward I discovered Miss Hastings' body with the actual killer, a previously unknown gentleman. You will be free to do as you wish."

"How am I to guarantee you will not return for another payment?" Morris asked, thoughtfully stroking his chin.

Benjamin paused a moment, contemplating the question, then leveled his gaze at Morris and spoke in an even tone.

"I will help you kill Miss Hastings."

Miss Hastings gasped and fainted, her limp form slumping against Morris. Surprised by the sudden weight in his arms, he dropped her, and she landed in a graceless lump at his feet. He stared down at her with disgust, yanking his foot out from under her immobile form.

Taking advantage of Morris' momentary distraction, Benjamin launched himself across the room and caught the man around the middle of his torso, knocking Morris off his feet. Morris reacted quickly to the sudden attack, punching Benjamin in the stomach. The two men rolled in a ball of limbs, sending the knife skittering across the floor.

Benjamin, stronger than Morris, used his weight to pin him to the ground. Morris swung wildly, connecting his left hand with Benjamin's chin, the crack causing stars to dance in front of Benjamin's eyes. Stunned, Benjamin rolled to the side as Morris made a desperate grab for the knife glittering ominously under Mrs. Hastings' ruined desk. Benjamin's hand closed around Morris' leg, yanking back. Kicking his free leg, Morris struck Benjamin's temple, then scrambled toward the desk.

Shaking his head to clear his vision, Benjamin rose, and chased after Morris. Morris' fingers grasped the knife handle and blindly slashed it backward in the air toward Benjamin. Benjamin jumped sideways to avoid the blade and crashed into an overturned chair. Pain detonated in his left leg, and Benjamin collapsed, tangled in the rungs of the chair. Morris descended with a depraved smirk.

CLICK!

The men paused and turned mechanically toward the sound. Frozen, Morris hovered over Benjamin, the knife raised to strike. Miss Hastings stood, pistol gripped tightly in both hands, glaring at them. Her terrifying expression sent chills racing down Benjamin's spine—a woman scorned.

Did she intend to shoot them both?

"Samantha, what are you doing?" Morris patronized as he lowered the knife. "You don't know how to use a pistol."

"Of course, I do." Miss Hastings laughed mirthlessly. "If

Edward was willing to teach me something as inappropriate as fencing, do you not think he would allow me the courtesy of learning to use a gun?" She tilted her head and smiled winningly. "Would you like me to show you?"

"You really shouldn't antagonize her," Benjamin said, his eyes trained on the barrel. Aidan's description of Miss Hastings' shooting prowess flashed through his mind. If she shot half as well as Alana, they were in extreme danger.

"Samantha, my dear cousin, you know me." Morris took a step toward Miss Hastings, his hand outstretched nonthreateningly, the knife hidden behind his back. "I am your family, your friend, and I have been since your birth."

"You are a murderer," she snarled.

Morris bared his teeth and lunged at Miss Hastings with a growl, the knife slicing through the air.

"No!" Benjamin yelled from the floor, still tangled up in the chair.

Miss Hastings squeezed the trigger. The bullet struck Morris in the right shoulder. Shock crossed his face as pain spread down his arm, causing him to drop the knife. Blood spurted from the open wound, his face paled, and he sank down onto the floor.

"Why Sammie?" he mumbled pitifully, his chubby face frozen in agony.

Miss Hastings plucked the knife from the floor before Morris could react, her eyes never leaving his face. She slid the penny knife closed, palming it in her left hand. The pistol she aimed directly at Benjamin's heart.

Benjamin slowly rose from the floor and with a grimace, limped toward Miss Hastings, holding his hand out.

"Give me the gun, Miss Hastings."

She scowled at him and shook her head. "No."

"Samantha." His voice strained. "Please, hand me the pistol."

She refused to lower the gun. Her hand quivered, and the air shimmered with her fury.

"You lied to me."

CHAPTER 7

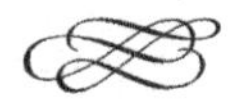

"I had good reason to lie, Samantha." Lord Westwood took a step forward.

Sam brought her second hand up, supporting the base of the pistol with both hands.

"You said you loved me."

"I do." He took another step.

"How can I believe anything you say?" She swiped at the angry tear sliding down her cheek.

"Sammie?" Edward's disembodied voice echoed down the corridor.

"Edward!" Sam called out, refusing to lower her weapon. "We're in the study."

The knob rattled, and a moment later, Edward burst through the locked study door, followed by Mr. Walton and Mr. Reid. Their eyes quickly scanned the scene. Edward whistled under his breath as he drank in the room's destruction. His gaze stopped on Sam, whose trembling arms pointed the gun at Benjamin's chest.

"Sammie, hand me the pistol." Edward moved to Sam's

side, wrapping his arm around her waist, and extricated the weapon from her shaky fingers.

"Perhaps you should confiscate the knife, too," Lord Westwood suggested, his arms still raised.

Edward nodded and held his hand out again. Sam relinquished the weapon with a scowl at Lord Westwood, who shrugged apologetically and lowered his hands.

"What did Benjamin do?" Edward swallowed his gasp as Sam turned toward him. She must look worse than she felt.

"I told Franklin I was ruined and only wanted to marry your sister for her fortune," Lord Westwood said, moving closer. Edward froze him with a glare.

"Are you?" he asked, his voice hard.

"Yes, are we?" Mr. Reid repeated, darting around Edward.

"Of course not." Lord Westwood shot his brother an annoyed glare.

"Prove it to me," Sam whispered, her heart breaking.

Prove that you love me.

"I will." Lord Westwood stared into her eyes.

"Prove it to me as well," Mr. Reid said, thumbing to his chest.

"I keep the business ledgers at my lodgings. Will that be sufficient evidence to verify my holdings?" Lord Westwood refused to break his gaze, speaking only to Sam.

"Yes." Her teeth sunk into her lower lip. Beside her, Edward nodded his consent.

"I would like to see them as well." Mr. Reid slipped between them, breaking Lord Westwood's intense gaze.

"If you are confirming your ability to remain a bachelor, who will stay with Morris until the constable arrives?" There was a less than subtle touch of exasperation in Lord Westwood's question.

"I will." Mr. Walton stepped from the doorway, accepting the pistol from Edward, and pointed it directly at Franklin.

Glaring at her cousin, Sam walked over and stared down at his heaving form. She kicked his shoe. "If he moves, shoot him through the heart."

"Without hesitation," Mr. Walton replied, upending and sinking into one of the chairs, the pistol cocked.

Edward joined Sam, hatred burning in his blue eyes. "It will be my pleasure to watch you hang, Franklin."

Spinning, Edward wrapped his arm around Sam and helped her hobble out of the study. They walked at a snail's pace, taking measured steps through the entranceway and down the stairs, every movement dragging an anguished moan from Sam's lips.

Sam felt Lord Westwood trailing behind. He passed them on the sidewalk, leaning heavily on Mr. Reid's shoulders. Both men maintained a silent stride apart from barely audible grunts which escaped Lord Westwood when he placed too much weight on his left leg.

He was injured...

With Edward's arm wrapped securely around her waist, Sam stumbled down the footpath, dark spots swimming in front of her eyes. She stopped, waiting for the darkness to recede from her mind, Edward anxiously hovering in her peripheral. Sam attempted to wave him off. Her stomach rolling, she slumped against the rough bark of a nearby birch tree, one of many which dotted the street.

"It would be easier if you allowed me to carry you," Edward said half-heartedly. It was the third time he made the suggestion.

"No," Sam replied, although her voice held none of the conviction she felt. "I would prefer to walk."

Edward glanced up. Lord Westwood paused several meters in front of them, his face conflicted. He took a step toward Sam, but Edward shot him an angry glare. Lord Westwood recoiled. He allowed Mr. Reid to turn him and continue their slow progress toward his lodgings. Mr. Reid whispered earnestly in his brother's ear as they walked.

Dizzy, Sam rested her head against the tree, hugging it closely. The world spun, colors flying past her eyes. Squeezing her eyelids shut, she vomited, and an acidic taste filled her mouth, remnants of the medication Franklin administered while she was unconscious. Her hands slipped from the tree trunk, and she collapsed, falling sideways into the road. Automatically, she tensed, bracing for the hardness of the street, but the pain never appeared.

She flew through the air, lifted by strong hands. Sam twisted angrily to admonish Edward, but it was not his arms holding her. Lord Westwood cradled her to his chest, his face contorted with agony. Mr. Reid lay supine on the pavement—wearing a similar grimace—knocked aside when Lord Westwood leapt to catch Sam.

"I have already informed Edward of my capability," she said indignantly, glaring at him.

"I am quite aware of your abilities," Lord Westwood replied, a cheeky grin pulling his lips. He squeezed her tightly and limped down the street again.

"We still have business to resolve," he said to Edward without breaking stride.

Sam wiggled unhappily, frowning at Edward and Mr. Reid over Lord Westwood's shoulder. Mr. Reid shrugged, smiled, and climbed to his feet. He clapped Edward on the back, who muttered objections under his breath. Mr. Reid shrugged again and offered Edward the same cheeky grin.

A gasp drew Sam's attention, her gaze sliding to Lord Westwood's profile. His jaw, set firmly, twitched with each step. A couple of words came to mind as she watched him struggle—stubborn, inflexible, and obstinate—definitely obstinate.

"This is ridiculous." She pushed her hands against his muscular shoulder, trying to slip out of his grasp.

"I am not setting you down," Lord Westwood replied, clutching her closer. He glanced down.

Sam glowered at him, folding her arms in aggravation. He returned her hard stare, his nose millimeters from hers—eyes blazing as they melted into liquid emerald pools of varying layers of annoyance and frustration. Sam exhaled loudly in acquiescence. Breaking their mutual glare, she twisted her head to check Edward's location. He maintained a respectable distance, grumbling at the modified traveling arrangements.

Mr. Reid whispered indistinguishable words of reassurance. His soothing tone and the iron grip on Edward's shoulder prevented Edward from physically ripping Sam out of Lord Westwood's arms.

"Thank you for saving my life," she mumbled begrudgingly, returning her gaze to Lord Westwood.

"That was much better than your first apology to me." He smirked. "Did Edward request that heartfelt sentiment of you?"

"No, though I suspect he will make that suggestion once he inspects your ledgers. He's very keen on proper behavior, and I would like to have the advantage over him, just once." The corner of her mouth pulled.

Lord Westwood raised his eyebrow. "Does that mean you believe me?"

"I believe you lied to me." She shifted again, causing Lord Westwood to readjust his hold, and a moan escaped his lips.

"Not one word," he called over his shoulder to Mr. Reid, who grinned and resumed placating Edward's irritation. Lord Westwood touched his forehead to Sam's. "I lied to save your life."

"I believed you," Sam hissed through clenched teeth. Her eyes moistened, threatening to spill angry tears. Closing her eyes, she took a deep breath, willing the tears away. Opening her eyes, she returned her blazing glare to Lord Westwood. "I'm not pleased with you."

"Nor I with you," Lord Westwood replied. "Did I not ask you to remain on the estate?"

"You did." She dropped her eyes to the street, watching the footpath shuffle slowly beneath her, and her fury deflated. This whole ordeal could have been avoided if she had just listened to Lord Westwood, not that she would ever admit that to him.

He pulled her chin back toward his face. "Do you not think I had reason to make that request of you?"

Of course, he had reason.

"Why do you want to marry me?" She bit her lip. Lord Westwood's cruel words had slashed scars through her heart.

Halting the crawling convoy, he tipped Sam's chin until they were nose to nose again. His burning green eyes captured hers with unparalleled intensity.

"I love you, foolish woman. If you can't remember anything else, remember that."

His mouth descended with the same passion he spoke with, demanding immediate satisfaction. Sam melted, wrapping her arms around his neck tightly, pulling him nearer. Her fingers twined in his hair, and a satisfied growl rumbled in Lord Westwood's throat. His lips nibbled the lightest of kisses on the corner of her mouth, and a tremor vibrated through her body.

"I hope this is not an indication of how you will respond to my future requests," he said as he pulled away.

"You seem extremely confident about your forthcoming role in my life," Sam replied breathlessly, leaning her head against his shoulder.

"I am." Resuming his slow pace, he took a misstep off the

pavement, and pain flashed across his features, the playfulness replaced by agony.

"Lord Westwood, I must insist you put me down before you injure yourself further." Sam struggled again, kicking her legs.

"I'm quite satisfied with your current location, Miss Hastings." Grinning wickedly, Lord Westwood responded by tightening his grip. "It allows me to keep a close watch on you, which apparently is a full-time occupation."

"Now, I'm an occupation?"

"More like a delightful diversion." He nuzzled her neck, sending a cascade of shivers down her back.

"Benjamin, I have no idea what quality you possess that gives you the ability to influence the fairer sex. Kindly stop endeavoring to seduce my sister until you can prove your intentions are honorable. I have not approved your continued engagement." Edward increased his pace, but Mr. Reid reacted quicker, strategically situating himself between Edward and his brother, giving Sam a jovial wink.

Sam smiled at Mr. Reid. "My brother has other ideas regarding the safety of my present position."

"Indeed," Edward bit off. "Benjamin, may we proceed with the task at hand?"

"Certainly," Lord Westwood replied with an obliging tone. He turned up the stairs to his townhouse, balancing Sam carefully in his arms. Unable to prevent herself, Sam pressed her face against the open collar of his shirt, inhaling his intoxicating scent, her eyes closing as her head spun.

"Have I ever told you that you are extremely distracting?" she whispered against his throat.

"On occasion," he replied, brushing his lips across her hair.

She moaned, nestling closer. "This is not an indication of my forgiveness."

"I would never make that presumption." Lord Westwood grinned, pushing open the door.

Whatever Mr. Davis thought regarding his employer's unexpected, ghastly appearance, he kept to himself. The butler spent his time fussing over Sam after Lord Westwood deposited her gently in the chair nearest the fireplace. He lingered near her for a moment, his fingers brushing softly against her cheek, circling the bruise carefully.

After muttering quick instructions to Mr. Davis, Lord Westwood led Edward and Mr. Reid to his desk. He gestured to the vacant chair, which Edward claimed after a silent battle with Mr. Reid, who took residence at Edward's shoulder. The three men perused the ledgers for proof of solvency, which must have been impressive since Edward murmured his assent after a few moments of research.

Glancing up at Sam, Mr. Reid grinned and winked. "It is a relief to learn I may continue my lecherous behavior."

Sam giggled.

"Thomas!" Edward scolded. "Samantha does not need to hear of your exploits."

"But they are so intriguing."

"Drink this," Mr. Davis said, startling Sam as he handed her a cup of steaming liquid. "I'm not quite sure what Mr. Morris gave you, but this should help alleviate some of the less pleasant symptoms."

Sam accepted the cup gratefully and took a tentative sip. The warm broth tasted sweet, sliding down her throat, easing her churning stomach. "Thank you," she said, taking a second, larger sip.

Lord Westwood appeared in place of Mr. Davis. He dragged a nearby armchair closer, so the arm touched Sam's chair. Wearily, he rubbed his forehead, leaving a streak of soot across his skin. His gaze lifted to the desk, watching Edward and Mr. Reid argue, sidetracked into a debate about appropriate female topics of conversation, then he turned his eyes to Sam.

"I would like to know the reason you decided to disregard my wishes for your safety." This question quieted the room. Edward and Mr. Reid paused mid-conversation, turning toward Sam.

Sam took a deep breath and set the teacup down.

"I found the threatening note from Franklin."

"I'm aware of that," Lord Westwood replied, holding up his hand to prevent Edward from interrupting. Edward pressed his lips together firmly, his narrowed gaze indicating his displeasure.

"How did you know?" Sam asked, ignoring her brother's mounting anger.

"I discovered your hiding place."

Sam glanced at her hands. "I was in a hurry."

"Did you already know you were going to the townhouse when I spoke with you this morning?" he asked, his voice soft.

"No." Sam shook her head adamantly. "I didn't."

"How did you come to find the note?" Edward asked, unable to remain silent. He rose and crossed the room, kneeling next to Sam's chair.

Her gaze slid to him. "I discovered it on the floor outside my chamber this morning."

"My chamber." Lord Westwood corrected her with an amused grin.

Edward scowled.

"Yes," Sam answered with a small smile. "I found it right after you stormed off."

"I did not storm," Edward bristled.

"Yes, you did, directly after calling me a child."

Mr. Reid choked on his laughter.

"Please continue, Miss Hastings." Lord Westwood silenced his brother with a wave of his hand.

"I opened the door to apologize for my inexcusable manners," Sam said, fluttering her eyelashes. Edward rolled his eyes. "The note was on the carpet. I picked it up but couldn't find Edward to return it."

"Why did you not relinquish the note to me?" Lord Westwood asked, his face expressionless.

Sam bit her lip, trying to communicate the truth behind the actual location of the letter.

"I'm sorry. I didn't think to seek you out. Franklin arrived unexpectedly to repair Father's watch. I hastily shoved the missive under the inkwell, so no one else would discover it, then raced downstairs. When Franklin opened the back of Father's watch, a scrap of paper fell out." Sam looked directly into Edward's eyes. "It was in Father's handwriting."

Edward placed his hand over Sam's arm, careful not to disturb its current position. "Do you remember what he wrote?"

"Fortune lays forgotten in a house that is not a home. Treasure waits for discovery in a place Sammie has outgrown." She closed her eyes as she recited the words.

"I have no idea what that means," Edward said. He and Lord Westwood exchanged a glance.

"I do." Sam stared earnestly at Edward. "Franklin explained the treasure referred to in the poem is the Hastings family heirlooms, like Mother's diamond and sapphire necklace."

"Did you figure out the rest of the clue?" Lord Westwood leaned forward in his chair, a muffled groan accompanying the movement.

Sam nodded. "Lucy helped me."

Lord Westwood's face cleared suddenly. "The dollhouse... Lucy told me you went to the townhouse to fetch her dollhouse."

"The dollhouse which used to belong to me when I was a little girl."

"Why did you not wait for me to return?" Edward asked, pain in his voice. "We could have searched together."

"He threatened to kill you," Sam replied, twisting her fingers into knots.

A tear rolled down Edward's cheek. He quickly turned away, pressing his palm into his cheek as he focused his attention on the crackling fire.

"Yes, I am well aware of what kind of woman I agreed to marry," Lord Westwood murmured, his eyes flicking to Edward.

"Where is the dollhouse right now?" Mr. Reid asked. He snapped the ledgers closed, setting them carefully on the desk.

Sam thought for a moment. "I left it under Mother's desk at the townhouse. I'm not sure what happened to it during the struggle with Franklin."

"It should still be somewhere in the study. Miss Hastings, perhaps it would be best if you and Benjamin rest while Edward and I fetch the dollhouse," Mr. Reid suggested as he rounded the desk.

"I would prefer Sammie stays with me." Edward corrected Mr. Reid's plan with a glare at Lord Westwood. "Not all your intentions are honorable."

"I'm not waiting here. I figured out the clue, so I'm going with you." Sam rose from the chair, wobbled, and collapsed backward onto the plush cushion.

"You're too weak to walk," Edward said, a smug grin on his face. Sam stuck her tongue out.

"Mr. Davis can drive all of us in my coach," Lord Westwood replied and stood, holding his hand out to Sam.

Edward shot him a dark look, rising and holding his arm out as well. It was Lord Westwood she favored, leaning against his muscular frame as she recovered her equilibrium. He snaked one arm around her waist, holding her closer than necessary. When she laid her forehead on his chest, Edward nearly bit his tongue in half.

"You are not carrying me," Sam stated firmly, her voice muffled against Lord Westwood's shirt.

He laughed, lightly stroking her hair. "I had no intention of asking."

Sam looked up at him with a smile and extricated herself from his grasp. "I'm pleased to hear that."

She gingerly inched across the study, unsteady on her legs, her eyes focused on the open door. As she reached out her hand to grasp the door frame, a wave of dizziness overtook her. She froze, breathing deeply.

"Stubborn, is she not?" Edward muttered.

"Indeed, she is," Sam replied over her shoulder, stepping into the hallway, her hand outstretched for the nearest table.

Lord Westwood appeared behind her, sweeping her into his arms without comment, and continued his labored pace toward the front door, Sam tucked against his upper body.

"Put me down," she commanded with as much dignity as she could muster in her current position. "Did I not just state you wouldn't be carrying me?"

"You did." Lord Westwood dropped a feathery kiss on her forehead. "However, I told you I had no intention of asking permission."

Edward snarled, his displeasure echoing in the hallway.

"Would you please stop antagonizing my brother?" Sam jerked her head toward Edward.

Lord Westwood leaned closer, his warm breath tickling her lips.

"I enjoy it."

He positioned her carefully in the coach before climbing in and taking residence on the bench across from Sam. Edward followed in a huff and plopped next to Sam, scowling at Lord

Westwood. Mr. Reid, taking the last empty seat, pulled the door closed with a flourish and winked at Sam.

She giggled, and Edward and Lord Westwood rolled their eyes, a simultaneous display of annoyance. Within a few minutes, the coach arrived at the Hastings townhouse. It was eerily quiet. An involuntary shudder traveled the length of Sam's spine.

Something felt off.

"Sammie, I want you to remain in the coach while we fetch the dollhouse," Edward said.

He must feel it, too...

"Mr. Davis will wait with you," Lord Westwood added as he climbed from the coach. He nodded to the aforementioned man, who scrambled down from the driver's seat and stood guard outside the carriage.

The three men entered the house cautiously, calling out Mr. Walton's name. There was no response. Shouts echoed from inside the house. Edward's ashen face appeared first. He sprinted to the carriage, his chest heaving, eyes wide.

"Sammie, I want you to leave right now."

"What happened?" she asked, anxiously peering around Edward.

"Now," he replied, shoving Mr. Davis toward the front of the coach.

"Miss Hastings shouldn't travel alone. Someone must go with her." Mr. Reid yelled from the front door of the townhouse.

"I will." Lord Westwood slid past him and stumbled down the steps, flashes of agony dancing across his brow.

"Edward." Sam tried to climb from the coach, but Edward pushed her back into the cabin with more force than he intended. She bounced once on the cushion and propelled herself forward toward Edward.

"Sammie, for once, please listen to me," he pleaded, swinging the coach door.

"What happened?" she repeated her fearful question, her foot blocking Edward's attempt to close the door.

"Mr. Walton has been killed." Lord Westwood huffed as he rounded the rear of the coach. He leaned against the rear wheel, bent at the waist in anguish.

"Benjamin!" Edward wrenched his head in the direction of Sam's pale face, peeping out the open door.

"She's bound to discover the news when Mr. Walton doesn't return with us, Edward," Lord Westwood slashed his arm toward the townhouse.

Sam scrambled out of the coach. "Where's Franklin?"

"He vanished."

"Benjamin!" Edward's visage purpled.

"Edward." Sam pulled his face toward hers, interrupting the impending argument. "Franklin told me someone else helped him set the townhouse fire, and I heard another voice at Franklin's lodgings."

All color drained from Edward's face.

"Can you remember anything about the second man?"

Sam shook her head despondently, fuzzy memories obscured by Franklin's drug.

"We need to move quickly."

Mr. Reid appeared with the dollhouse tucked under his arm.

"Edward, they can't be more than ten minutes ahead of us. With Morris injured, they shouldn't be too difficult to locate."

"Sammie, do you remember where Franklin's lodgings were?" Edward asked, his gaze sliding back to her.

Sam shook her head.

"No matter," Mr. Reid said. "We will find them."

Edward pinched the bridge of his nose, his internal struggle violent. Sighing, he turned to his left.

"Benjamin, as the most injured of the three of us, I must ask you to travel with Samantha to your mother's estate. Your presence will only hinder our search."

Lord Westwood bristled at Edward's statement.

"It's against my better judgment to allow this unchaperoned activity; however, the situation calls for lax decorum." Edward stepped to Lord Westwood's shoulder, narrowed his eyes, and growled, "Whatever you do to her, I will do to you, understand?"

Lord Westwood clamped his jaw tightly in annoyance and didn't respond. Sam wondered what waspish comment he chose to swallow. Considering Edward's current emotional state, Lord Westwood's silence was wise.

"Samantha, please climb back into the coach and close the door *completely*."

Sam complied without protest. The door swung closed with a tiny click, and all sound was cut off. Through the carriage window, she could see the three men talking animatedly and wondered what other pieces of information Edward was keeping from her. She very much doubted she would be able to pry the information from Lord Westwood during their unsupervised drive to the country.

Alone with Benjamin. The words danced happily through the empty cabin, despite Edward's creative threat and Franklin's disappearance.

No, she firmly told herself. This was not the time for passion, but she couldn't deny the montage of memories filtering through her consciousness. Sam bit her lip in anticipation, twitching anxiously. She tried to distract her mind by focusing on the ash-covered tips of her shoes, but her mind replayed the previous evening's pleasurable activities with Benjamin.

"You are in extreme danger," she stated, her voice echoing in the coach. "Franklin tried to kill you this morning." She tried to realign her brain with the peril of their situation. It refused. Her eyes unconsciously rose to seek Lord Westwood.

She caught him watching her over Edward's shoulder, his head tilted with an amused expression. Could he read the carnal thoughts preoccupying her mind? He winked; he knew. A blush exploding across Sam's face, she jumped away from the window, anticipation crawling down her spine.

Unchaperoned...

CHAPTER 8

"We'll discuss this matter later." Edward yanked open the carriage door, gesturing to the empty bench, and placed his other hand on Benjamin's back, shoving him toward the coach. "My sister is in need of rest, and you look a frightful sight."

"Do I?" Benjamin asked, turning to Miss Hastings, whose pale face peeked out the open carriage door.

"You are..." She paused, debating the word. "Horrific."

Edward snorted.

Benjamin offered a half-smile. Climbing slowly into the carriage, he settled himself on the opposite bench with a grunt. Thomas slid the dollhouse along the coach's floor, stuffing it under the bench as his eyes flicked up to Benjamin, no humor lighting his face. He bobbed his head once, a sharp movement, which was returned by Benjamin.

In case I never see you again...

Thomas vanished.

"We will meet you at your mother's estate." Edward grabbed Benjamin's arm, twisting it toward him. "Take care of her."

"I will."

Edward turned toward Miss Hastings, taking her hand. She dropped from the bench to the carriage floor, wrapping her arms around him.

"Please be careful, Edward," she whispered in his ear. "You're the only brother I have."

"I will see you soon." Patting her arm, Edward untangled himself from her grip and slammed the carriage door.

Benjamin lit an oil lamp and hung it from a hook inside the coach. Sliding the curtains closed, he leaned back and groaned, adjusting his leg and combing his fingers through his hair.

"Horrific, am I?" he teased, lifting his heated gaze to Miss Hastings. She sank her teeth into her lip.

The air vibrated between them, tensely wound passion threatening to incinerate them. The moment the carriage lurched forward, Miss Hastings flew off her bench. Benjamin opened his arms and enveloped her, crushing her body against his chest, his arms wrapped tightly around her waist. She straddled him, accidentally jarring his left leg. Benjamin cussed, and she froze, unsure if she should move.

"I'm sorry," she whispered, her blue eyes wide. She tentatively laid her hand on his shoulder. "I don't know where you are injured."

"Everywhere." Benjamin redistributed her weight, touching his forehead to hers. "But holding you eases the pain." His thumb skated across her lower lip, and her mouth parted, her teeth nipping lightly on the pad of his finger.

"Edward will be extremely irritated with you," Miss Hastings murmured as Benjamin tipped her chin.

"Let him." His mouth brushed across her lips.

She was safe, here in his arms, and he would never let her go again. Ever. Morris would pay with his life for what he did to Miss Hastings.

Growling, he drew her closer, the heat between them burning through his clothes. His lips devoured every visible inch of her skin, nibbling along her collarbone, over her throat, and down to the swell of her breast. She shifted her hips, grinding against his erection.

His hands wandered down her body, slipping under the hem of her skirt. Sliding one finger up her leg, he caressed the soft skin and skimmed up her thigh. His finger sought her warmth, slipping between the slit in her drawers, and brushed against her sex.

"Please." She panted against his mouth, rocking her hips against his invading hand.

Benjamin captured her lower lip and bit lightly as he thrust his finger deeper. She quivered against him, crying out in ecstasy. His mouth captured hers, swallowing her screams as she trembled uncontrollably.

Unbuttoning his trousers, he slid them low on his hips, freeing his erection. Grasping her hips, he lifted her, angling himself between her legs, and lowered her onto his lap, inch by inch. She gasped as he sheathed himself completely. Sliding his hands leisurely down her back, he gripped her firmly and pulled hard against his hips.

"Benjamin," Miss Hastings moaned, her body falling into his guided rhythm. His lips danced across her soft skin, etching a trail of fire on her neck.

"I should make you suffer for all the worry you caused me this morning," he murmured. "Maybe you'll learn to listen to me."

"Please," she pleaded, her voice straining as she ground her hips into him.

"Whatever you desire, my lady." Tugging down the edge of her chemise with his teeth, his mouth grazed her breast, drawing another moan from her lips. Grabbing her hips, Benjamin thrust deep, driving into her until she came apart.

His name echoed through the coach as she released, and Benjamin followed quickly, burying himself in one thrust as he tumbled over the edge. Wrapping her tightly in his arms, he shuddered several times before his breathing returned to normal. Miss Hastings collapsed onto his chest, drawing a finger over the sensitive skin peeking out from between his shirt collar, and sighed, her eyes fluttering close.

"Infinitely better than my last carriage ride," he said, pressing his mouth against her forehead.

BENJAMIN'S EYES SNAPPED OPEN, his arms tensing around Miss Hastings. She was curled into his chest. *Safe.* He twitched the curtain aside. The carriage bounced down the drive toward Westwood Estate. Thankfully, the engagement luncheon had dispersed several hours prior.

"Have we arrived?"

He glanced down. Miss Hastings gazed up at him with a sleepy smile and nuzzled closer, shivering from the chilly air seeping under the carriage door. His mouth finding hers, her eager response reignited his earlier passion. Hooking her arms around his neck, she pressed her body into him, and Benjamin lifted her onto his lap, his arms wrapped low around her waist. He brushed the lightest of kisses across her bruised lips, which parted expectantly.

"I fear this will be the last of our privacy for a while," he said, pressing a final kiss on her mouth.

A cacophony of sound exploded from outside the carriage as Benjamin spoke those words. Miss Hastings's gaze flicked to the closed coach door, her mouth pulling into a grimace.

"Miss Hastings, I must warn you." Depositing her on the bench next to him, he lifted her hand to his mouth. "Over the next few weeks, I shall endeavor to seduce you every chance I encounter."

The carriage door was ripped open, and Benjamin was yanked from the coach, swallowed by a crowd of ladies, both old and young. They shunted him aside with several clucks concerning his haggard appearance. Miss Hastings, they favored with many exclamations of shock and sympathy regarding her appalling condition. Benjamin wondered how the exuberant well-wishers would affect Miss Hastings' psyche. She looked overwhelmed by the concentrated attention. Only Miss Clemens remained on the exterior of the group, awkwardly out of place as she hovered near Benjamin.

"Thank you for finding Miss Hastings, Lord Westwood," Miss Clemens whispered shyly before an arm snaked out of the huddle and sucked her into the group of women.

Edward's wife succeeded in convincing the other ladies to allow Miss Hastings to climb from the carriage without assistance. However, she stumbled on the footstep, tumbling forward into the group, and several hands righted her—none of them his, he mused sourly as he watched the ladies fret over Miss Hastings. She disappeared in a sea of colorful frocks, carried toward the house.

Mr. Davis materialized by Benjamin's side. "Miss Hastings will be well cared for." His gravelly voice was surprisingly filled with emotion.

Benjamin didn't flinch at the sudden appearance of his manservant. He did, however, arch an eyebrow. "Sentiment, Mr. Davis? I'm surprised by your attachment."

"She is to be the future lady of the house, is she not, my Lord?"

"She is." Benjamin nodded, catching sight of Miss Hastings' chestnut hair in the light from the lanterns hanging along the veranda. She turned to search him out, offering a tiny wave before the gaggle ushered her into the entrance hall.

"A fine choice, my lord," Mr. Davis added nonchalantly.

"Were you concerned regarding my ability to select an acceptable companion?" Benjamin chuckled, glancing to his right.

"I'm no longer in doubt as to the state of your mind," Mr. Davis replied as he gathered the horses' reins, then climbed onto the driver's bench. Before driving the horses to the stables, he allowed one final comment to slip. "I would have been less satisfied to be reacquainted with my prior employer."

Silent, Benjamin watched the sun slide slowly below the horizon. He reflected on Mr. Davis' final remark. Even the servants disliked the family. Mr. Davis refused to speak about his previous employment, making Benjamin wonder what had driven Mr. Davis to resign from the Shirely household. Benjamin's thoughts sifted through the day's atrocious events, a frown pulling the corner of his mouth.

Would he have risked his life for Miss Shirely?

"You seem perturbed," his mother called from the veranda, her silhouette flickering in the lamplight.

"I was unaware you could observe my expression from such a great distance," he replied, strolling toward her.

She laughed. "Benjamin, you've been standing in the exact same position for the last five minutes. Something is on your mind."

The whinny of horses caught Benjamin's attention. His eyes scanned the drive, straining in the darkness to make out two shadows approaching through the gate. A few minutes later, Thomas and Edward appeared, wearing grim expressions. Thomas shook his head as he dismounted, stalking the last several meters to Benjamin's side, and blew out an exasperated sigh. Benjamin glanced at the veranda, but his mother had discreetly disappeared. Edward slid from his horse and approached, his jaw set.

"Thomas and I have been discussing a situation."

Thomas remained unusually silent, an indication of a disagreement between the two men.

"Your brother believes we need to inform the female members of our families of the circumstances regarding our safety."

"And you are in disagreement with this suggestion?" Benjamin asked, his voice even. Edward would be against anything which involved telling his sister the truth.

"I am." Edward folded his arms.

"Miss Hastings is already aware of the impending danger, having experienced much trauma at Morris' hand," Benjamin replied, using the same logical tone he'd employed in their youth whenever he wanted to convince Edward of a particular course of action. "She looks frightful, and the ladies are bound to question her injuries."

Several emotions rolled across Edward's face—denial, anger, and lastly, guilt.

"I know."

"You can't protect everyone unless they are localized." Benjamin indicated the house. "We need to remain here until Morris is captured."

"The ladies will want to know why they have been restricted to the country estate," Thomas interjected.

Edward scowled at him. "My daughters do not need nightmares."

"He isn't suggesting we scare the children." Benjamin placed his hand on Edward's shoulder. "However, your wife deserves to know the truth."

"As does your mother," Edward replied, smacking away Benjamin's arm.

"We told her."

"What about Aunt Abigail?" Thomas' gaze shifted to the house, watching silhouettes dance in front of the parlor window.

"Mother would have informed Aunt Abigail," Benjamin replied. Thomas snickered.

"Even so, we should extend the invitation to Mrs. Stanton as well as Miss Clemens," Edward said. "We don't know how far Franklin's hatred will extend. However, we only reveal the most important details, agreed?"

"Miss Clemens knows more than you think," Benjamin said, struggling to keep his mouth from twitching into a wry grin. Edward looked as if he was going to murder Benjamin.

"Can no one keep a secret?" Edward threw his hands in the air.

"Nope." Thomas draped a friendly arm over Edward's shoulders, leading him toward the house. "Do you suppose there's any food left over from the luncheon?"

Rolling his eyes, Edward glanced back at Benjamin. "How can you have dealt with this for almost thirty years?"

"It has been extremely trying at times." Grinning, Benjamin limped after them, reaching them when Edward slowed his gait. Thomas punched him in the arm.

As they entered the house, Mrs. Hastings sailed to Edward, nearly knocking him over in her relief. He wrapped his arms around her, swinging her in a wide circle to maintain his balance. Shamelessly, he kissed her, a display of affection Benjamin rarely witnessed from the proper couple. He ached for Miss Hastings.

"I would like to have a discussion with the members of both families," Edward said as he set his wife on her feet. He refused to release her, one arm remaining locked around his wife's waist. "Where is Sammie?"

"She's in the dining room with Lady Westwood and Mrs. Stanton. They are plying her with food." Mrs. Hastings sighed as she laid her head against Edward's chest.

"Excellent. I thought I might faint from starvation."

Thomas bowed, then strode down the corridor toward the wafting smell of food.

Edward and Mrs. Hastings followed, whispering soft sentiments to each other. Benjamin lagged, his eyes scanning the courtyard one last time before he closed the front door.

"Do you know the length of our stay?" Mr. Davis asked unobtrusively from the shadows of the entrance hall.

"Indefinitely," Benjamin replied, wrenching the lock.

"I shall need to travel to town tomorrow to collect some necessities," Mr. Davis said, stepping forward.

"Meet with me the morning prior to your departure. I have an errand for you." Benjamin turned toward him.

Producing the dollhouse, Mr. Davis held out the grimy toy. "I collected this from the carriage."

Benjamin nodded his approval. "Place that on my desk in the study."

"Yes, my Lord." Mr. Davis bowed and retreated, leaving Benjamin to hobble across the entrance hall to the dining room.

Miss Hastings' eyes instantly rose to Benjamin's face when he entered the room. He offered her a lopsided grin and limped to the foot of the table where the only empty chair remained. Edward sat at the head of the table, to his right and left his wife and sister, respectively. Aunt Abigail and his mother conversed animatedly to Benjamin's left. Thomas, seated to Benjamin's right, mumbled something around a mouthful of food and stabbed his fork at the two ladies across from him. Benjamin smirked.

Between Thomas and Miss Hastings, Miss Clemens sat quietly, picking at her plate, invisible in her misery. She furtively glanced sideways at Thomas several times but remained mute. Miss Hastings leaned over and whispered something to the younger girl, who smiled gratefully in return.

Edward cleared his throat, and silence blanketed the room. He looked over the expectant faces and spoke solemnly.

"I realize I have been less than forthcoming regarding the recent events affecting our families. It has been pointed out that perhaps the lack of information may have led to Sammie's abduction."

Thomas bent over his plate, shoveling food into his mouth as quickly as possible, refusing to look at Edward. Benjamin glanced at Thomas oddly, wondering what other parts he missed from the unpleasant conversation between his brother and Edward. Out of the corner of his eye, Benjamin noticed Miss Hastings placed her hand on Miss Clemens' trembling arm.

"Therefore, I have a few pieces of information I'm compelled to share. First, I wish to express my gratitude to Lord Westwood and Mr. Reid for bringing Samantha back to us alive." Edward paused and nodded to both men. An unspoken conversation occurred among them, a permanently forged connection between the families—Edward had given his official consent to the marriage. He cleared his throat and resumed. "Second, the person responsible for Samantha's abduction, the attempt on my life, and the murder of my father was Mr. Franklin Morris. We have alerted the authorities."

"As well as the society papers," Thomas said, causing Edward to wince.

Ah, that was the other part of the disagreement. Thomas realized the only way to protect Miss Hastings' reputation from vicious gossip—regarding her absence from the engagement party and her unchaperoned escapade—was to admit to the kidnapping. It was not a terrible scheme. By including the ton in their tragedy, they gained a lot of supporters—and their eyes. Edward, being an extremely private individual, would have vehemently rejected that plan. Benjamin was shocked the discussion hadn't come to blows. He glanced at Thomas, who returned to his plate without another word.

"It's important we are vigilant until Franklin is brought to justice. Also, Samantha has informed us Franklin was not working alone. There is an unknown person who assisted with his escape this afternoon, and in doing so,"—Edward paused, his gaze sliding over the faces at the table—"killed Mr. Walton."

There were several gasps, including Mrs. Hastings, who paled considerably. Miss Hastings continued to pat Miss Clemens' arm reassuringly, a monochromic rhythm of tranquility. The younger girl looked on the verge of falling out of her chair.

"I'm thankful everyone realizes the severity of the situation in which we now find ourselves. With the upcoming union between Benjamin and Samantha, both families are in grave danger. Therefore, we,"—he indicated himself along with Benjamin and Thomas—"believe it would be best for everyone to remain here."

"I would be delighted to have everyone as my guests." Benjamin's mother beamed. "We have more than enough rooms to accommodate everyone."

"Are we to remain prisoners on this estate indefinitely?" Aunt Abigail asked, her wizened eyes narrowed.

"Not at all," Edward replied with an easy smile. "We're merely asking, for your safety, you don't travel outside these grounds alone for the next few weeks."

"I have a busy social schedule to uphold," Aunt Abigail replied, adding a thump of her cane.

His mother snorted and demurely covered the sound with a ladylike cough. "I regret to inform you, my dear Abigail, you may have to forgo some of those activities."

"Especially now that Mr. Flannery is mucking about with

a loaded rifle," Benjamin muttered, shoving away his plate of food.

His mother's head whipped up. "Why is Mr. Flannery wandering around with a weapon? I heard his son was caring for him."

"He is," Benjamin replied, adding a curt nod when Thomas pantomimed eating Benjamin's food. "I had an encounter with the two of them earlier today. Aidan offered their assistance."

"Was that wise?" Concern seeped through his mother's question. "Mr. Flannery has had an extremely difficult time since the death of his wife."

"Touched," Aunt Abigail said, pressing her fingertips to the side of her head. "Poor man, he loved Noreen deeply."

"Alana is returning to assist Aidan with that particular situation," Benjamin said quietly, his gaze flicking to Thomas, who flinched, his fork scraping the plate.

Thomas glanced up from his hunched position, his eyes quickly scanning the table, then his gaze skipped to Benjamin. A myriad of wild emotions danced across Thomas' face, threatening to unravel him. Without speaking, Thomas bent his head and put another forkful to his mouth. Mechanically scraping and chewing, the resolute activity took most of Thomas' concentration. Perturbed, Benjamin looked away from his brother's forced façade. Alana's timing was dreadful.

"Cousin Alana taught me how to shoot one summer," Miss Hastings whispered noisily to Miss Clemens, whose brown eyes lit with delight.

"Perhaps we can convince her to instruct me as well." She smiled shyly.

"A wonderful way to pass the time," Aunt Abigail said with a wink. "How delightfully inappropriate."

"We will not be shirking our social obligations either,"

Edward added with a slight frown, owing to the direction of the conversation. "The whole of society is aware of Franklin's crimes. It's highly doubtful he will attempt anything in public."

Miss Hastings glanced at Edward suspiciously. "What upcoming social obligations do we have?"

"The Shirely masque is six days' time," Miss Clemens murmured to her lap.

Miss Hastings groaned, slumping in her chair. Benjamin caught her eye and winked, causing the delightful blush he thoroughly enjoyed. Quickly, she glanced down, hiding her rouged face.

Thomas looked up from his near-empty plate, his face a mixture of confusion and curiosity. "I was unaware you enjoyed social functions, Miss Clemens."

Miss Clemens blushed from Thomas' direct attention. "I don't, Mr. Reid. However, since we have received an invitation, it would be impolite to decline."

"I wonder if her fingers caught fire while addressing those invitations," Miss Hastings muttered, just loud enough for the entire table to hear. Miss Clemens giggled.

"Samantha!" Mrs. Hastings admonished. "Your opinion of Miss Shirely doesn't need to be shared with your elders."

"Even when they agree with you," Abigail said, smirking.

Miss Hastings didn't respond. She set her fork next to her plate, her skin paling, and her eyes rolled. Benjamin was on his feet before she slipped out of the chair.

"What did Franklin give her?" Edward bellowed as he flew to his sister's side.

"Mr. Davis thought it might be an overdose of laudanum," Benjamin replied grimly, lifting Miss Hastings from the floor. "However, the effects should have worn off by now."

She stirred. Opening her eyes, Miss Hastings seemed

surprised to find herself in Benjamin's arms again. "I would like some fresh air," she mumbled thickly.

Edward reached out, but Benjamin twisted away, refusing to release his hold. "I will take her," he growled.

Mrs. Hastings appeared beside her husband and placed a restraining hand on his arm. "Let him go, Edward."

Miss Hastings gagged. Benjamin spun in haste, navigating the corridor in mere seconds. Ripping open the door, a cool breeze smacked him in the face as he raced outside. Gently, he set her down on the wooden steps, and she took several deep breaths with her eyes squeezed shut. He dropped beside her and wrapped an arm over her trembling shoulders.

"If you would rather decline the Shirely ball, I would happily make our excuses."

A faint smile crossing her lips, Miss Hastings opened her eyes. Tilting her head, she contemplated his words. "I would be extremely disappointed to sacrifice an opportunity for a moonlit walk with my fiancé."

"Your guardian may not agree to those terms," Benjamin said, capturing her hand and drawing little patterns in her palm.

Miss Hastings shivered and leaned against him. "I thought," she paused and choked on a tiny sob. "I thought I would never see you again."

"I will always come for you," he replied, cupping her face.

"Is that a promise?"

"Yes," he rumbled and pressed his lips to her mouth. She sighed his name, sliding her arms around his neck, and drew him closer.

He knew to expect the interruption, yet although it was inevitable, he was still irritated when Thomas' buoyant voice reverberated from behind them on the veranda.

"If Miss Hastings is feeling better, Edward would like to open the dollhouse."

"Thank you, Thomas." Benjamin ground out his displeasure through clenched teeth. He glared at his brother, who grinned, hovering a respectable distance from them. "We will join you once Miss Hastings has regained her composure."

"I'm well enough to view the contents of the dollhouse." Miss Hastings' wispy voice came from his right.

Thomas snickered and stepped forward to offer his arm. "Allow me to assist you, Miss Hastings."

"Thomas," Benjamin warned menacingly, a rumble growing in his throat.

Thomas held up his hands playfully. "I shall inform Edward of your imminent arrival." He flashed a cheeky grin and disappeared.

Benjamin blew out an exasperated breath. "I suppose we shouldn't keep Edward waiting."

"We could..." Miss Hastings smiled.

Sliding his arms around her waist, he nuzzled his face against her neck, his mouth placing a searing kiss on her throat.

"May I carry you inside, Miss Hastings?"

She pulled away and frowned. "No, you may not, Lord Westwood."

"Ah well," he shrugged and slipped his arms beneath her, lifting her from the steps, "I did ask."

CHAPTER 9

The faded dollhouse sat innocently in the center of Lord Westwood's desk, unaware of the tragedy it had caused. A light coating of soot dusted its peeling roof, falling onto the desk and circling the dollhouse with a morbid gray ring.

Three pairs of eyes looked up as Lord Westwood entered the room. Sam wriggled discontentedly in his arms, her mouth screwed up in frustration. He set her lightly on her feet near the doorway.

"Stay," he murmured, turning to close the door.

Sam rolled her eyes and pushed off the door frame, slogging across the floor. She was halfway to the desk when Lord Westwood caught her, scooping her back into his arms.

"My brother will hear of my displeasure." Sam shoved Lord Westwood's shoulder.

"As your brother has given consent for our marriage, your happiness is no longer his concern." Lord Westwood grinned, placing his forehead to Sam's. "It's mine."

"I'm unhappy." Sam jutted out her chin, folding her arms.

"Noted," Lord Westwood replied, carrying her to the desk. He lowered her to the floor, cupping her elbow to steady her.

"All of this trouble for such a decrepit plaything," Wilhelmina said, wrinkling her nose in disgust. She poked one of the grimy windows.

"It's not the dollhouse itself, but what is hidden inside," Sam replied. The words carved up her raw throat, and her stomach rolled. She leaned forward, planting her hands on the desk, and inhaled slowly. She waved away Edward, who had rounded the desk to place his hand on her back, and lifted her head, turning it toward Wilhelmina. "What you cannot see, what is hidden inside this dollhouse, is our family ancestral jewelry."

Bile rose in her throat. She swallowed. Cobwebs crawled into the corners of her mind, and the world tilted. Reaching behind her, she fumbled for Lord Westwood's hand. He materialized next to her, pushing Edward aside and wrapping a comforting arm around her waist. Sam curled into him, exhaling softly.

Edward's eyes narrowed at their intimacy. Stiffly, he turned toward the desk, struggling to hold his tongue, and focused on the dollhouse.

"How do you propose we open it?" he asked to no one in particular.

"Is there a key?" Wilhelmina asked, glancing at Samantha, her brown eyes hopeful.

Sam shook her head. "It was lost years ago."

"We could smash it open," Edward said, tapping on the roof with his knuckle.

"Lucy would prefer we try to save her dollhouse," Sam replied with a tremor. Lord Westwood's thumb skated over the nape of her neck, drawing small circles over her spine.

"I can open it," Mr. Reid said, winking at Sam as he

rounded the far side of the desk. Humming, he bowed to the dollhouse as one would do prior to a duel.

"Watch this," Lord Westwood whispered in Sam's ear, his mouth sending shivers over her skin.

Edward studied Mr. Reid with a skeptical frown. "Is this one of your less-than-desirable abilities Benjamin warned me about?"

"Could be," Mr. Reid replied absently, his tongue trapped between his teeth.

"It has come in handy on more than one occasion," Lord Westwood murmured, nibbling on her ear. She moaned, the sound drawing Edward's irritated glare.

Clearing her throat, Sam straightened and craned her head toward the desk.

"Mr. Reid, I would be keen to learn that particular skill if you would be a willing instructor."

"Whether he is willing is not the matter under discussion," Edward said, his exasperation seeping through the room.

"Actually," Wilhelmina chimed in, her eyes glowing as she watched Mr. Reid fiddle with the small lock, "I would like to learn as well." She winked at Sam.

"The female members of this family do not need an education in the art of lock picking," Edward roared, purple coloring his face.

"Edward, you sound a bit overwhelmed. Perhaps you would like to lie down." Mr. Reid glanced up from his task with a grin.

The lock clicked, and Edward swallowed his waspish response. Mr. Reid swung open the front of the dollhouse, and the hinges creaked, protesting forced movement after so many years of inactivity. The upstairs was a menagerie of faded furniture and little dolls, sitting forlornly in their abandonment. However, in the downstairs area, crushing the dining room table against a large picture window, was a lady's purse.

"That's Mother's," Edward and Sam said simultaneously.

Edward tugged the velvet bag free, carefully brushing the soot and dust from the sack. Pulling the strings until they loosened, Edward gently opened the top of the purse, then turned the bag over, spilling its contents onto the desk.

"Oh," Wilhelmina breathed, her face coated in brilliant colors.

Sparkling in the candlelight was a mound of jewelry. Necklaces, bracelets, and rings painted rainbows over the study walls and the rooms' inhabitants. In the center of the pile rested the diamond and sapphire necklace Mrs. Hastings wore the evening of her husband's murder.

Sam took a tentative step closer to the desk, reached out slowly, and brushed her fingers over the necklace. Edward laid his arm over her shoulders, drawing her into his embrace and effectively separating Sam from Lord Westwood, who acquiesced his position without complaint.

Sam lifted the necklace, holding it to her throat, and glanced at Edward with gleaming eyes. Franklin wanted the jewelry, and they had it. If they wanted to catch him, they needed a way to communicate that fact to him.

"I have an idea," she said, her voice pitched with exhilaration.

"No!"

Edward's head snapped up. Lord Westwood's palpable anger rolled across the desk like thunder, his dark face focused solely on Sam.

"No!" Lord Westwood repeated, slamming his fist on the desk.

Sam offered him a partial smile and a shrug. "It would work."

"I'm not concerned with the efficacy of your plan." His green eyes flashed. "The answer is no."

"I don't believe I asked for your permission." Sam rose on

her toes, attempting to match Lord Westwood's stature as the air crackled between them.

Edward's head swiveled between Lord Westwood and Sam. "Did I miss something?" he asked Wilhelmina, who shook her head with a similar puzzled expression.

"Actually, Benjamin, it is an excellent idea," Mr. Reid interjected thoughtfully.

Lord Westwood looked as though he would murder his brother where he stood.

"I said it was out of the question."

"Are you forbidding me?" Sam asked with raised eyebrows.

"Careful, Benjamin," Edward warned with a grin, clearly, enjoying Lord Westwood's frustration.

"You will not find the situation as amusing in a few moments once you grasp the details of her plan," Lord Westwood replied, his voice thick with anger. He glared at Sam, who returned his hard stare unblinkingly.

"It is my life!" Sam stamped her foot. The corner of Lord Westwood's mouth twitched. He was laughing at her! She longed to strike his smug face, her annoyed fingers curling in response, but she settled for a seething glare.

"If your brother agrees to your proposal, I will withdraw my objection," he said, crossing his arms over his chest.

Damn.

"Miss Hastings." Lord Westwood bowed and gestured widely. "We are all patiently waiting to hear the details of your brilliant idea."

Sam took a deep breath and turned her attention to Edward.

"The Shirely masque is approaching."

"We don't expect Franklin to make social appearances in the near future," Edward interrupted.

"I remember the discussion." Sam cut him off, earning a

reproachful glance from Wilhelmina. "However, the accomplice working with Franklin may attend."

"That is a possibility." Edward nodded his agreement. "Please continue."

"The only way to draw Franklin out of hiding would be to show him we have what he wants." Sam laid the necklace on top of the glittering jewelry piled in the center of the desk.

"How do you propose we get the message to Franklin?" Edward touched the largest stone with his fingertip.

"I will wear Mother's necklace to the masque." The words hung between Sam and her brother.

"No." This time the refusal came from Edward.

"Are you forbidding her?" Lord Westwood goaded, his quiet anger unnerving Sam.

"I am." Edward crossed his arms in finality, his stance mirroring Lord Westwood's. earlier posture.

Lord Westwood's eyes slid to Sam. "Your brother has also refused your plan. Would you care to appeal to anyone else?"

"I shall wear it." Wilhelmina's determined voice surprised everyone. Edward's head nearly popped off his shoulders as he whipped around to stare at his wife, his state of shock so great, no sound came from his hanging mouth.

"If both of you wore pieces from the collections, that would definitely garner someone's attention," Mr. Reid said. He had moved to the other side of the desk, out of reach of both Edward and Lord Westwood.

"Thomas, think very carefully about which position you favor," Lord Westwood cautioned, his voice dangerously soft.

"The position which feeds me," Mr. Reid said evenly.

"Wilhelmina and Sammie would be putting their lives at risk," Edward replied, his anger equal to Lord Westwood's.

"Our lives are already in danger." Wilhelmina placed her hand over Edward's. "Our children's lives are in jeopardy. I refuse to spend the rest of my days hiding, sequestered in a country estate. I'm certain you would never allow anything to happen to Samantha or me."

Edward stood quietly for some time, contemplating his wife's arguments. He locked eyes with Lord Westwood and shrugged. "From a logical standpoint..." His voice trailed off as the dark cloud over Lord Westwood's features detonated.

Lord Westwood stormed from the room, slamming the study door behind him. The crash resonated through the house, windows vibrating with his fury. Sam took three steps after him and paused in hesitation. She turned toward Mr. Reid, a question in her eyes. Mr. Reid nodded and disappeared out the study door.

"I should return the dollhouse to Lucy," Wilhelmina said quietly, breaking the silence suffocating the study. She gathered the toy from the desk and followed Mr. Reid's exit.

Edward pulled Sam into a tight hug, resting his chin atop her head. They remained motionless for several minutes, lost in their thoughts, until Edward broke the silence.

"It's exceedingly difficult for a man to allow his heart to walk around outside of his body. He wants to protect it at every moment. Give him time, Sammie. We have asked too much of him. Today was one of the worst days of Benjamin's life, and it may not be the last."

Sam lifted her gaze to Edward. "We must try to capture Franklin before he has the opportunity to murder someone else."

Before he kills you or Benjamin...

"I realize that, Sammie. However, offering yourself as bait, hours after Benjamin risked his life to rescue you is like slapping him in the face. Does his sacrifice mean nothing to you?"

"Of course, it does, Edward. I have already expressed my gratitude."

Edward pursed his lips, and his eyes narrowed as he contemplated Sam's statement.

Realizing her admittance, Sam rushed on. "I can't sit here and wait for Franklin to attack again." Sam swallowed a mournful lump, fighting the tears springing to her eyes, and buried her face in Edward's checked waistcoat. "I cannot endure your death nor his."

"It appears Benjamin cannot bear yours either," Edward replied softly, stroking her head.

"What should I do?" she asked, her muffled voice hiccupped.

"Allow Thomas to handle this matter. He understands Benjamin best." Edward rested his chin on Sam's curls. "You've had an extremely long and trying day, Sammie. Perhaps you should go upstairs to rest."

Nodding, she squeezed Edward once, then released him with a heavy sigh. She dragged toward the study entrance and paused in the doorway.

"Mother hid some letters in her desk. When Franklin and I struggled, they scattered all over the study. Do you think you could send someone to fetch them? I would very much like to read them."

"I will see to it," Edward said, giving Sam a little shove toward the staircase. "Now, please go to bed. At least I will not have to worry about you there."

"Are you certain about that? It is Lord Westwood's chamber," Sam murmured as Edward closed the study door. She darted up the staircase in the moment of silence she was afforded before Edward ripped open the study door.

His thunderous voice rippled through the entrance hall.

"If he touches you, I *will* kill him prior to the wedding, Samantha!"

CHAPTER 10

He watched her sleeping form, restless and tense, evidenced by the continual clenching of her hands as they twisted the sheets. She whimpered, agony echoing around the room, and jerked, flinging a pillow to the floor. Screaming, Miss Hastings shot up, nearly falling from the bed. Her arms flung out, covering her face as she twisted away from her invisible attacker.

"No!"

The word vibrated down his spine, breaking his heart.

He'd failed her.

Lowering her arms, Miss Hastings took several deep breaths to slow her heart rate and swiped the tendrils clinging to her sweaty forehead. He remained motionless in front of the door so as not to startle her. She glanced around the bedroom, her expression a mixture of terror and mortification, gasping when she caught sight of him—bruised and broken—hidden in a half-shadow. He held up a hand, the gesture more to prevent Miss Hastings from flying off the bed than as a greeting.

Interestingly, she obeyed. Pressing her lips together, she

wordlessly waited for an explanation why he chose to visit her at such a late hour, no hint of surprise or shock at his appalling appearance, as though she expected him.

His tongue tied in knots. Pacing in front of the door, he muttered unintelligible words. He jiggled the door handle twice to ensure the door remained locked, then glanced toward the fire, still flickering around a single log. On his third pass, he finally looked at Miss Hastings. She studied him curiously, her hands folded on top of the blanket.

"You are late," she announced, her tone calm but slightly peeved.

He laughed and approached the bed. Sitting on the edge, he lifted her hand to his lips and placed a chaste kiss on the back of her fingers.

"Please accept my most humble apologies for my tardiness, my dear Miss Hastings. I shall endeavor to correct my egregious behavior in the future."

"Thank you," she replied with amusement, tucking the sheet around her hips.

The movement captured his attention. Tilting his head, he regarded her for a moment, her hand trapped under his, its warmth traveling through his fingers.

"Was it a nightmare?"

Darkness passed through her blue eyes, a cloud covering the sun. "Yes," she replied, her face haunted. "How long were you watching me sleep?"

"For some time," he replied and squeezed her hand, falling silent. His thumb rubbed circles on the inside of her wrist, the softness of her skin distracting him. He allowed the memory of other soft parts of her body to divert his thoughts.

A tear landed on his thumb, and his head snapped up. Miss Hastings blinked rapidly and turned her head, staring at the curtains. He reached out and gently tugged her chin until she stared into his eyes, sadness pouring from her eyes.

"When are you leaving?" Her whispered question pierced his heart.

"In a quarter of an hour." He didn't ask how she already knew his intentions.

"Thank you for coming to say goodbye." She tried to remain aloof, but a second fat tear escaped the corner of her eye. Wanting to hide her face, she attempted to turn away again, but he still held her chin.

"Please," she begged softly, and he released her. Twisting away, Miss Hastings scrubbed the betraying tear. She hiccupped but refused to turn back, glaring unhappily at the pillow, which had been flung to the floor during her horrifying dream. He stroked his fingers tenderly over her hand.

"I will only be gone a few days. You will have plenty of activities to distract you. I doubt you will notice my absence."

She lifted her gaze, sinking her teeth into her lower lip. "I will notice."

He brought her hand to his mouth, dropping a light kiss on her palm, then relinquished possession. She shivered and offered him a partial smile, and he grinned in return.

"Had I more time, I would properly take advantage of you in your current state of undress."

"It is not quite morning." Her eyes gleamed.

"I want more than tonight," he replied softly, brushing his lips over her forehead. "I want forever." Rising with conviction, he walked slowly to the door, each step carrying him further and further away from her. Resting his hand on the door handle, he paused and glanced back. "Tell me not to leave."

"You will not listen," Miss Hastings replied, eerily calm.

"I know." He smiled, a rueful crook of his lips. "Tell me, anyway."

"Please stay."

"I cannot," he replied heavily, watching her heart shatter.

He couldn't turn away from her pain, nor could he return to her side. He stood frozen, conflicted.

"Benjamin."

He was losing his battle to remain disconnected. That one word—his name—was a whisper from heaven. He could stay. He could wait for Morris to show his hand, as Thomas suggested earlier that evening. In doing so, Benjamin would spend many blissful hours in the pursuit of seduction. The idea was exceedingly tempting.

Yet... he would not.

He couldn't allow Miss Hastings to place herself in such a precarious situation. Her stubborn temperament, so much like his, gave him no other option. She would move forward with her dangerous proposal to tempt Morris out of hiding. If it cost her life, Benjamin would morph into Mr. Flannery's twin, madly searching the hillsides for Miss Hastings' spirit, drawn by her scent, her whispered voice—forever bound to her memory.

"Benjamin," she called again, her voice sensing his hesitation, feeling his need.

His wild eyes raked over the girl residing in his bed, the heat rising in his veins simmering precariously. She possessed the power to force him to forgo his quest. Immobile, fighting his desires, he realized Miss Hastings knew. An invisible chain linked them—he would not survive without her.

Thoughts shifted mercurially across his features. Miss Hastings watched the migration thoughtfully, immobile in her contemplation. Folding her hands in her lap, she tilted her head, capturing his gaze until the smoldering heat growing between them threatened to erupt. She nodded her consent.

"Do you know where to find Franklin?"

The corner of Benjamin's mouth pulled up at her question, relief ebbing into his veins and releasing him from purgatory. He stepped forward from the shadows.

"We received information claiming he was hiding east of here on an old family farm."

"You heard this from a reliable source?" she asked, arching a skeptical eyebrow.

Benjamin grinned faintly. She sounded very much like Edward.

"We believe the letter is truthful."

"We?"

"Mr. Davis and myself."

"What does Edward believe?" she asked, curiosity lighting her face.

"Edward would prefer not to spend his time chasing rumors."

"Was that a direct quote?" Miss Hastings smirked.

"It was."

"I see." She swallowed her grin. "And Mr. Reid, what was his opinion?"

Benjamin's face darkened considerably. "Mr. Reid,"—Benjamin placed severe intonation on the first word—"believes your plan is an excellent idea and mine is a fool's errand."

Miss Hastings rose from the bed and approached Benjamin.

"It was not my intention to cause discord between you and your brother."

"Stop," he said, hungrily watching her movement. Slowly shaking his head to halt her progress across the room, he continued speaking only when Miss Hastings paused, halfway between the bed and him. "Thomas and I differ due to my inability to observe the situation rationally, or so he has accused."

She took a small step closer, hovering on the edge of an invisible circle, just outside his reach.

"Is Mr. Reid correct in his assessment?"

"He is."

The heat consuming Benjamin burst into flames, licking enticingly across his skin. Miss Hastings glided closer, a moth drawn by the inferno.

"Samantha." He whispered the warning through the rising fire blinding his senses.

She reached out her hand, tentatively stroking one finger tenderly across his full lower lip. Moaning, Benjamin sprang forward, wrapping his arms around her, pulling her against the hard length of his body and inhaling her scent. Without a thought, his mouth descended, attacking her lips with fervor. She sighed, molding herself to him. Tightening her arms around his neck, she pulled him closer, allowing Benjamin to consume her breath.

"Benjamin." The siren voice called again, filled with longing. Her eyes glittered brightly, alight and energized. Her body warmed, rouging until she glowed from his touch.

Growling, Benjamin lifted her easily, wrapping her legs around his waist as he carried her back to his bed. His mouth wandered over her lips, nibbling down the side of her throat until she cried out his name. They collapsed together.

She tugged at his shirt, skimming her hands over his exposed chest. He sucked in a sharp breath and bit down gently on her lower lip. Wiggling impatiently underneath him, she slid her palms over his muscles. His shirt disappeared, flung unceremoniously across the room. Her fingers danced across his bare skin, sending tremors vibrating through his skin in every direction. Smiling at his reaction, Miss Hastings' lips curved sensuously. Her hands wandered across his stomach, lightly brushing the top of his pants.

"Slow down, Samantha." He inhaled shakily, gathering and pinning her arms over her head. His tongue traveled wickedly along her jawline until she writhed beneath him, her body bowing in anticipation.

His hands inched their way to the hem of her nightdress, whipping the garment over her head. She was still, holding her breath. Benjamin's green eyes hardened to steel. Bruises of varying sizes decorated her pale skin, previously hidden—a map of torture. Benjamin roared and slammed his fist into the wall.

Miss Hastings' hands hastily covered the worst contusions, but Benjamin easily captured her arms again and moved them out of the way. His narrowed eyes inspected every mark as Miss Hastings watched him warily.

"Does Edward know the extent of your injuries?" Benjamin looked up from his examination when Miss Hastings did not answer.

She bit her lip hesitantly. "No."

Benjamin brushed his thumb tenderly down the side of her cheek.

"Why did you not tell him?"

Miss Hastings returned his gaze with melancholy.

"He would have left with you," she whispered. "I couldn't take him from Wilhelmina and the girls."

Releasing her arms, Benjamin encircled Miss Hastings' face with his palms, forcing her to hold his stare, his voice rumbling thickly.

"I will return to you."

Languidly he lowered his head until his lips were millimeters from hers, her warm breath tickling his skin. He grazed his mouth across her lower lip, sucking it gently. Her hands slid through his hair before she tightened her grasp around his neck and roughly pulled him against her.

The urgency that possessed him earlier returned in full. He needed to feel her, to be surrounded by her. His hand slipped between them, unfastening his pants. Quickly tugging his trousers from his hips, he shoved them down his legs and kicked them from his feet. He pushed her thighs further apart, then lowered himself in agonizingly slow increments until he filled her completely. She moaned, and her eyes half-closed. Leaning back, she exposed her neck to his sinful ministration. Obliging, Benjamin's mouth nipped her sensitive skin, caressing a path to the midpoint of her chest.

Fully sheathed in her warmth, he ground his hips into her. She cried out his name, her hands gripping his waist, wanting more. He slowly pulled back, pausing before sliding into her again and stilling, his tongue wandering wickedly across her exposed breast. His teeth closed around the nub, tugging gently. She growled with frustration, writhing again, begging for release. He complied, slamming into her with every ounce of the desire coursing through his veins. Her sapphire eyes glowed wildly as she rose to meet his thrusts. Benjamin lost the last shred of his control, increasing the rhythm of his hips as they moved together in unison.

She trembled beneath him, her fingers gouging into his back, and leaving red marks. His name tumbled from her lips, swallowed by his greedy mouth. Once more, he pushed deeply into her, reaching his own climax as she vibrated uncontrollably beneath him. He shuddered and collapsed on top of her twitching form, then rolled to the side, pulling her with him.

They lay entwined, trying to slow their breathing. The blush of passion slowly faded from her alabaster skin as she curled into Benjamin. He dropped a light kiss on her neck, eliciting a tiny shiver. She pushed up, resting on her arms, and smiled at him.

"You truly are the World's Most Wicked Rake."

"I believe you used the word *Notorious*."

"So, I did." Miss Hastings idly drew a pattern on Benjamin's chest with her fingertips.

"Samantha," Benjamin warned her with a playful smile, removing her hand. "There is nothing I would like more than to spend the next twenty-four hours showing you how truly wicked I can be. However..."

"You cannot." She sighed heavily. "Will you at least stay with me until I fall asleep?"

"That I can do," Benjamin replied, softly stroking her hair. She purred contentedly, her head resting in the crook of his arm.

He glanced around the room. An old traveling trunk resided at the foot of the bed. Aside from that intrusion, very little of Miss Hastings' personal belongings permeated his space, yet she had always been there. His eyes flicked to the loose brick in the fireplace. With the pistol and watch both removed from the cubby hole, only one other delicate item remained. Actually, two items, he corrected himself—letters from his past. One letter was the last correspondence he ever received from Miss Hastings and the other, his long belated response.

He peeked down at her. She slept dreamlessly, her face buried in his chest. Slowly sliding out from under her, Benjamin rose from the bed, retrieved his pants from the floor, and yanked them over his hips. Padding to the hearth, he carefully loosened the brick, pulling it free from the fireplace. Reaching into the cubby, he grasped the two letters and extricated them from the recesses of his hiding place. He carefully replaced the brick, checking to make sure the noise didn't wake Miss Hastings.

The letters were folded neatly together, their worn creases an indication of the frequency with which he had read them. Taking a seat in the armchair next to the dying fire, Benjamin unfolded the two letters and began with the last letter from Miss Hastings.

Dear Mr. Reid,

I HATE YOU!
P.S. Why did you stop writing me?
Sincerely,
Miss Hastings

THE CHILDISH WRITING OF A TWELVE-YEAR-OLD. Benjamin's mouth twisted into a wry grin. He'd expected this particular response once he was forced to cut all communication with her. After ignoring several letters, Miss Hastings finally wrote this last attempt to regain his attention. At the time, she didn't know Uncle Ephraim and Edward had demanded Benjamin discontinue any future contact with the impressionable little girl.

The letter behind hers—his response to her unanswered missives—was never delivered. Edward ensured that. However, Benjamin continued to hold on to it. So many years it remained hidden, for what purpose he never understood. He perused the letter, debating old wounds.

DEAR MISS HASTINGS,

I am sorry to hear your good opinion of me has changed. I regret I will not have the opportunity to convince you otherwise. However, there are circumstances outside my control that require me to terminate our friendship. Before I never speak with you again, there are three points I wish to make.

First, my correct title is Lord Westwood. It has been my salutation for some time now. Mr. Reid, to whom you consistently write but have never met, is my brother. However, rest assured, I have not shared any of our correspondence with him.

Second, I see no reason why a girl should not learn how to shoot. As you have already mastered the fine art of fencing—a skill from which I still bear the mark—I believe learning to use a pistol would be suitable to your temperament. You may share with Edward my sentiments on the subject.

Third, if I had the ability, I would pursue our acquaintance further. However, I am not your guardian and as such, do not have the right to make that particular judgment. I have enjoyed our discussions and regret they will not continue.

Sincerely,

Lord Westwood

BENJAMIN FOLDED both pieces of paper again, staring at the fire as it crackled. A bird chirped outside the window, announcing the early morning hour. Rising from the chair, he stuffed the papers back into the cubby and pressed the brick flush, a shower of dust sprinkling to the ground. Discreetly, he scraped the brick residue into the fireplace grate with the side of his foot. He took one last look at Miss Hastings' sleeping figure, silhouetted in the firelight, her delicate skin glowing with bruises.

Franklin would never touch her again.

CHAPTER 11

Day 1

Emptiness oozed into her bones. Without opening her eyes, Sam felt Lord Westwood's absence. It permeated the room, seeping under the sheets, leaving her with icy chills. Refusing to confirm the truth she already knew, she stretched her arm out to her side. Her fingers slid along the cold linens, searching for his warmth, agonizingly aware her action was fruitless. With a sigh, Sam retracted her hand and opened her eyes, staring at the ceiling.

He was gone.

"Samantha," she said aloud. "Get out of this bed. You already know he departed early this morning. You heard the door shut."

She had half hoped Lord Westwood would change his mind. However, the light click of the door woke her. She sat up, recognizing the sound of the latch. Racing to the front-facing window, Sam ripped the drapes aside, hovering impatiently as her eyes scanned the grounds. After a few minutes, she saw a flash of light in the darkness near the gate to the main road. It lingered, dancing like a firefly in the night. Sam imagined Lord Westwood raising the lantern as a final farewell. Pressing her hand against the smooth glass, she watched as the light disappeared, swallowed by darkness.

Two hours later, she relinquished her post at the window. Lord Westwood didn't return. Shivering, Sam climbed onto the bed and slid under the coverlet, but sleep eluded her. In an attempt to trick her mind into slumbering, she squeezed her eyes tight and breathed deeply, concentrating on each breath... one... two... three, but the endeavor failed. Now, as the first beams of the morning crept across the floorboards, she abandoned the idea. Rolling off the bed with a grunt, she paced the room, her bare feet carving circles in the decorative rug.

The room suffocated, its walls closing around her like a cage. Deciding fresh air would be the best remedy for her melancholy, she dressed quickly, needing to escape the prison she now found herself in. Nearly tearing the seams on the muslin dress as she yanked it over her head, Sam rushed from the room as if it were ablaze. Slipping quietly down the stairs, she scurried toward Lady Westwood's extensive gardens.

The sun warmed her frozen skin but didn't penetrate the surface, leaving ice chunks swimming in her blood. Her hands clutched at her shoulders, and she frowned. The missing shawl, draped carelessly over an armchair, waited forlornly in her chamber. Sighing, she shivered and wrapped her arms tightly around herself. Her sigh, visibly frosting, tingled icily on her lips. She really should retrieve her shawl, Sam argued silently with her melancholy. As she dissented, she wandered toward the gazebo situated in the center of the gardens. When she reached the wooden stairs, she glanced into the shadows of the gazebo and gasped.

"Benjamin!" She bounded toward him, knocking him backward onto the floor of the gazebo. Her zeal carried her forward as well, and she landed on top of his supine body.

"Wrong brother," Mr. Reid replied, detangling himself from Sam's enthusiastic embrace as he gently rolled her to the side. Sitting up, he brushed dirt from his coat.

"Mr. Reid," Sam replied with chagrin, mortification burning her face. She flung her arm over her eyes and laid face-up on the floorboards. Her heart sank, splintering on its descent. "Please accept my apologies for my exuberant behavior," she mumbled through her sleeve.

"I think I prefer Benjamin's greeting," Mr. Reid teased. He climbed to his feet and offered Sam his hand. "Would you like some assistance, Miss Hastings?"

Sam debated remaining on the gazebo floor. It was not the most comfortable place to rest, but it made it easier to hide her embarrassment. Grimacing, she sat up.

"Am I that horrible to converse with?" Mr. Reid asked, a grin tugging at the corner of his mouth.

"Not at all, Mr. Reid." Sam shook her head, the heat of her embarrassment flaring in her cheeks.

He studied her for a moment, his head tilted to the side. "This must be extremely difficult for you. I look just like him."

"You truly do," Sam replied, offering him a tiny smile, and accepted his aid, rising—almost gracefully—from the floor.

"Benjamin left early this morning," Mr. Reid said, his brown eyes holding none of their usual twinkle. "I was unable to dissuade him."

"He would not allow his mind to be changed," Sam replied softly, feeling the need to ease Mr. Reid's guilt.

He took a step nearer and spoke forcefully, "Benjamin will be cautious. Of the two of us, he is the most pragmatic."

She was unsure if he was trying to convince her or himself. "This particular idea of his seems a bit reckless."

Several emotions crossed Mr. Reid's face. "Would you not agree your plan is also somewhat dangerous?"

"I would." Sam nodded, her gaze flicking toward a row of rose bushes. Her plan was extremely dangerous.

"And do you still intend to move forward with this scheme?" Mr. Reid moved closer, dropping his voice to a low murmur.

A spark of fury raced through Sam's veins, and her gaze flicked back to Mr. Reid.

"I do."

"Good. You have my full support." He paused, nose lifted in the air like a dog, then grinned. "Would you care to join me for breakfast?"

Despite her glum mood, Sam giggled. "How can you smell breakfast all the way out here in the gardens?"

Mr. Reid tapped the side of his nose. "I have an excellent sense of smell when it comes to food."

"Just food?" Sam laughed.

"Yes," he replied, winking.

"Samantha!" Wilhelmina yelled from the front of the house. The veranda creaked softly as she stalked its length.

Sam groaned. Wilhelmina—no doubt—was already planned a whirlwind of activities for the day, and chances were, they were all wedding-related.

"Mr. Reid, I regret that I must decline your offer for companionship. Please inform Mrs. Hastings you have seen me this morning, and I was walking toward Mr. Flannery's estate."

"That's in the completely opposite direction from the gardens," Mr. Reid replied, his mouth twitching.

"Indeed, it is." Sam waved airily.

"Samantha Hastings!" Wilhelmina bellowed. "Do not think you can hide from me all day!"

"Miss Hastings, I will deliver your message." Mr. Reid bowed low, exiting the gazebo. He took the nearest path to his right but paused before the path joined the main walkway around the house. "I must ask you not to leave the grounds, Miss Hastings."

Sam shot him a peculiar look. "Is that your demand or your brother's?"

"It is my request." He bowed low, flashing her a debonair smile.

"I shall endeavor to comply with your request." Sam curtsied.

"Thank you."

"Enjoy your breakfast."

"Oh, if you do decide to head in that direction, watch out for Mr. Flannery. He is wandering about with a loaded rifle." Mr. Reid gestured toward the Flannery estate, then waved cheerily and disappeared around the front of the house, leaving Sam alone in the gazebo.

She trembled in the shadows. Without the sun to warm her skin, the chill returned full force. Wrapping her arms around her waist, she glided down the stairs and followed a different footpath toward the rear of the house.

Sam wasted her morning wandering through the meadows. True to her word, she didn't leave the estate. However, she did find herself turned back on several occasions. Surrounded by a well-worn wooden fence, the property's edge ran along the road leading to the Shirely's country manor. Several times, she came across Mr. Reid, who, like her, was avoiding the ongoing wedding planning. He strolled beside her for several minutes, silently trudging through the grass. Sam was grateful for his company even though his doppelganger appearance caused painful squeezing in her chest.

"Damn," he muttered suddenly and melted into the scenery. Sam spun around, shocked by his disappearance.

"Ah-ha! Intruder!" A voice accused from behind, the thick brogue unmistakable.

"Hell," Sam said, turning to stare at a loaded rifle. Three more curse words slipped from her lips.

The old man squinted, studying her intently with his faded blue eyes. He tilted his head before lowering the gun with a smile.

"There are only two ladies in this entire world who would dare to speak such terrible blasphemies to me. As you are not my delightful daughter, you must be my niece."

"Uncle Aengus." Sam smiled as she darted forward and hugged him, the smell of stale tobacco wafting from his clothes.

"It is good to see you again, m'girl. I hardly recognized you with all those marks." He held her at arms' length, his gaze sliding over her battered face. "You look as though you were attacked. What happened?"

Sam pulled out of his grasp and crossed her arms, self-consciously covering the bruising on her throat.

"I ran afoul of an old friend."

"Some friend." Aengus snorted, stroking his beard thoughtfully, his fingers tangling in the strands. "I suspect Edward has already dealt with the matter."

"He is attempting to rectify the situation."

"Would this be the same cause for Benjamin's distress earlier this morning?" Aengus arched an eyebrow.

"Lord Westwood rescued me from my attacker." A stabbing pain shot through Sam's chest when she said his name.

Where was he? Was he safe... was he alive?

"He's a good boy." Aengus smiled, his eyes flicking over Sam. "I wish you would have given us some advance notice of your arrival. We could have prepared a formal dinner for your visit. No matter, you shall dine with us tonight." Aengus clapped his hand around Sam's wrist, leading her down the rise toward his house. In the distance, smoke puffed continually from one of the chimneys.

Sam planted her feet, pulling against him. "I appreciate your kind offer, Uncle. However, I'm currently Lady Westwood's guest. It would be rude of me to make plans without first consulting my host."

Aengus glanced back in confusion. "Lady Westwood isn't family."

"Not yet," Sam muttered.

"What did you say, m'girl?" Aengus took a step closer. "My hearing isn't what it used to be."

"She said, 'Not yet,' Da," Aidan replied from Sam's shoulder.

"Aidan!" Sam whipped around to greet her cousin, joy radiating through her body.

He embraced her tightly. "It is a pleasure to see you again, Cousin."

"How is Alana?" Sam asked as he released her.

"Stubborn, just like every other member of this family," Aidan replied, grinning widely. "She's due home later today."

"Since we can't tempt you this evening, I do hope you will arrange to dine with us in the near future," Aengus said, shifting his gun to his shoulder. "It gets a little lonely with only Aidan and Noreen to keep me company."

Sam raised her eyebrows, but Aidan shook his head subtly. His blue eyes ached with unspeakable anguish.

"I would be delighted," Sam replied, adding a curtsy.

Aidan narrowed his eyes. "What are you doing wandering about by yourself?"

"I was strolling with Mr. Reid, but he vanished several meters ago." Sam gestured behind her.

"Hmph. Never got over her, did he? That boy still refuses to cross the boundary lines." Aengus shook his head in pity.

"Da," Aidan warned softly. "There is no need to dredge up old wounds."

Aengus tipped his head, his eyes rolling with delight. He

held a wizened finger to his lips. "Listen. The pianoforte," he whispered. Whooping, Aengus lumbered down the slope, moving much quicker than Sam believed possible considering his age.

Aidan sighed heavily as his father raced toward the house, wildly swinging the rifle with glee.

"I must take my leave, Cousin. Enjoy the rest of your afternoon." He turned and trudged down the hill after his father, a mere speck dancing in the distance.

Sam watched Aidan thoughtfully as he caught up to his father at the gravel pathway leading toward their garden. It was not quite as large as Lady Westwood's gardens, but it possessed a quaint charm she enjoyed on her last visit. Aidan flung an arm around his father's slight shoulders, extracting the gun from Aengus' grip. Together they stood in front of the parlor's open window, Aengus swaying along with an inaudible tune. Aidan remained stoic, his back stiff.

Straining her ears, Sam listened intently to the breeze which ruffled the ends of her curls, hoping to hear Aengus' invisible torment. Nothing. Her heart broke for Aidan. He was forced to watch his father slowly descend into madness, possessing no ability to prevent his father's worsening condition. Perhaps Alana's presence would ease Aidan's burden.

Retracing her path, Sam returned to the main house by nightfall, the muddy hem of her dress dragging on the ground, torn during her exploration. As she slowly ascended the veranda, an irate Edward met her on the steps.

"Where have you been?" he demanded, nearly apoplectic.

"I was walking about the estate," Sam replied mildly, trying to scoot around him.

He blocked her passage. "I was worried. Wilhelmina was worried. Everyone was worried."

"Mr. Reid was not." Sam slid to her left, attempting to edge past Edward again.

"Samantha." Vibrating with annoyance, he pinched the bridge of his nose. "Mr. Reid is not your guardian."

"Yet he is the only one who knew exactly how Miss Hastings spent her day." Mr. Reid joined them on the porch, appearing out of the darkness with a jaunty grin.

"Mr. Reid, it is a pleasure to see you again." Sam offered him a dazzling smile.

"Miss Hastings, I believe I can smell something delicious wafting from the kitchens. Would you care to join me?" Mr. Reid offered his arm, which Sam gratefully accepted.

"Thank you, I would be delighted."

Edward growled his displeasure when Sam and Mr. Reid skirted around him and disappeared into the house.

"Is he gnashing his teeth?" Mr. Reid whispered as they entered the dining room.

"Yes," Sam replied with a grin.

Mercifully, Edward didn't chase her down the hallway. As the earliest to the dining room, Sam and Mr. Reid filled their dishes before the rest of the household arrived. Sam took advantage of Edward's tardiness to dash from the room with her dinner plate before he found occasion to restrict her to indoor activities. She paused in the corridor, her head swiveling between the staircase and the library. Unwilling to return to Lord Westwood's cold bedchamber, she opted to investigate the library in search of a distraction.

She picked at the food on her plate while she walked along the well-stocked shelves, her head craned sideways as she perused the bindings. Selecting three interesting titles, Sam snuggled into an armchair near the fire, stacking the books and her heaping plate on the table next to her. She read, undisturbed until exhaustion took hold. Her body slumped, the book resting in her lap toppling to the floor... and the nightmares began.

CHAPTER 12

Day 2

Franklin's black eyes burned menacingly, his fingers closed around her throat, squeezing until she choked. She clawed at his hands, digging her nails into his skin, as his deafening laughter rang in her ears. Screaming, Sam swung her arm at Franklin's smug face and fell out of the armchair, landing on the floor with a grunt. Her eyes flew open. She stared at the room, the nightmare fading from her mind like wisps of smoke rising from a dying fire.

She was in the library.

Someone shifted in the chair beside hers. Sam's head snapped to her left, terror hovering on her lips. Wilhelmina, her hands elegantly folded, waited patiently. Disapproval leaked from her eyes, which traveled slowly over Sam's disheveled appearance, landing on the muddied, ripped hemline of yesterday's tattered dress.

"I half-expected you would have already escaped out of the residence by the time I arrived." Wilhelmina gestured to the chair Sam fell off.

Sam struggled to her feet. The fire had died at some point during the night, and her stiff muscles ached in the frigid air. She grimaced, stretching her arms.

"That was my intention."

"Samantha," Wilhelmina's brown eyes softened, "I realize you have suffered through a horrific experience." She indicated the visible bruising on Sam's face.

Sam bit her lip, turning her back to Wilhelmina. Hugging her arms tightly around her chest, she moved in front of the fireplace, her body craving the paltry heat.

"I suspect there are some details you have chosen to withhold from myself as well as Edward." Wilhelmina paused, debating her next words. "You have my blessing to wander freely about the grounds today, just as you did yesterday."

Whipping her head around, Sam opened her mouth to defend her behavior. However, before she had a chance to speak, Wilhelmina held up her hand.

"Tomorrow, you are expected for a fitting. If we are to execute your plan to draw out Mr. Morris at the Shirely ball, you must be properly attired. Mr. Reid and I discussed this in great detail after dinner last evening."

"My brother—"

"Is reluctant to lend his support," Wilhelmina said as she rose. "However, he has no choice in this matter." She lifted a sack from a nearby table and held it out to Sam. "Inside, you will find some provisions for the day. Please return by the evening meal."

"What about Edward?" Sam asked. Untying the strings, she peeked inside, and her stomach rumbled.

"Edward is exceedingly concerned for your well-being. Therefore, if I were you, I would take my leave before he discovers me in the library. Don't bother changing your clothing. That dress is ruined." Wilhelmina raised her eyes heavenward and shook her head, mouthing a silent prayer, then returned her gaze to Sam. "You might as well complete the job. Go now before Edward wakes."

"Thank you." Sam leapt forward and enveloped Wilhelmina, who returned the embrace fiercely.

After extracting herself from Sam, Wilhelmina smoothed her skirt, her head held regally, and walked to the door. She stopped at the threshold, her hand on the door handle, and spoke quietly, keeping her eyes forward.

"When Edward disappeared, I was lost without him. I had no relations and three little girls to support. You showed me incredible kindness during that time. I would like to do the same for you." She spun around, her eyes moist. "It would be an honor to wear your mother's necklace to the Shirely masque."

She cracked the door and glided through the small space without another word, her sentiments swirling around Sam's head in dizzying circles. Heeding Wilhelmina's advice, Sam hefted the sack over her shoulder and followed her out of the library, heading toward the entrance hall.

"Samantha!" Edward's voice echoed upstairs, his shoes stomping down the corridor toward her bedchamber.

Freezing, Sam glanced to her right and left. She wouldn't reach the door without Edward catching her trekking across the entrance hall, which left only one other option.

Tiptoeing toward the rear of the house, Sam snuck toward the kitchens as Edward's footfall announced his rapid descent of the staircase. She quickened her pace, her breath caught in her throat. Shoving through the kitchen door, she crashed into Mr. Reid, biscuit in hand, and screamed, her hand flying to her mouth the moment the sound left it. Ignoring Mr. Reid's shock, she twisted around and pushed the door ajar, peering through the opening. Edward had vanished. Exhaling slowly, she released the door and turned around again.

"Good morning, Mr. Reid," she murmured, hoping his usual boisterous tone wouldn't draw Edward's attention.

Mr. Reid pressed a finger to his mouth and leaned closer, his voice as quiet as hers. "You didn't see me this morning."

She arched an eyebrow, her mouth quirking. "If that is such, then you didn't see me, either."

"Indeed, I didn't." He winked, bowed, and vanished into the corridor.

Not a soul crossed her path in the morning. No sound interrupted her reverie, save the crunch of her shoes on the grass. Removing her stockings and shoes, Sam wiggled her toes in the warm blades of green. She sprinted toward the meadow, allowing her hair to whip freely behind her, then flopped down in the pasture, and the long stalks sprung up around her body, hiding her from view. Buzzing insects droned around her, the sound oddly soothing, and her eyelids fluttered close.

"When Benjamin mentioned your dislike of footwear, I had no idea he meant you intended to wander barefoot about the estate."

Sam's eyes flew open. Squinting into the afternoon sun, she placed a hand up to her forehead to block the light. Mr. Reid, on a tan-and-white stallion, paced a lazy circle around her hideout. He lifted his hat as a friendly greeting.

"We almost stepped on you." Mr. Reid patted the horse's neck, murmuring a few gentle words before he slid from the saddle with surprising grace. Deftly landing on his feet, he wrapped the reins loosely around a thick patch of grass.

"I didn't expect to meet anyone." Sam sat up hastily, grass and flower bits stuck in her unbound hair, then collected her shoes and stockings, reluctantly pulling them over her naked feet.

"Don't feel the need to be proper on my account," Mr. Reid replied, dropping beside her. Kicking off his boots, he stretched his long legs and wiggled his toes in an exaggerated fashion. "Ahhh," he breathed, "I see the attraction."

Sam giggled as Mr. Reid flopped back onto the meadow grass, rolling back and forth, with his hands tucked into his chest like an exuberant puppy. He sat up, his tousled hair embedded with weeds.

"Now we match."

"I'm not sure that is a good thing." Sam laughed. "I've been accused of lacking certain ladylike qualities, and I'm certain my most recent state of undress wasn't appropriate for a gentleman."

"Miss Hastings, I too am lacking certain ladylike qualities," —Sam snorted— "however, rest assured, nothing you do would ever compare with the improper activities which color my background." He grinned.

"Which are?" Sam asked, curiosity raging through her. Perhaps the rumors surrounding Lord Westwood and his brother were more accurate than she assumed.

"Definitely not suitable for discussion in mixed company." Mr. Reid winked.

"I would expect nothing less."

He leaned closer, dropping his voice to a whisper. "Not every piece of gossip is true, Miss Hastings." He paused and grinned again. "Unless it's about Benjamin."

"I shall try to keep that in mind." Sam laughed.

Mr. Reid collapsed onto his back, tucking his hands under his head, and stared at the sky. "You had a visitor earlier today," he said, his mood shifting mercurially with the statement.

Sam glanced at him, perplexed. "Who?"

"Your cousin, Mr. Aidan Flannery," Mr. Reid said, his usually playful tone greatly subdued. "The entire household has been invited to a luncheon to celebrate the return of his sister in one week. I informed him I would pass the message along."

"That was very thoughtful," Sam said, thinking back to Uncle Aengus' off-hand comment about Mr. Reid's prolonged absence. She peeked sideways at him. "Do you plan to attend?"

Mr. Reid maintained his vigil on the sky. "I have a prior engagement."

"That is unfortunate." Sam laid down next to him in the long grass and lapsed silent, watching gray clouds seep toward the afternoon sun. The hazy glow kissed the meadow with melancholy.

"Rain is coming." Mr. Reid sat up suddenly, tugging on his boots. "We should return to the house."

"I would prefer to walk," Sam said, unwilling to relinquish her sanctum.

Mr. Reid shrugged as he rose. Untangling the horse's reins from the grass, he lithely leapt atop the mare and forced a half-smile.

"If I was Benjamin, I would pluck you from the ground, drape you over my saddle—despite your stubborn nature—and force you to return to the house."

She sat up, tilting her head as she considered his threat.

"However, you are not."

"I am not, and I prefer not to do what is expected of me. Which means I must encourage you to do the same."

Sam grinned.

"Try not to get too wet," he said as the horse stamped the ground impatiently. "Mrs. Hastings' opinion of me will not improve if I allow you to return in a bad state."

"Yes, sir." Sam saluted him.

Mr. Reid attempted a second smile but failed dismally. Digging his heels into the horse's flanks, the horse whinnied and galloped toward the stables without further direction from his rider.

Judging the distance of the clouds, Sam calculated she had

at least a half-hour before the rain began, but the storm moved quicker than she anticipated. Just as the house appeared over the rise, rain fell in sheets, pelting her with thick drops. Instantly soaked, Sam raced for cover. Losing her footing, she slipped on the wet grass and skidded down the final hill in a decidedly inelegant fashion, and a large tear—hem to waist—appeared with a deafening rip.

Stunned, Sam lay on her back, raindrops stinging her face. Rolling to her side, she pushed up on her arms and climbed to her feet, scraping soggy curls off her cheek. She wrapped the skirt tightly around her waist, covering the tear, and hobbled toward the house. As she approached the veranda, her pace slowed until one foot barely shuffled forward an inch. She debated the ruined dress.

How would she sneak into the house?

"Samantha, would you at least move under the roof while you finish your daydream?" Wilhelmina yelled from the doorway, startling Sam from her trance.

Sam nodded, slogging her way toward the veranda. Two sodden shoes left a trail of muddy footprints across the wooden porch boards. She stopped in front of Wilhelmina, shivering and dripping on the floor, her hand still clasping the torn skirt.

"I see you followed my instructions." Wilhelmina clucked. "It's a shame you can't have that kind of tenacity with all my directions." Shaking her head, she reached out and lifted an edge of the ripped dress. "Edward is in the study. If you hurry, you can change without anyone else discovering your complete lack of propriety."

Sam bowed her head and squeezed past Wilhelmina, who shrank away from Sam's sopping clothes. Dashing across the entranceway, Sam's feet squished with each step, her shoes barely touching the staircase as she raced up them. Before Wilhelmina entered the house, Sam rounded the corridor corner and scurried into her chamber, slamming the door.

Peeling off her drenched clothing, Sam left the ruined dress and her underclothes drying in front of the crackling fire and stretched her hands toward the heat. Droplets of rain slid down her back, freezing her skin. The warmth from the fireplace did nothing to melt the cold block that settled in her stomach. The silence pressed in. Despite all her work at distraction, she still thought of nothing but Benjamin.

Was he safe?

She couldn't stay in the room, not without Benjamin. His absence amplified the despair crawling through her body. Even Edward's lectures were a better option than the endless quiet.

Rooting through her trunk, she yanked out fresh clothing and dressed quickly, then hooked her shawl off the lid of her trunk and fled the chamber, creeping downstairs. She glanced down the corridor. A light emanated from under the closed study door, and Edward's muffled voice rumbled in the room. Gliding past the door, she snuck into the library. A silver tray laden with food and a small handwritten note waited on the small table. Sam snatched the note, her eyes flying over Wilhelmina's handwriting.

There has been no news from Lord Westwood.

Dejected, Sam hefted an armchair over to the library window and propped her stocking feet on the ledge, watching the rain fall in torrents.

"Benjamin, where are you?" she whispered, wrapping her shawl tightly around her arms. Lulled by the steady drum of raindrops, her heavy head drooped against her chest as Franklin's voice swirled around her, laughing.

His hands tightened around her neck.

CHAPTER 13

Day 3

"What exactly am I?" Sam asked, her eyes flicking to Wilhelmina as a dressmaker fluttered around Sam's feet, stabbing portions of the dress with pins. Mrs. Silverthorne jerked the hem of the blue gown, signaling her disapproval of Sam's constant movement. Removing a pin from the bunch clamped between her lips, Mrs. Silverthorne shoved it through the material, sticking Sam for the third time in the past ten minutes. Sam's ankle throbbed. She scowled at the dressmaker. Mrs. Silverthorne turned her head to Sam, the pins rolling in her mouth as her lips stretched into a dreadful smile.

Sam shuddered. The woman enjoyed her work a bit too much.

"You are a peacock," Wilhelmina replied, unwrapping a parcel. She produced a glittering mask in the same shade as Sam's gown, plumage decorating the top in a crown-like arrangement.

"Oh, that is lovely," Miss Clemens gushed from her stool.

She stood in a similarly uncomfortable position, confined to a tiny stool with her yellow dress pinned up in various sections. Although since she'd been remarkably still during her turn, Sam doubted Miss Clemens' legs were covered in bleeding pinpricks.

Sam touched a large discoloration on her forearm, her mouth twisted unhappily. "How do you plan on covering the contusions on my arms," she asked, her self-consciousness growing increasingly worse with the reveal of capped sleeves.

"With these." Wilhelmina laid a pair of long gloves next to the mask. "Miss Clemens, I have a pair for you as well."

"Thank you for your kindness," Miss Clemens replied with a graceful curtsy. Clearly, balance was not an issue for Miss Clemens. Sam frowned and wobbled, earning another poke from Mrs. Silverthorne.

"Miss Clemens, I hope you don't mind my selection of a canary for your costume. Yellow looks lovely with your coloring." Wilhelmina offered her a smile, which the younger girl failed to return.

"I wonder what hue Miss Shirely decided to wear," Miss Clemens murmured with a nervous hitch in her voice. Her eyes followed Mrs. Silverthorne as she moved to the back of Sam's gown.

"I believe she has selected pink," Wilhelmina replied, laying a feathered yellow mask and matching gloves next to Sam's blue pair.

"She has chosen to dress as a pig," Sam muttered under her breath, causing a giggle to burst from Miss Clemens. She coughed to cover her gaff and turned away from Sam.

"Samantha!" Wilhelmina chastised without looking up.

Sam rolled her eyes. "Please excuse my inappropriate comment."

"I would much more prefer you meant the apology.

However, I suppose that was a beginning." Wilhelmina lifted a third mask and gloves, each white.

"Miss Shirely has alleged much worse," Miss Clemens murmured, causing Wilhelmina to glance up with an arched eyebrow.

"About Samantha?" Wilhelmina inclined her head in Sam's direction.

"Yes," Miss Clemens whispered, her eyes unable to meet Wilhelmina's.

"I'm afraid every bit of it was true." Sam stretched out her arm and grasped Miss Clemens' trembling hand, squeezing gently.

The ladies burst out laughing. Miss Clemens breathed a deep sigh, accepting the yellow gloves Wilhelmina offered. After pulling them up her arms, Daphne rotated slowly on the stool, her arms outstretched to prevent herself from falling.

"You're beautiful." Aunt Abigail spoke from her position on the sofa. She and Lady Westwood quit their quiet conversation when Miss Clemens mentioned Miss Shirely's name.

"I would like to see the entire costume," Lady Westwood said, gesturing at the yellow mask.

Wilhelmina passed the mask to Miss Clemens, who dutifully pulled it over the top part of her head and posed atop the stool, a statue of elegance. Mr. Reid chose that exact moment to peek his head into the parlor.

"Would any ladies—" He stopped, his eyes traveling over Miss Clemens as his mouth hung open in shock. Lady Westwood and Aunt Abigail exchanged a knowing glance.

"Miss Clemens, you are exquisite," Mr. Reid finally said when he remembered himself.

"Thank you, Mr. Reid." Miss Clemens glowed. She tried to curtsy, but her apparent nervousness at his presence caused her to lose her balance, and she toppled forward, crashing to the ground with a groan. She flushed, embarrassment crawling through her face.

Mr. Reid leapt forward and knelt, offering his hand to assist Miss Clemens to her feet. Righting the stool, he held her hand until she returned to her original position atop the small pedestal, giving it a tiny squeeze before releasing her fingers. The matrons in the family exchanged a second glance, and Sam was quite certain they were plotting to bring Mr. Reid and Miss Clemens together.

"Thomas, it's lovely to see you, but I must ask the purpose of your interruption." Lady Westwood folded her hands. "Ladies' fashion doesn't generally interest you."

"I was wondering if any of the ladies present would care to join me fishing tomorrow morning if the rain has ceased by then." Mr. Reid spoke directly to Sam, who gleefully grinned at Wilhelmina.

Wilhelmina sighed and glanced out the window, watching the thick, dark clouds pensively, and nodded. "You have no obligations tomorrow. You may occupy yourself however you wish as long as the weather is favorable."

"I would be delighted to join you, Mr. Reid," Sam replied, bouncing on her stool in uncontainable excitement.

"Miss Clemens, would you care to join our outing tomorrow morning?" Mr. Reid turned his gaze to the younger girl. She nearly fell again.

"I don't know how to fish," she replied quietly, blushing again as she dropped her eyes.

"It's not a difficult activity to learn, Miss Clemens. I can teach you," Mr. Reid said, gliding closer to her.

Miss Clemens hesitated, chewing her lower lip, and glanced up. "Mother said it was inappropriate for a lady to learn a man's sport. 'No gentleman wants a wife who behaves like a man,'" she said, replicating her mother's shrill tone.

Wilhelmina snorted. "Edward taught Samantha a slew of

improper activities, and she still managed to receive a marriage proposal."

"More than one if you include Mr. Lockhearst's feeble attempt at the Leveret's ball." Lady Westwood winked at Aunt Abigail.

"I heard Miss Hastings shredded his hopes with her sharp tongue." Aunt Abigail leaned over, loudly whispering to Lady Westwood. Sam blushed.

"It wasn't that sharp," she muttered to Miss Clemens.

"I think he cried," Lady Westwood added, her face glowing with delight. Aunt Abigail snickered.

Mr. Reid's eyes flicked over his aunt and mother. Shaking his head, his amused gaze returned to Sam.

"I am curious to know what other unsuitable pursuits in which you have experience, Miss Hastings."

"Edward has sworn me to secrecy as my inappropriate tutoring lands squarely on his shoulders." The corner of Sam's mouth lifted into a half-smile. "However, I have a query for you in return, Mr. Reid. Have you ever been bested by a woman?"

"Miss Hastings, I'm intrigued by your confidence." He raised his eyebrows at her challenge. "Would you care to make a wager?"

"One shilling on Miss Hastings," Aunt Abigail announced with a deft thump of her cane.

"Please, don't allow Edward to discover you are betting again," Wilhelmina said, her lips puckered into a frown. She glanced at the parlor door.

"Just because you lost the last wager—" Sam swallowed the rest of her comment when Wilhelmina shot her a sharp scowl.

"What was the bet?" Miss Clemens asked, her voice filled with curiosity.

Frowning, Wilhelmina turned to Miss Clemens. "A proper lady doesn't place bets."

"Does that mean you are no longer a refined woman?" Sam goaded. She moved to step off the stool but was pinched by Mrs. Silverthorne, who continued her work unobtrusively.

Wilhelmina narrowed her eyes. "Nor does a lady gleefully point out the faults of others."

"By that definition, I cannot say I have met more than four ladies during my entire time in society," Sam replied, debating kicking her foot back into the dressmaker.

"Dear me, only four?" Feigning shock, Aunt Abigail's hand flew to her chest. "I hope you count me as one of those ladies."

"Most certainly not," Lady Westwood replied and lifted her teacup to her lips, her eyes sparkling.

"Thomas," Aunt Abigail said, her devious face mirroring that of Lady Westwood's. "Would you consider me a lady under Miss Hastings' terms?"

"Ladies,"—Mr. Reid held his hands in the air—"before this becomes a dangerous situation, I must take my leave. Have a pleasant evening. I shall meet you both in the library tomorrow at daybreak." He bowed and escaped into the corridor.

"Why the library?" Miss Clemens asked, her eyes on the parlor door as if she hoped Mr. Reid would return.

"Samantha has a tendency to wake up there," Wilhelmina replied without humor, collecting the blue mask and gloves and holding them out to Sam.

Sam frowned.

"A fact is not a reason to be angry, Samantha," Wilhelmina said, her gaze dropping to the offered gloves and mask.

"You don't have to point it out," Sam replied. Snatching the gloves from Wilhelmina, she yanked them up her arms.

"Mr. Reid isn't attending dinner with us tonight?" Miss Clemens asked, a melancholy undercurrent in her question.

"He has a prior obligation," Wilhelmina replied. She indicated for Sam to lean down, then slipped the mask over her head.

"Which has absolutely nothing to do with the unexpected arrival of a certain young lady." Aunt Abigail murmured to her sister.

"Abigail!" Lady Westwood admonished her. "We do not discuss that matter."

"That matter," Aunt Abigail said, enunciating the word, "occurred eight years ago."

"Eight years ago, today," Lady Westwood replied softly.

"Oh, I see." Aunt Abigail patted Lady Westwood's hand, her tone exceedingly sympathetic. "I forgot the date. I do apologize for my insensitivity, Katherine."

"What are they discussing?" Sam whispered to Wilhelmina.

Wilhelmina glanced back at Lady Westwood. "It's not my place to discuss Mr. Reid's past."

Lady Westwood raised her eyebrows and stared at Wilhelmina. "I was unaware Thomas shared this information with anyone outside our family."

"Edward told me about it," she admitted, taking a step toward Lady Westwood. "We were engaged at the time. I was acquainted with both Lord Westwood and Mr. Reid. Edward wanted to share the good news with me."

"It was the fastest engagement in history," Aunt Abigail muttered.

"It's also not common knowledge, and I would prefer it remains that way until Thomas decides otherwise." Lady Westwood indicated Mrs. Silverthorne, who labored around the hem of Sam's skirt.

"I have completed the necessary adjustments," Mrs. Silverthorne announced from her crouched position, giving no impression she'd overheard any portion of the hushed conversation.

"When will the alterations be completed?" Wilhelmina asked as she passed her gown to Mrs. Silverthorne.

"I will have them completed by Friday. They will be delivered in the afternoon." She turned to Sam and Miss Clemens, still perched upon their footstools. "Ladies, if you would remove your gowns for me, please?"

"Would you also be able to repair this dress as well?" Wilhelmina handed Mrs. Silverthorne a ragged dress. Sam recognized it immediately as the ill-fated outfit from her previous day's adventures.

Mrs. Silverthorne stroked a weathered thumb over the material, mumbling to herself as she inspected the split. "I may be able to save this garment. I will do my best, Mrs. Hastings."

"Wonderful," Wilhelmina replied, arching an eyebrow at Sam as if she was astonished Samantha hadn't managed to completely destroy her clothing.

"It was my pleasure to assist you today." Collecting the dresses, four in total, Mrs. Silverthorne bobbed her head to each lady in turn. "Please let me know if there is anything else you require."

"Not at this moment, Mrs. Silverthorne," Lady Westwood replied, rising from the sofa. "Thank you for coming on such short notice."

"I was surprised to learn you declined your invitation, Lady Westwood. I hope you are not ill," Mrs. Silverthorne said as she returned her materials to her basket. "The Shirely masque is an exceptionally popular event."

"Indeed, it is. However, Mrs. Stanton and I have other business to attend to that evening. Thank you for your concern, Mrs. Silverthorne."

"My Lady." Mrs. Silverthorne nodded again to Lady Westwood. Without another word, the seamstress hefted her basket of supplies off the floor, draped each dress over her arm, and scooted through the parlor door.

"I believe it is time for more tea," Aunt Abigail said, refilling her teacup.

A flash of color over Sam's right shoulder captured her attention. She squinted out the window through the rain-streaked glass, her eyes searching the gray soup. A second burst of color appeared in the distance—a horse and atop the horse, Mr. Reid. He rode full-bore across the drive, rocks flinging under the horse's wild hooves.

Sam didn't draw attention to the ghostly sight of Mr. Reid, subtly shifting toward the window and blocking it with her body until she was sure he was no longer in view. Joining Wilhelmina on the settee, she accepted a teacup and saucer.

The ladies moved on to discussing the less interesting topic of fashion. Sam felt her mind wandering, jumping over rain-soaked bushes and brambles on horseback with Mr. Reid. Periodically, her eyes flicked sideways in the hopes of observing his intriguing horsemanship, but he never reappeared. The afternoon plodded on in dull fashion, rolling into an evening of ennui and cards.

When the other ladies retired, Sam wandered toward the library again, unable to sleep. Neither Edward nor Mr. Reid invaded her sanctuary, although she heard their voices in the house, resonating from the entrance hall sometime after midnight. She strained her ears, endeavoring to translate their mumbles into viable words, but she couldn't. The footsteps of both gentlemen faded as they ascended the staircase, resulting in an abrupt end to the hushed conversation. Sighing, she picked up her book and waited for sleep... and Franklin.

His laughter echoed in the library, poisoning her peaceful dreams.

CHAPTER 14

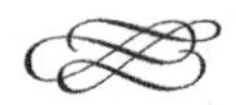

Day 4

"Is there a legitimate reason why you voluntarily abandoned a perfectly good bed in favor of these stiff chairs?"

Sam's eyes popped open, and her head snapped up. Lord Westwood resided in the adjacent armchair, his long limbs folded in a reclined position, his lips curved in a pleasant smile. The bruising on his face, diminished over the past few days, was replaced by dark circles under his eyes—an indication of sleeplessness.

"I have terrible dreams," Sam replied, still reeling from the sudden shock of discovering Lord Westwood sitting beside her in the library.

"I'm quite aware of your nocturnal difficulties... everyone in the house can hear you scream." His weary voice held an edge of concern.

Sam's mouth opened into a tiny "o." She flushed but refused to look away for fear he might vanish. Her hands twisted in her lap. Wilhelmina had said there was no word from Lord Westwood, but someone had communicated the depth of her suffering to him. Had Edward lied to her?

"Who told you?"

"Thomas." Lord Westwood lifted a glass of what Sam assumed was brandy from the nearby table. He sipped it slowly, watching her over the rim.

"Is that why you returned?" Guilt blossomed in her chest. She missed him, craved his presence like the sunlight, but interfering with his task to capture Franklin wasn't her intention. The realization he'd given up his pursuit to ascertain her well-being sent a considerable shame rippling through her body.

"That is one of the reasons." He dropped the glass lightly on the table, turning his full attention to Sam. "Are they always of your cousin?"

She nodded and shivered as Franklin's leering face floated into her mind.

"If I was here, do you believe they would desist?" he asked, his eyes glowing.

She wanted to lie, wanted him to stay. She bit her lip and dropped her gaze from his intense stare to his boots, muddied from the recent storm.

"No," she whispered miserably.

The chair groaned as Lord Westwood leaned forward, reaching out his hand to tip Sam's chin up. Before he could touch her, she shrank away from him, vehemently shaking her head.

"Please, don't. If you're a dream, you will disappear as soon as you touch me, and if you are truly here," she paused and exhaled slowly, "I cannot bear to watch you leave again."

His green eyes burned as a myriad of emotions passed through them. With a sigh, he retracted his fingers and relaxed into the chair. "I'm an illusion."

"For a dream, you look exhausted," Sam murmured.

"It stems from not sleeping in my bed." A hint of wickedness tinted Lord Westwood's half-smile. "However, that shouldn't keep you from its decadent softness."

Sam crossed her arms. "I refuse to sleep in your chamber until you do."

"Is that a fact?" Lord Westwood arched an eyebrow. "I'm intrigued by your scandalous request. However, I'm surprised to learn your brother has not required you to discontinue this nonsense." He gestured at the room.

"Wilhelmina has been distracting him," Sam replied with a small smile.

"I see." Lord Westwood nodded once, his eyes roving over her. "You're quite distracting yourself. Had we more time, I would accept your offer and put you to bed properly."

A tingle ran the length of Sam's spine, pooling in her abdomen. She cocked her head to the side, considering his statement.

"Would that convince you to stay?"

"Would you forgo your inane plot to ensnare Morris?" Lord Westwood volleyed in a dark whisper.

"No," she replied and frowned. "Have you no faith in me?"

"I have no doubt your plan will work, Miss Hastings." His face hardened. "However, I have no intention of sacrificing my fiancée to prove that fact." He scooted forward again, reaching across the distance between them. His fingers stopped short of her cheek, heat radiating from his skin.

Sam closed her eyes, leaning into his hand. "If I open my eyes and you vanish, I am going to be extremely angry with you."

He chuckled, his thumb brushing over her lower lip. She shivered under his caress, her lips parting. His hand skimmed over her jaw, sliding behind her neck and tugging gently. Sam slid out of her chair, sailing across the small space between them, and landed on his lap. Wrapping his arms around her, he surrounded her with his intoxicating scent. She opened her eyes, a smile tugging at her mouth. He bent his head, pressing his lips to hers, and she moaned, skimming her hands up his arms. Her fingers encircled his shoulders, digging into the skin as she arched against him.

"I missed that sound," he murmured as he pulled away, his eyes gleaming. "It's my second favorite sound that comes from your mouth."

"What's the first?" she panted. Her heart sputtered erratically.

"My name."

A wicked grin split his face. His mouth claimed hers, his tongue pushing past her lips, teasing. Shivers raced down Sam's spine. She shifted on his lap, desire pulsing through her body. His hand clamped down on her legs, pinning them, and he broke the kiss.

"You must stop wiggling." Passion raged behind his eyes. "Your brother won't appreciate discovering you in a compromising position."

"You are my fiancé," Sam replied, purposefully wriggling in his lap, his arousal pressing into her.

His grip tightened, and he leaned his forehead against hers.

"I'm pleased you still wish to bestow that title upon me, but tempting Edward's ire is not something I wish to do at this moment."

A door echoed directly above them, and both glanced at the ceiling.

"That must be Thomas." Lord Westwood expelled a heavy sigh. "His chamber is directly over the library."

"When will you return?" Sam asked, her voice cracking. Tears gathering in the corners of her eyes, she blinked rapidly.

"Three days' time, unless we capture Morris sooner."

"You will miss the Shirely masque."

"Such is my loss." Lord Westwood chuckled. "I do enjoy moonlit strolls with my fiancée. However, since I can't convince you to abandon your foolish plan..." He paused, studying her. "I can't convince you, correct?"

"Correct."

"Then I shall have to miss the masque." He drew his finger down her cheek. "Will you promise me something?"

"Yes," Sam replied hesitantly, drawing out the word.

"Please be cautious. I much prefer my fiancée remain alive."

A second door sounded in the house. Sam glared at the ceiling in annoyance. It appeared both Mr. Reid and Miss Clemens had awoken for the fishing excursion. The morning approached, bringing the impending end of her unexpected rendezvous with Lord Westwood.

"I must take my leave," he said and rose, depositing her on the armchair and brushing the barest of kisses on her lips. She slid her fingers through his hair. Clasping her wrists, he lowered her arms to her sides, tucking her into the chair. "Close your eyes."

She complied. His lips brushed hers in a chaste kiss, then he pulled away, taking his warmth with him. When she opened her eyes, Lord Westwood had evaporated, although his scent lingered in the library. Moments later, the door cracked open to reveal Mr. Reid, his brown eyes sparkling in the firelight.

"Miss Hastings, I'm pleased to find you awake and ready to depart." He stepped into the room, leaving the door open. "Will Miss Clemens be joining us this morning?"

"Yes, she will," Miss Clemens replied from the corridor, her soft voice floating over Mr. Reid's shoulder.

"Excellent." He grinned, turning to greet Miss Clemens with his alluring smile. He seemed to have recovered his usual buoyancy. Sam assumed Lord Westwood's late-night visit included alleviating some of his brother's anguish.

The three of them set off, fishing gear in hand, toward the sunrise and a nearby stream that passed through the country estate. Mr. Reid wandered obscurely, backtracking several times and crossing through a particular meadow three times before they emerged through the trees lining the riverbank. The journey took almost an hour due to his chaotic path.

"My secret spot." Mr. Reid gestured grandly at the gurgling stream. "Please don't speak of its location."

"Mr. Reid, how could you possibly expect us to find this place again?" Miss Clemens asked breathlessly. She stopped to adjust her hat, knocked askew by a low-hanging branch.

"Beautiful," Sam murmured, watching the sunlight glitter on the river's gentle current.

Mr. Reid spent the first hour assisting Miss Clemens since she truly had no idea how to use the fishing equipment. That allowed Sam the leisure to reminisce on her earlier conversation with Lord Westwood—although his actual presence remained in question. *Was it all just a dream? If not, how could he have escaped from the library without meeting his brother and Miss Clemens in the hallway?* She pondered several possibilities about Lord Westwood's ability to vanish soundlessly, but none of them made sense.

As Sam mulled over his disappearance, she watched Mr. Reid. Standing partially behind Miss Clemens, he instructed her on the finer points of casting. Interestingly, he was a good teacher, patient and encouraging. Miss Clemens flourished under his tutelage, learning the sport quickly. She managed to cast her own line and by mid-morning, remained the only person to reel in a catch. Squealing, Miss Clemens glowed with delight as the trout popped out of the water. Mr. Reid grabbed the slippery fish, unhooked it from the line, and carefully placed it inside a basket. Miss Clemens' skill was apparent as two more fish quickly joined the first.

After another hour of little nibbles and a few delightful shrieks, Mr. Reid leaned over the basket to determine the winner, his head bobbing absently as he counted fish. He glanced up with a grin.

"Miss Hastings, while you may not have bested me this morning, I will admit defeat to a woman." He took an exaggerated bow toward Miss Clemens. "Miss Clemens, I declare you the official champion of today's contest. Aunt Abigail will be extremely pleased with your progress on inappropriate talents."

Miss Clemens giggled and curtsied awkwardly, a blush crawling through her skin. "Thank you for your kind words. However, my proficiency can only be attributed to your excellent instruction, Mr. Reid."

He glowed at her compliment.

Fatigued and hungry, they abandon their sport in favor of lunch. With Mr. Reid leading the way, taking a much more direct route due to his grumbling stomach, they arrived at the house within twenty minutes. Dropping the fishing gear at the rear kitchen entrance, they wandered in single file through the dining room. Mr. Reid snagged a tray of sandwiches off the sideboard and headed for the parlor, following the voices of his mother and aunt. Miss Clemens trailed behind, blushing as she entered the room under Mr. Reid's boisterous announcement of her newfound fishing ability.

"Sammie," Edward called. He popped his head out of the study, blocking her progress with his body. "You have avoided me for the past few days with much success."

Sam grimaced. "I have been extremely busy."

Edward's eyes narrowed. "I'm given to believe you've been wandering about freely at all hours."

"Not at all hours," Sam muttered, her eyes sliding to the inviting sanctuary of the parlor.

"I told you to remain on the grounds." He grabbed her arm, twisting her toward him.

"I didn't stray off the estate! Mr. Reid would attest to that since you requested that he follow me," Sam replied in a huff. Her stomach groaned, protesting the slight amount of food she'd consumed the past few days.

"Thomas' behavior is outside of my control," Edward bit off.

"So is mine." Sam ripped her arm out of his grasp.

"Samantha," Edward warned, his tone aggravated.

"Yes, Edward," she replied sweetly, sending him a winning smile, forcing herself to swallow her venomous reply.

He pinched the bridge of his nose and closed his eyes.

"I received a missive from Benjamin while you were larking about this morning."

Sam's heart leapt. *Could they have already captured Franklin?*

"What did he say?"

"He and Mr. Davis have been unable to locate Franklin. The original source which claimed he was hiding at an old family farm was correct. They followed him from the farm to his country estate, chasing him south from the estate this morning, but they lost his trail. They believe he is circling back in this direction. Therefore, I must ask you not to leave the house without a chaperone." Edward's eyes belied the worry he was attempting to keep from his face.

"I suppose I will be spending most of my time in the library." Sam sighed, knowing it was useless to argue with Edward.

"If you would prefer a change of scenery, you could return to your chamber," he suggested, tilting his head.

"Lord Westwood's chamber," she said, unable to resist the

opportunity to rankle him, especially since he'd confined her indoors.

A dark cloud crossed Edward's face. "It is *your* chamber, and I expect you to remain in it this evening and every evening until we depart. If I hear of you sleeping anywhere but that room, I will lock you in myself."

"Don't leave the house without an escort, and don't sleep anywhere but Lord Westwood's bed." Sam fluttered her eyelashes. "Have I missed anything, dear brother?"

"Samantha, this is serious," Edward growled.

"I'm locked in a house with two gentlemen, numerous servants, and a pack of wild children." She flung her arms wide. "I'm safe."

"You admitted Franklin had an accomplice." Edward leaned forward, dropping his voice to a whisper. "Who do you think that person is, Sammie?"

She chewed her lip, disturbed by Edward's grave tone. "I don't know."

"Neither do we." Edward gestured at the entrance hall. "What if that person is already inside these walls?"

CHAPTER 15

Day 5

"Samantha, in an effort to divert your focus from your involuntary imprisonment, I have invited your cousin for tea this afternoon." Wilhelmina forced a tired smile at Sam over a plate of steaming eggs the next morning.

She had been screaming again. The maid told her this morning when she came to stoke the fire in Lord Westwood's chamber, "We could hear you in the servant's quarters, Miss."

"I look frightful." Sam protested, indicating the slowly healing bruises on her face.

"Alana has seen worse. She has brothers," Edward said from the head of the table. "Your condition will not surprise her in the slightest. Aidan already informed her of Franklin's violent actions against you, and she is concerned for your well-being."

As much as Sam detested any social activity, she enjoyed Alana's company and was extremely pleased to hear she was arriving for tea that afternoon. A small party of ladies was much easier to digest than the large societal functions normally foisted on her. Besides, Alana hardly qualified as a condescending society member, having caused a few scandals in her own right.

"Perhaps we can take a stroll about the gardens after breakfast." Miss Clemens spoke from Sam's left. She, too, found the splendor of the gardens enchanting. Sam discovered her meandering dreamily through the flowers on several occasions over the past few days.

"I think that would be a lovely idea," Wilhelmina replied, placing a silencing hand on Edward's arm.

"What would be a lovely idea?" Mr. Reid asked as he seated himself in front of an overflowing platter of food.

"I'm surprised at your tardiness this morning, Mr. Reid." Sam grinned at him. "Typically, you are the first to arrive when any type of refreshment is offered."

"I was unexpectedly delayed," he replied but didn't elaborate, then took a large bite of bacon, chewing slowly.

"The ladies are planning an intimate luncheon this afternoon. Would you prefer to accompany me on an errand?" Edward asked, sharing a meaningful glance with Wilhelmina. Sam wondered if Edward's unexpected engagement was motivated by Mr. Reid's disastrous relationship with Alana.

"Most definitely." Mr. Reid gulped down a cup of coffee. "Will we be leaving shortly?"

Edward nodded, rising from the table. "I will meet you in the stables in five minutes."

"Shall we save you some sandwiches?" Lady Westwood asked with a knowing wink at her son. He chuckled.

"That would be most appreciated, Mother." Mr. Reid grabbed several pieces of toast, swallowed the last of his coffee, and departed, flashing his lopsided smile.

Lady Westwood waved to her son, then returned her attention to Aunt Abigail. They bent their heads together, their whispered voices a mere hum at the table. Sam's eyes narrowed—they were plotting something.

Finishing her meal swiftly, Sam rose with Miss Clemens, who seemed grateful for the excuse to retreat from the dining room. Arms linked, they strolled through the gardens toward the gazebo, choosing a path that ran the length of the flower beds. As they sauntered down the walkway, Miss Clemens paused unexpectedly and spun toward the house.

"My room is right there." She pointed at a window centered on the second floor. "Every night, I get the pleasure of viewing these beautiful gardens by moonlight."

"What a fortuitous location," Sam said, her eyes traveling over the side of the house.

"How so?"

Sam smiled, a blush creeping into her cheeks. "Ever since Wilhelmina forced me to attend all those tedious social functions, I developed a habit of seeking out the best escape route."

Miss Clemens offered a tiny smile, her gaze flicking back to the window. "How would you flee from my room?"

"Should we find ourselves hosting a luncheon in your chamber?" Sam immediately regretted her comment when Miss Clemens' crestfallen face dropped to the pebbles along the pathway. Sam patted her arm, drawing the younger girl's attention.

"I would climb down the trellis." She indicated the wooden, ivy-covered lattice that split the wall between two windows. "There are plenty of footholds, and it's easy to reach from your window."

"There are many occasions when I wish I could escape," Miss Clemens said, her faint voice nearly overpowered by a light breeze. Her eyes searched Sam's face for reassurance.

"The next time I intend to run off, I shall take you with me." Sam winked.

"Could we forgo the masque?" Miss Clemens asked timidly. "Miss Shirely finds great enjoyment in my suffering."

Sam contemplated Miss Clemens' distressed expression.

"I must attend the masque. Plans are in motion which cannot be changed. However, Wilhelmina and I will be near you the entire evening."

Miss Clemens swallowed and nodded, her voice a mere squeak.

"Are you frightened?"

"Petrified," Sam admitted, worry squeezing her chest.

ALANA ARRIVED NOT long after Sam and Miss Clemens returned from their promenade, greeting them on the veranda. Alana looked exactly as Sam remembered—long red hair, which fell past her waist, and the same twinkling blue eyes as her father. Alana's laugh carried across the courtyard as she enveloped Sam in a tight embrace. Her contagious spunk lifted Sam's spirits.

"It has been far too long, Samantha."

"Indeed," Sam replied, gasping against Alana's strong grasp. "I would like to introduce you to Miss Daphne Clemens. She and Mrs. Stanton are guests of Lady Westwood as well. Miss Clemens, may I present Mrs. Dubois?"

"Miss Clemens." Alana curtsied politely, then laughed again. "Unfortunately, that is the extent of my manners."

"Mrs. Dubois." Daphne curtsied shyly, overwhelmed by Alana's boisterous personality.

"Now, we will have none of that formality," Alana said, waving her hand. "Please address me as Alana. I have no desire to be remembered by any other name."

"Certainly, Alana," Miss Clemens replied in a dutiful tone. "It's lovely to meet you."

"I heard you completed the Parisian finishing school." Sam escorted her into the house, Miss Clemens trailing behind them. "What happened to all the etiquette lessons foisted upon you?"

"I forgot those autocratic teachings as soon as I left the grounds." Chuckling, Alana flung a wayward tendril over her shoulder. "I still hold the record for the most demerits in one school year."

"Your father must have been thrilled."

"That he was." Alana laughed.

"Alana is the only person I know who is less proper than me," Sam half-whispered to Miss Clemens as she joined them in the entrance hall.

"I heard about the dog incident." Alana arched an eyebrow. "Getting into trouble without me, dear cousin?"

Sam snickered. Alana's company was exactly the distraction she needed.

"Hopefully, you will have the opportunity to meet Miss Randall."

"It would be my pleasure to introduce myself to the other woman involved in your shameful brawl." Alana's eyes sparkled with mischief.

"Do you intend to remain at your father's house for an extended holiday?" Sam gestured toward the parlor.

"I have no plans to leave." Alana moved toward the open doorway. "Da and Aidan need me."

"Poor Mr. Reid." Miss Clemens murmured barely loud enough for Sam to hear.

"Well, I'm pleased you have returned. I sorely missed your company," Sam replied with a smile, hoping Alana hadn't heard Miss Clemens.

She strode into the parlor behind Alana, finding Wilhelmina, Aunt Abigail, and Lady Westwood assembled around a low table, covered in various dishes of sugary refreshment. She took a seat between Miss Clemens and Alana and was reaching for a teacup when a messenger arrived at the door with a missive for Miss Clemens, who rose from her chair and accepted the note, perusing it quietly. Her face paled.

Alana glanced at her in concern. "Miss Clemens, are you ill? You look quite agitated."

"The letter is from my sister." Miss Clemens' eyes flicked to Aunt Abigail.

"Let us hear what she has to say." Aunt Abigail set her cup down, her expression grave.

Miss Clemens swallowed and read aloud, her voice trembling.

"Dearest Daphne, I am troubled regarding Mother's well-being. She has been distraught since you abandoned her in favor of less desirable company. I do not understand why you have chosen to be so willful and can only attribute your appalling behavior to the influence of your new acquaintances."

"I seem to remain extremely popular among your family," Sam muttered. Wilhelmina silenced her next comment with a warning glance. Sam pursed her lips and allowed Miss Clemens to continue reading.

"Mother has informed me she managed to arrange a fiancé for you, which is no small feat, considering your lack of acceptable attributes. If you return home, you will finally enjoy the same happiness as me, to be a wife. I will not tell you the name of the gentleman as I have sworn not to reveal his name. However, I will give you a hint. We would be sisters two times over. Love, Delilah."

A collective gasp echoed through the room, apart from Sam, whose head bobbed between Wilhelmina and Miss Clemens in confusion.

"I do not understand," Sam whispered to Wilhelmina. "Why is everyone distressed? Who is the proposed fiancé?"

Wilhelmina leaned over, murmuring, "Miss Clemens' sister is married to Mr. Alexander Shirely II."

Sam's eyes flew to Miss Clemens, and they exchanged a grimace. "What is his brother's name?"

"Mr. Robert Shirely," Wilhelmina replied with such contempt, Sam's head whipped around to stare at her.

"A vile young man," Alana added with equal vehemence. "I had the misfortune to encounter him last year at a friend's wedding."

"How shall I respond?" Miss Clemens' wide eyes pleaded with Aunt Abigail.

"We will discuss this matter properly," Lady Westwood said with authority. She set her cup down on the table as well and angled her body until she faced Miss Clemens directly. "Miss Clemens, you have received an offer of marriage from Mr. Robert Shirely. Do you accept his proposal?"

"No, I do not." She shook her head so hard, it nearly popped off her neck.

"You realize, rejecting this proposal, you may not receive another one," Lady Westwood said severely.

"I do."

"Good. We shall write to your sister with your response." Lady Westwood smiled encouragingly at Miss Clemens.

Sam glanced around the group of ladies. "I will acknowledge I don't favor Miss Shirely's company, although I've heard nothing of her family."

"You won't either." Wilhelmina's curt response surprised Samantha. Her sister-in-law usually kept her opinions more guarded.

"At least not in polite society," Alana added, retrieving her teacup.

"Which we are not." Aunt Abigail winked at Lady Westwood, who struggled to keep a grin from her lips.

"Abigail, I'm shocked." Lady Westwood's voice dripped with amusement.

Lifting her teacup from the saucer, Aunt Abigail sipped, the mirth fading from her face. When she set down her cup, there was only sadness in her eyes.

"There have been rumors surrounding Robert since his youth. The Shirely family used to have four children, three boys and one girl. The youngest boy, an adorable child by the name of Jeremiah, was about six at the time of the incident." Aunt Abigail looked to Lady Westwood for confirmation. She nodded and picked up the story where her sister had left off.

"Jeremiah and Robert were playing outside one summer day. Their governess left them alone for several minutes for some murky reason. It is even rumored young Robert bribed the governess for the few moments of privacy with his little brother."

"True or not, the Shirely's sacked the governess immediately after the investigation," Aunt Abigail interrupted.

"By the time the governess returned from her walk, Jeremiah lay unconscious on the ground, bleeding severely from his head. He died before the doctor arrived. Robert claimed Jeremiah fell and hit his head on a rock while they were playing." Lady Westwood's tone revealed she didn't believe his words.

Aunt Abigail shook her head. "The doctor stated it looked as though Jeremiah's skull had been bashed in with a rock, more damage than could be explained by Robert's story. Whatever the truth may be, the Shirelys buried it along with their son." She discreetly dabbed at her eyes with a handkerchief. "Poor little Jeremiah, he had the kindest heart."

"Didn't Mr. Davis work for them during that time period?" Aunt Abigail asked. She glanced around the circle for confirmation.

"He did," Lady Westwood replied, glancing toward the

entrance hall, as if the man they were discussing would somehow appear, despite his accompanying Benjamin on the journey to capture Franklin. "Mr. Davis left their employ shortly after the incident, working for several families over the next few years before he took the position with Benjamin. However, I have never heard him mention one word about the Shirely family."

"One of the lighthouse keepers who works with my brother Patrick was at university with the eldest Shirely brother. Patrick wrote to me that they learned the younger Mr. Shirely was expelled for attempting to beat another student to death, and I shouldn't encourage his attention." Leaning forward, Alana picked up a cookie, broke it in half, and placed one piece in her mouth.

"He tried to assault me," Miss Clemens admitted quietly, twisting a napkin into knots. All heads snapped in her direction.

"When did this occur?" Aunt Abigail asked, her face dark.

"Five days ago, when you sent me to fetch Mr. Reid from the gentlemen's club," Miss Clemens replied, her voice barely audible.

"I will kill him myself." Aunt Abigail rose from her chair, angrily knocking the table aside as she grasped her cane.

"Mr. Reid intervened on my behalf." Miss Clemens attempted to calm Aunt Abigail. Lady Westwood placed a restrictive hand on her sister's arm.

"Abigail," she said firmly. "Thomas dealt with the incident, and I am given to believe Mr. Shirely is sporting some fresh bruises due to my son's interference."

Aunt Abigail allowed herself to be cajoled back into her seat. "Daphne, I forbid you to marry Mr. Shirely."

"I shall be sure to note your objections to the union in my response to Miss Clemens' sister," Lady Westwood said, her tone surprisingly austere.

"Thankfully, Mr. Reid will be escorting you to the Shirely masque tomorrow evening." Wilhelmina offered Miss Clemens an encouraging smile.

"Will you be attending?" Alana asked politely to Aunt Abigail, ignoring the mention of Mr. Reid.

"Most certainly not!" Aunt Abigail replied with venom. "I never attend their functions."

"Yet you continue to receive and decline their annual invitation," Lady Westwood said, her mouth twitching.

"Societal decorum must be observed," Aunt Abigail replied, slamming her cane on the ground again. "Even when one is dealing with a family as vile as the Shirelys."

Samantha shuddered and wrapped her arms around her waist.

If Mr. Shirely killed his own brother, what else was he capable of? Could he be Franklin's accomplice?

CHAPTER 16

Day 6

"I believe I explicitly told you to sleep in your bedchamber." Edward peeked into the library and frowned when he caught sight of Sam pacing in front of the fireplace, her fingers tangled together in worry.

The Shirely's country estate wasn't far. If Mr. Shirely was assisting Franklin, he had an excellent—and alarming—location to hide her cousin. No one would suspect Mr. Shirely, and the Shirely family apparently held little regard for Samantha. *Did their hatred extend to Edward?*

"I'm not tired," she replied, tugging the shawl around her arms with a shiver.

With a shake of his head, Edward entered the room, shutting the door with a light click. "Everyone has gone to bed, Sammie."

"What time is it?" She paused in front of the fireplace, warming her frozen body.

"Late or early, depending on your definition of the

words," Edward replied, gliding across the room, and dropped into the nearest armchair.

"I think late is better." Sam spun around, her arms folded across her chest, pinning the shawl in place. "Where did you go today?"

"I ran an errand," Edward said, fiddling with a book on the table beside him.

"I know that," Sam grumbled.

Glancing up, Edward smiled. "Then why did you ask me?"

She growled.

"That particular behavior is not ladylike."

"Is there a specific reason you disrupted my evening or was it simply to mock me?" Sam snarled, rubbing her arms for warmth.

Edward rose, wrapped her in his arms, and rested his chin on the top of her head. He sighed, ruffling the strands of hair that escaped her braid.

"Much of my life has been spent protecting you. Tomorrow, you will deliberately place yourself in harm's way, and I can do nothing to prevent it."

"I'm already in danger." She tried to push him away, but Edward refused to release his hold. "The only change to my situation will be my locale."

"It's against my nature to allow both you and my wife to shoulder such a heavy burden," he replied, ignoring her outburst.

"You would look extremely silly in Mother's jewelry."

"Yes, I would." Edward released her and turned away, his gaze falling on the fire crackling in the grate. "Thomas and I will remain beside both of you throughout the entire evening. He and I will be carrying pistols."

"Pistols at a masque? How uncivilized," Sam said. Her flippant tone belied her true sentiments. If Edward thought carrying a weapon was necessary, he suspected the worst.

"You would be surprised how many 'fine' gentlemen are concealing weapons," he replied without any humor.

"You think Franklin will attend this evening!" The accusation flew from her lips.

"No, I don't. However, it's best we are prepared since Benjamin won't be in attendance. In that vein, I wish you to carry this with you tomorrow evening." Edward passed her an object which winked in the firelight—Franklin's penny knife.

Sam accepted the weapon with uncertainty. Heavy in her hand, she wondered how much blood the blade had drawn over its lifetime. Unfolding it curiously and inspecting the metal, it flashed ominously.

"I don't anticipate you will need the knife. However, I prefer you take every precaution."

"Have you received news from Lord Westwood?" she asked with a hopeful tone, refolding the dangerous blade. Her eyes flicked up to Edward's pinched face. *Something was wrong.*

Edward turned and paced several feet away, keeping his back to Sam. She chased him across the room and stepped in front of him, grabbing his face with both hands and twisting his head until she forced him to stare directly into her eyes, a mirror image of her own worries.

"Where is Benjamin?" she asked, a hysterical edge in her voice.

"We lost contact," Edward said after a long pause. "The last missive we sent was returned unopened."

"Is he alive?" She wobbled, her legs trembling.

"Thomas assures me Benjamin is fine." Edward grabbed her arm, steadying her. "I'm not sure of the mechanics of being a twin. Thomas simply stated he would know if something happened to Benjamin."

"Do you believe Mr. Reid?"

"Implicitly."

Sam took a deep breath, then exhaled slowly and nodded. "I'm terrified for all of us."

"I am as well," he whispered, his voice choked with emotion.

A second knock at the library door startled them. The door opened gradually to reveal Miss Clemens. Wrapped tightly in a shawl, she glided into the room and offered a tiny smile.

"Please accept my apologies for the intrusion." Her quiet voice wavered. She curtsied to Edward. "Mr. Hastings, if you would care to spend the rest of the evening with Mrs. Hastings, I will keep your sister company."

"That is quite generous of you, Miss Clemens."

"It is no trouble, Mr. Hastings." She offered him a small smile. "I'm having my own difficulties sleeping and would prefer not to spend the remainder of the night in solitude."

Edward glanced at Sam, who nodded her consent, shooing him from the room with a small gesture. Edward bowed to both Sam and Miss Clemens.

"Ladies, please do try to get some rest."

"I'm surprised to find you awake at this hour," Sam said as Edward disappeared behind the ajar library door.

Miss Clemens flushed. She took a seat in the armchair nearest the fire, chewing on her lip. When she glanced up, her hands were twisted into knots.

"How did you convince Lord Westwood to fall in love with you?" Her timid voice cracked on the last word.

"I didn't do anything," Sam replied with a hard edge, dropping into the empty armchair. "The man is frustratingly stubborn and refuses to listen to one word of reason." As the comment slipped from her lips, she realized the motive behind Miss Clemens' strange inquiry and offered her a kind smile, softening her tone. "Would this question have anything to do with Lord Westwood's brother?"

"Yes," Miss Clemens said faintly, her gaze focused on the dancing flames in the fireplace. When she spoke again, her distant voice addressed the burning logs. "I hoped my affection was mutual, especially after the lovely morning we spent fishing together. However, I fear Mr. Reid doesn't harbor any special attachment for me."

Sam sat silently for several minutes, her mind feverously devouring Miss Clemens' admission. "I suppose it would be best to involve Wilhelmina."

"Oh, no, please don't tell Mrs. Hastings." Miss Clemens' hand flew across the space between the chairs and grabbed Sam's forearm. "I can't bear the embarrassment if everyone knew of my fondness."

"Wilhelmina would never reveal anything delicate to anyone," Sam replied, withdrawing her arm from Miss Clemens' grip. "Of the three of us, she has the most experience with courting. I hardly have one season."

"Do you think it feasible Mr. Reid might regard me as a potential match?" Miss Clemens asked, returning her hand to her lap, a light pink tinge coloring her skin.

"I believe anything is possible," Sam replied, thinking about the shared glance between Lady Westwood and Mrs. Stanton the previous day. It seemed highly probable the two matrons were scheming on this very subject.

"As do I." Miss Clemens relaxed into the armchair, snuggling her shoulder blades into the plush cushion, her eyelids fluttering close. "He called me exquisite," she murmured dreamily. Light breathing following her comment as Miss Clemens slept peacefully, free of her secret.

Sam contemplated Miss Clemens' predicament. Surely, Aunt Abigail and Lady Westwood were plotting to bring her and Mr. Reid together. There was no other excuse for their recent behavior. However, Mr. Reid's abrupt temperament change at the mention of Alana's name proved he may not be a willing participant in their machinations.

Sam rose and padded over to the window, sliding between the heavy curtains. The material flowed around her until she was completely hidden. Pressing her forehead against the cold glass, she stared into the night, brightly lit up by the moon.

"Come back to me," she whispered, her warm breath feathering across the window.

Sam held her post until the sun broke the horizon. Disentangling from the curtains, Sam's eyes flicked over the unchanged library. Miss Clemens, still curled in the armchair, snored lightly. Sam covered her with her shawl. Miss Clemens mumbled incomprehensibly and sighed again, sinking deeper into the cushion.

Slipping from the room, Sam shuffled to the dining room, following the smell of food. She hoped to speak with Mr. Reid regarding his curious brotherly connection to Lord Westwood, but only an empty dining room greeted her. Mr. Reid didn't appear. She mechanically chewed, barely able to swallow a piece of toast, then abandoned her breakfast in favor of the gardens.

Wilhelmina's arm snaked out of the parlor as Sam passed by the opening and grasped Sam's sleeve, closing with an iron grip.

"We have much to do before tonight's plan can transpire, Samantha."

"Lord Westwood..." Sam said in a hollow tone.

"Is away on business," Wilhelmina replied with a note of finality. "Now, you have a final fitting this morning, and I can't allow you to disappear again. Get on your stool."

The day of the Shirely masque flew by in a blur of color and anxiety. Too soon, Sam was dressed for the occasion. She fidgeted with the gold choker which bound her throat in a sparkling band interwoven with diamonds and pearls, hiding the bruising around her neck. A comb, equal in decadence, decorated her hair, an enticing invitation to Franklin and his accomplice.

Adorned with the largest piece of the collection—the diamond and sapphire necklace—Wilhelmina vibrated restlessly, pacing the entrance hall, her eyes glancing toward the study at every pass. Next to the staircase, Miss Clemens remained pale and motionless, trying to fade into the background.

As the grandfather clock chimed in the hallway, Edward and Mr. Reid appeared by Wilhelmina's side, Edward slipping his arm through Wilhelmina's with a silly grin. She returned his smile and leaned against him as if drawing strength from his presence. He kissed the top of her head before escorting her to one of the carriages waiting, a firm hold on her waist.

Mr. Reid offered his arms to Sam and Miss Clemens with an exaggerated bow. Miss Clemens giggled uneasily, pressing her gloved hand to her mouth. Sam barely managed more than a tight smile, the sentiment not extending beyond her lips. She adjusted the necklace again, fiddling with the clasp, then took Mr. Reid's arm. Her heart hammered, pumping fear through her veins.

The short ten-minute ride to the Shirely country estate did nothing to ease Sam's worries. Her eyes darted about the carriage. Mr. Reid, catching her gaze, offered a half-hearted grin, meant to be comforting but only added to her nervousness. He thumped on the carriage wall, encouraging the driver to increase the carriage's speed. With a crack of a whip, the horses responded, jerking the coach forward. Light pressure clasped Sam's hand. Miss Clemens' gloved hand squeezed Sam's, a nervous yet comforting gesture. Sam squeezed back.

They overtook Edward's carriage—at Mr. Reid's

continued urging—passing it easily, and arrived at the Shirely estate several moments prior to Edward. Sam grimaced; Edward detested any alteration to his plans. She wondered if antagonizing Edward was a favorite pastime of the Reid brothers. Miss Clemens leaned forward, distracting Sam from her brooding, and twitched the curtain aside to peer out the window.

Taking advantage of the full moon, the Shirely's chose to host their masque in the gardens adjoining the drive. Candles flickered invitingly from their posts above the garden path, and a maze of hedges, immaculately trimmed, awaited those couples daring enough to attempt to solve the labyrinth. According to Wilhelmina, a gorgeous marble fountain wrapped in ivy and several marble benches waited at the center, but deciphering the labyrinth proved extremely difficult since the Shirely's altered the pathway each year.

Lanterns swung merrily, tickled by a gentle breeze, bathing the garden in speckled light. Small groups of costumed guests murmured among themselves, the exuberant mood of the party increasing with each new arrival. Masks of all colors, highlighted by nearby torches and the bright moon, glinted at Sam as she peeped out the window over Miss Clemens' shoulder. Sam's stomach flipped over… twice.

Swallowing, she glanced at Mr. Reid for reassurance. He pulled down his mask—identical to Edward's—black with white accents, but it couldn't hide the worry in his brown eyes. Sam donned her peacock mask, effectively hiding any remaining injuries Franklin had administered on her fragile skin. Miss Clemens repeated Sam's actions with her canary mask and drew in a shaky breath.

The coach door ripped open, causing a tiny shriek to escape from Miss Clemens. Edward's zebra mask appeared, and Sam imagined the face underneath was quite vexed.

Several quietly hissed words were exchanged between Mr. Reid and Edward before Mr. Reid climbed from the carriage. He turned, holding out his hand to Sam.

"Let's make some people angry."

Sam stepped from the safety of the carriage.

CHAPTER 17

Benjamin waited, tapping the toe of his shoe in a rapid tempo as his eyes scanned the horizon. Dusk inched its way across the sky, trailing a coat of stars behind. Out of the approaching darkness, a coach barreled, pursued closely by a twin black carriage as if the drivers were racing each other. The first coach skidded to a halt, kicking up a plume of dust. Hidden in the shadows, Benjamin studied the guests milling about the garden, several of them taking note of the newly arrived carriages.

None of them looked like Morris, but he was here or would be at some point this evening. Miss Hastings' plan would draw him to the masque, as well as the unknown accomplice, who could be anyone in attendance.

Benjamin inched forward to the edge of the black circle cloaking him. One man emerged from the second carriage, a scowl gracing his mouth, visible below the demi-mask, a scowl Benjamin knew quite well. Only Edward could grimace in that particular fashion, which meant Thomas must be occupying the first coach. After helping Mrs. Hastings from their carriage, Edward stomped to the open door of the other carriage, leaned into the cabin, and a hushed row ensued.

Thomas emerged a few moments later. As he bounded easily from the coach, Thomas clapped Edward on the shoulder with a playful grin, Thomas' infectious smile causing Mrs. Hastings to chuckle. She looped her arm through Edward's and led him to a small group at the forefront of the expansive gardens, effectively ending the argument. They all murmured as she neared, their comments regarding the beauty of her necklace carrying across the grounds toward Benjamin's hiding place.

Spinning on his heel, Thomas bowed low to the inhabitants in his carriage. Benjamin recognized Miss Hastings as soon as her arm slid into view. The breath of air he'd held over the past ten minutes whooshed from his lungs when she appeared. Accepting Thomas' hand, she floated to the ground, her beautiful face concealed by a blue mask. She turned toward Benjamin's shadow as if she could feel him lurking in the darkness and shivered under his intense gaze. The elegant necklace decorating her delicate throat shimmered in response.

His heart swelled. Fighting his desire to fly to her side and embrace her, Benjamin tore his eyes from Miss Hastings, studying the guests in attendance. Not one offered any recognition of the jewelry worn by either Mrs. or Miss Hastings. Sighing in frustration, Benjamin adjusted his mask, a triplicate of Thomas' and Edward's, and sauntered out of the night, slipping among the guests unnoticed.

It was quite easy pretending to be Thomas. Benjamin and Thomas had employed this deception on a handful of occasions with much success. Their mother—the only exception to this ruse—had no difficulty determining their true identity. However, neither she nor Aunt Abigail intended to make an appearance at tonight's masque. Thomas called their decision to refuse the Shirely's invitation an ongoing social snub.

The atypical shade of blue of Miss Hastings' dress caught Benjamin's attention. She, Thomas, and Miss Clemens—Benjamin assumed that was who the other girl must be—stood near the entrance of the garden maze, having a lively discussion regarding the best method to solve the labyrinth. Benjamin scooted closer, eavesdropping on their conversation as Edward and Mrs. Hastings joined them.

Thomas and Edward shook hands, agreeing to an unspecified bet. Each man selected a path and turned toward the ladies waiting under the rose-covered archway. Mrs. Hastings chose Edward's direction, Miss Clemens chose Thomas' direction, and Miss Hastings remained rooted to the spot, her head oscillating between both paths. Benjamin slipped next to the hedge unnoticed, listening intently.

"Honestly, I'm not certain either one of you knows the correct direction." Miss Hastings, hands on her hips, looked earnestly down each path.

"Sammie, you cannot create your own trail through the hedge," Edward said impatiently, earning a glower from his sister.

She glanced at Thomas, then back at her brother. "Edward, I'm extremely sorry, but I must choose Mr. Reid's path."

Thomas snickered. "Even your sister thinks you're mistaken."

"She frequently believes that," Edward said with a shrug. "Alright, Samantha, if you think Thomas is correct, I will meet you at the center. Good luck."

Edward and Mrs. Hastings wandered down the left path while Thomas, Miss Hastings, and Miss Clemens followed the path to the right. Before they disappeared around the first corner, Edward and Mrs. Hastings waved.

Benjamin pursued Thomas, Miss Clemens, and Miss Hastings down their trail, remaining out of sight by favoring the shadowy corners. Several meters down the path, a second split appeared. Miss Clemens and Miss Hastings decided on a different course. Thomas found himself torn between the two women. He stood at the crossroad, his brow scrunched with indecision.

"I think it best to wait here," he stated finally, a decision Benjamin agreed with. "Each of you can travel down your path and report back if you think the path will lead to the center."

After a brief discussion, Miss Clemens and Miss Hastings agreed to his plan. Nodding a quick farewell, each lady vanished around a nearby hedge, losing sight of Thomas. Thomas called out to Miss Clemens as she rounded a second bend, reminding her to remember the direction from which she came.

Benjamin approached Thomas from behind, passed him, spun around, greeting his twin with a salute, and walked backward down the path Miss Hastings chose without breaking pace. Thomas inclined his head and headed down the path Miss Clemens selected.

Five minutes later, Miss Hastings turned her third corner and froze, her breath catching. *She had heard his footsteps echoing from behind her.* Whipping her head around, Miss Hastings spotted him hiding in the shadows and gasped. Light emanating from lanterns hanging along the path glinted off the black and white mask.

"Mr. Reid, I thought you were planning to wait for Miss Clemens," Miss Hastings managed, her hand flying to her chest. She took a deep, calming breath.

Benjamin shook his head slowly. "I'm not Mr. Reid."

Miss Hastings gulped and backed away, but her progress was stopped by a thick hedge wall. She looked around wildly, searching for a plausible escape route. Sidling to the side, she found an opening in the hedge and continued her shuffle backward. Her elbows scraped against another hedge wall, the opening led to a dead end.

"Who are you then?" Miss Hastings demanded, her voice carrying across the small alcove.

"I'm surprised Mr. Reid allowed you to wander off by yourself." Benjamin took a large step forward, corralling Miss Hastings in the dead end.

"He will be joining me shortly." Miss Hastings lifted her chin, daring him.

"I would prefer he did not interrupt our privacy. It's a rare occasion that I find myself alone with you, and I intend to take full advantage of the solitude," Benjamin's deep voice rumbled. He took a second step forward and removed his mask.

"Benjamin!" Miss Hastings leapt into his open arms. He enveloped her, the scent of honeysuckle wafting over him as she snuggled into his chest, and the icy block in his stomach melted. He drew her onto his lap as they sank onto an ornamentally carved wooden bench, one of three decorating the recess.

"You look beautiful this evening," he murmured against her hair, unwilling to loosen his embrace.

Miss Hastings pulled away, stroking her hand down Benjamin's face. Her gloved thumb brushed over his lips as if she feared he might disappear in front of her.

"I missed you."

"And I, you," he replied softly.

Capturing her mouth with his, Benjamin thrust his tongue past her lips. Miss Hastings moaned, her fingers entwining in his hair. He deepened the kiss, his body clenching and flooding with desire. Arching her back, she pulled him closer. Lifting her, he twisted her a quarter-turn until she straddled him, his arousal pressed between her legs.

His lips caressed her fevered skin, and Miss Hastings moaned again, grinding into him with urgency.

"Benjamin." Her passion-filled voice begged for release.

Roughly, he pushed the hem of her dress up, pulling her hips against his erection. His fingers wandered over her thigh, intent on making her cry out his name. They worked through her underclothes, sliding across her center and dipping inside. She cried out, her hips rolling against his fingers, which froze in their wicked ministrations. Benjamin jerked his head up.

Footsteps crunched on the gravel walkway.

"Someone is approaching," he hissed, yanking Miss Hastings' gown into place. Reluctantly, he deposited her beside him on the bench, giving her a moment to collect herself. The delightful blush faded from her skin, cooled by the night air, and his entire body protested in frustration.

"Miss Clemens, since you have had much success this evening, I think it best to allow you to select the next direction." Thomas' cheerful voice carried through the hedge directly behind the bench.

Benjamin groaned, his eyes rolling upward. "Good evening, Thomas," he called through the bushes.

"Benjamin?" Thomas' surprised voice came closer to the hedge. "Where is Miss Hastings?"

"She is sitting next to me," Benjamin replied with a final nuzzle against her neck as they rose from the bench.

"Miss Hastings." Thomas' voice moved slightly. "Could it be that Benjamin is helping you cheat?"

"How so, Mr. Reid? Isn't Miss Clemens assisting you?" Miss Hastings replied with a grin.

"Miss Clemens, it is a pleasure to see you again and so soon after our last meeting. May I say you are looking ravishing this evening?" A sneering voice joined the conversation. "How fortuitous I have found you wandering alone in this maze."

"She isn't alone," Thomas replied, gravel crunching under his shoes as he moved toward the voice.

"Indeed." The drawled word oozed through the hedge. "Let us guess your name, shall we? You don't carry yourself as if you hold a title. Therefore, you can't be of great importance."

"Neither do you," Thomas growled.

This was rapidly turning into a dangerous situation.

"Who is that?" Miss Hastings whispered. Benjamin shook his head. The voice sounded vaguely familiar, and Benjamin had a nasty suspicion regarding the identity of its owner.

If it was Mr. Shirely, a fight was coming.

The cool voice continued undeterred. "You seem intent on separating my betrothed from me."

Miss Clemens gasped. "Your offer was refused."

"Your mother has overruled your unfounded sentiments," the voice blithely continued.

"Mrs. Clemens disowned her daughter," Thomas said, his voice hard. "She's no longer responsible for Miss Clemens. She's now under the care of Mrs. Stanton. It is Mrs. Stanton who determines Miss Clemens' future."

The unmistakable sound of knuckles cracking followed. "That situation will be corrected shortly."

"Miss Clemens will never be joined with your family, Mr. Shirely," Thomas snarled.

"I didn't realize you had staked a claim to Miss Clemens."

"I have no privilege with her."

"Then I'm surprised by your attention to Miss Clemens' welfare. As you are neither her fiancé nor her guardian, I can only imagine what your true interest could be," Mr. Shirely said coldly.

"Mr. Reid has remained a gentleman in all his interactions with me," Miss Clemens' soft voice replied from beside the hedge, where Thomas must have placed her when Mr. Shirely appeared.

"Miss Clemens, since you don't know the reputation of Mr. Reid as well as I do, you should hold your tongue." Mr. Shirely's voice neared her. "Unless you would like to hear of his exploits? It might lower your esteemed opinion of his good nature."

"He is still more of a gentleman than you."

Benjamin was surprised by her forceful words. He glanced at Miss Hastings, who seemed unperturbed—almost pleased —by Miss Clemens' retort.

"Mr. Reid, it appears you have a champion," Mr. Shirely mocked. "I believe I owe both of you an injustice." A twig snapped behind him. "Gentlemen, I'm pleased you've joined me this evening. The man before you is preventing my union with this lovely lady, and I crave her tonight."

Miss Hastings glanced at Benjamin, her eyes wide with fear.

"What can we do?"

Without hesitation, Benjamin shoved his hands into the brambles, hauled himself to the top of the hedge, and heaved himself over, landing with a soft grunt. Benjamin glanced at the scene. On his right, Mr. Robert Shirely and three of his acquaintances blocked the path. On the opposite side stood Thomas—fists clenched—with Miss Clemens partially hidden behind him. Her pale face washed with relief at the sight of Benjamin.

"The odds seem a bit unfair." Benjamin's menacing voice barely carried the distance between Mr. Shirely and himself.

"Lord Westwood." Mr. Shirely greeted him with a genial nod. "How wonderful you were able to attend our soiree. I heard you were away on business."

"My apologies for my unannounced appearance. I shall

attempt to be more obliging next time you wish to assault my brother."

Mr. Shirely shrugged as he glanced at the men gathered next to him. "We will be more than pleased to accommodate both of you, won't we, gentlemen?"

"What about the three of us?" Edward's angry voice boomed from behind Miss Clemens. He and Mrs. Hastings approached quickly, Edward joining the rank between Thomas and Benjamin. Mrs. Hastings wrapped Miss Clemens in a tight embrace as they moved several steps away.

Mr. Shirely blanched and took a step back. "Perhaps now is not the time for this discussion."

"Perhaps not," Edward said coldly.

"Gentlemen, I'm in need of some refreshment." Mr. Shirely inclined his head, indicating a desire to retreat.

"Mr. Shirley," Thomas called as Mr. Shirely scooted backward. "You would do well to remember Miss Clemens is now under the protection of both our families." He gestured behind him. "Any business you have with her must first be discussed with us."

"You will regret your interference, Mr. Reid," Mr. Shirely growled and disappeared around a hedge.

"Miss Clemens, I hope you will forgive our intrusion in this matter." Thomas bowed low to her.

"You are forgiven, Mr. Reid." She smiled at him gratefully, returning his bow.

Edward glanced around at the group, silently accounting for each person. "Where is Samantha?" he asked with a note of panic.

A scream answered his question.

CHAPTER 18

Sam placed the side of her face against the cool leaves of the hedge, brambles poking against her skin as she strained to overhear the conversation. Focused intently on the argument stemming from the other side of the thicket, she failed to notice the pebbles softly crunching behind her. A cold hand grasped her upper arm between the seam of her long glove and the edge of her sleeve. Icy chills speeding through Sam's skin, she screamed in terror.

"Miss Hastings, please accept my apologies. I didn't intend to alarm you." Miss Randall, swathed elegantly in a shimmering black gown, lifted her whiskered mask and smiled.

"Miss Randall," Sam stammered, her pounding heart overpowering her senses, leaving a rushing sound in her ears. This evening had her jumping at shadows.

"Samantha!" Edward yelled from the other pathway.

"I'm fine," Sam called back sheepishly. "Miss Randall startled me."

"Good evening." Miss Randall cupped her hand around her mouth and yelled her greeting with a bemused expression. She neared the hedge, stopping when she reached Sam.

Leaning over, Miss Randall whispered, "Who is on the other side of the wall?"

"Lord Westwood, Mr. Reid, my brother, his wife, and Miss Clemens," Sam replied, ticking their names off on her fingers.

"Why are they all over there?" Miss Randall smiled curiously and gestured to the solid bush wall in front of them.

"They have all chosen the incorrect path," Sam said loud enough for her voice to carry.

"Miss Hastings, are you admitting you are no longer confident in my ability to select the correct direction?" Mr. Reid's playful question floated through the leaves.

"I believe that was my original argument earlier this evening, Mr. Reid. As both you and Edward have converged, I can only conclude I was correct. Neither one of you is capable of finding the path to the center." Sam grinned at Miss Randall.

"Since you don't trust my judgment, would you care to switch partners?" Mr. Reid asked, without any trace of annoyance at her teasing. "Miss Randall may know how to solve this labyrinth."

"Do you?" Sam mouthed.

"Not in the slightest," Miss Randall whispered and winked. "However, I'm certain two clever women can determine the correct pathway."

"Mr. Reid, Miss Randall and I shall meet you at the center of this maze," Sam said with false conviction.

"Sammie, would you not prefer Wilhelmina and I accompany you on your quest to best Mr. Reid?" Edward's worried voice echoed.

"It will take you too long to backtrack," Sam replied, "Mr. Reid will have beaten us to the center by then." *Not to mention it would send Edward and Wilhelmina in the direction of Mr. Shirely and his "gentlemen" friends.*

"I can scale the wall again," Lord Westwood said, sticks breaking.

"Look at your hands." Wilhelmina's concern halted the cracking of branches.

"It's nothing," Lord Westwood replied, removing his hands from the hedge. "Only a few scratches from the brambles."

"A few?" Mr. Reid scoffed. "It looks like you attacked him with your epee again, Miss Hastings."

"Mr. Reid!" Sam choked in embarrassment. "I have already made amends for that particular slight."

"Don't you mean slice?" He snickered.

"You learned how to use an epee?" Miss Randall asked, her eyes wide.

Sam nodded and encouraged by Miss Randall's awe, admitted, "I can shoot a pistol as well. Edward wanted me to learn how to defend myself."

"That's incredible." Miss Randall gestured toward the hedge. "I wish I had the opportunity to learn such exciting subjects."

Sam leaned closer, lowering her voice. "There are other parts of my education which suffered."

"Such as?"

"I have no skill with a needle and thread."

Miss Randall laughed, her musical voice reverberating in the alcove. "I believe that particular ability is overvalued."

"What are the two of you ladies discussing so earnestly?" Mr. Reid asked. His voice was so loud, Sam thought he must have pressed his face into the hedge.

"The direction we intend to go," Miss Randall replied demurely, flashing a smile at Sam. "If we are to best you, Mr. Reid, we must have a plan."

"Sammie, will you at least promise to be cautious?" Edward asked, his worried voice floating closer.

"I will try." Sam rolled her eyes at the hedge. *How much trouble could she and Miss Randall discover inside an overgrown garden?*

"That wasn't what your brother said." Lord Westwood's growl sent a burst of desire ripping through her body, and her stomach clenched. "Say the words, Samantha."

"You're learning," Edward muttered, an approving tone in his smug voice.

"I promise to be cautious," she ground out, crossing her arms in annoyance. Both men would receive her unfettered opinion of their overprotective behavior once they were alone.

Miss Randall tugged Sam's left arm, touched her finger to her lips, and gestured to the maze with a tilt of her head. The two ladies dashed down the path, giggling. Edward's nagging voice followed them around the first bend, but it was lost among the other parties attempting to find the center of the maze.

After several meters at their fast pace, they slowed, then stopped altogether when Miss Randall halted to catch her breath. She plucked her shoe from her foot with a grimace. Upending the shoe, a tiny pebble lodged in the toe tumbled to the ground.

"I find it extremely difficult to run in these shoes." Miss Randall's melodious voice drifted from her bowed position as she rubbed a sore spot on the pad of her foot. "Would you mind if we walked for a bit?"

"Not at all." Sam took a moment, studying the labyrinth to determine their current position. From her right, orchestra music and gossiping voices drifted from the lawn. She glanced ahead at the lantern-lit path.

Miss Randall watched her silently, still attending to her foot. "What are you thinking?" she finally asked.

"We will need to take a left to realign our direction. I

believe we have drifted too far to the right." Sam pointed over Miss Randall's shoulder.

Miss Randall's gaze flashed to the path behind them. "I don't recall seeing a turn behind us."

"Nor do I." Sam chewed her lower lip. "Perhaps, we should press forward until we reach another opening."

"I agree." Miss Randall slipped her shoe on. "Grass made a much more delightful pathway."

"What do you mean?"

Miss Randall strolled to Sam's side, looping an arm through Sam's, and ambled down the path, dragging Sam with her.

"Several years ago, Mrs. Shirely demanded all the labyrinth paths be changed from soft grass to this harsh dirt walkway."

"Why?" Sam glanced down and kicked a pebble with the toe of her shoe.

"There was quite a scandal following the masque which occurred three years ago." Miss Randall offered a wry smile. "Even though this is your first season, I'm surprised you haven't heard of it."

"I have been hiding out in the country." Sam grinned. "Rumors rarely reach me."

"A fine place to avoid all types of society." Miss Randall squeezed Sam's arm, then leaned in, lowering her voice to a whisper. "The scandal involved Mr. Alexander Shirely II and Mrs. Delilah Reece. Apparently, they were carrying on and didn't hear her husband approaching down the path. He caught them in a most embarrassing position."

Sam gasped. "The grass muffled his footsteps."

"Exactly."

They walked in silence for a few moments, listening to the telltale crunch of their shoes on the gravel path. Sam couldn't keep the inappropriate question from tumbling from her lips.

"What happened when Mr. Reece discovered his wife's infidelity?"

Miss Randall paused. "Mr. Reece demanded satisfaction."

"Was there a duel?"

"There was," Miss Randall replied grimly and exhaled a heavy sigh. "Mr. Reece lost his life."

"That's dreadful," Sam gasped, her hand clasped her chest, her heart breaking for Mr. Reece. "How did his wife accept such a terrible loss?"

"She married Mr. Shirely." Miss Randall snorted.

"Mrs. Reece is Miss Clemens' sister?" Sam stopped walking.

"The very same," Miss Randall replied, her face unreadable.

"How was this quieted?" Sam felt indignant for the unfairness of the situation. "Surely a duel and subsequent death would be news."

"The Shirely family is involved in various industries and exert tremendous control over those businesses, including the printing of societal pages. The entire affair was hidden, people were paid, and witness accounts changed—it disappeared." A ghostly smile curved across Miss Randall's lips.

"How did you come to learn of this disgrace?" Sam's mind spun around the Shirely's scandalous history—two murderous brothers.

"Aunt Hattie likes to gossip." Miss Randall shrugged. "Even when it is about her own family, she has no qualms. Although Aunt Lillian guaranteed nothing was repeated outside of the family."

Sam raised an eyebrow. "How did she do that?"

"She threatened to expose the truth behind Aunt Hattie's inability to bear children."

"Which you cannot repeat," Sam said when Miss Randall fell silent.

"Please, don't hold my family's lack of morals as a reflection of my character. I realize it's difficult to imagine where I fit into the family dynamics," Miss Randall added with a grimace. "I pray you judge me by your past experience with me and not by my name alone."

Sam thought immediately of her cousin, Franklin Morris, a man more horrendous than any member of the Shirely lineage. She nodded and offered Miss Randall a smile.

"You were so kind to assist me with the Bernard incident earlier this year. The luncheon was mortifying. I never would have recovered my shoes without your help."

"Aunt Hattie was livid when she discovered us wrestling Bernard to the rug in the middle of the dining room." Miss Randall giggled.

"As soon as she opened the door, Bernard bolted from the room, my shoe dangling from his mouth." Sam laughed. "He knocked aside several ladies in his joy, including Wilhelmina, who nearly lost her balance. There we were, still tangled on the ground, sweaty, hair disheveled, my right shoe missing, and the sleeve of your gown torn."

"Mrs. Hastings thought we were involved in a brawl." Miss Clemens doubled over with laughter.

"Wilhelmina assumed I started the whole fight," Sam choked out, wiping the tears streaming down her face.

"It certainly made the luncheon much more entertaining."

"Thankfully, Bernard brought back my slobber-covered slipper. He was so proud of himself, dropping the shoe at my foot and wagging his cute little tail with abandon."

"I'm sorry he ruined your shoe." Miss Randall tugged Sam forward, resuming their slow walk.

"I hated the pair. Bernard did me an enormous favor." Sam patted Miss Randall's arm.

"Miss Hastings, I believe we shall be great friends," Miss

Randall said and grinned, pointing ahead of them. "Look over there! We have found our left."

The break in the wall appeared suddenly, as if Miss Randall's presence had coaxed it out of hiding. Passing under a large wooden archway, Sam and Miss Randall marveled at the ivy intertwined slats.

"We are venturing in the correct direction." Miss Randall trailed her fingers over the leaves of a long vine that caressed the side of the arched trellis. "This is the entrance to the main garden. I remember it from last year. We should be close to the center."

"Is there only one entry?" Sam asked as they meandered down the path.

Miss Randall shook her head. "Typically, there are two, one on each side, so Mr. Reid may still arrive before us."

Sam flashed a grin. "He may also need to turn around."

Miss Randall laughed. "He very well may."

A pleasant splashing sound, muffled by the hedge, greeted them as they rounded the corner. A second arch indicated the opening to the interior garden and the center of the maze. Decorating the heart of the labyrinth, a stone fountain gurgled merrily, and lanterns flickered around the edges of the square, casting a mellow glow.

Sam rushed forward, bursting into the garden joyfully. Empty marble benches greeted her. On the opposite side of the garden was a mirror image of the white trellis that Sam had passed beneath a moment earlier. It, too, was bereft of guests.

"We have arrived first." Sam danced happily toward the fountain, her skirt whipping in wild circles.

A clap echoed in the night—once... twice... thrice. From the reverse side of the fountain, hidden behind a large statue, a masked man appeared, shuffling slowly toward Sam. He bared his teeth, gnashing them slightly, and flashed a pistol which glinted threateningly in the moonlight.

"Miss Hastings," he purred, "I'm delighted to see you again and so quickly after our last meeting. I feared it would be some time before we would be able to rekindle our acquaintance."

"Franklin," Sam gasped, stumbling backward. She'd underestimated Franklin's desperation. She'd promised to be cautious.

He approached slowly, favoring his right side, holding the weapon in his left hand. Sam wondered about the marksmanship of his less-dominant appendage. She kept her eyes focused on the barrel of the gun, suspecting the pistol was the same one employed in the demise of Mr. Walton.

Inclining his head in a tiny bow, Franklin removed the black mask, an audible groan accompanying the movement of his right arm. His greedy eyes swept over Sam's delicate throat and the necklace which decorated it.

"I see you have found my inheritance."

Sam's hand flew to her neck as she took a large step back. A few more meters and she would be able to disappear into the maze with Miss Randall. With any luck, they could outrun Franklin, owing to his physical condition. How would she communicate her intentions to Miss Randall without Franklin catching onto her plan?

Franklin shook his head subtly, clucking his tongue. Brandishing the gun, he pointed it directly at Sam's heart. Sam froze as Franklin's eyes flicked to Miss Randall, still partially hidden under the archway.

"Where are your manners, Miss Hastings?" Franklin admonished her with a sneer. "You have neglected to introduce me to your lovely friend."

Miss Randall took a brave step forward, aligning herself with Sam, grabbing her hand for encouragement. Squaring her shoulders, she glared at Franklin.

"My name is Miss Randall. I'm the niece of Mr. Shirely, your host this evening." Her regal tone only slightly wavered.

"Miss Randall," Franklin replied with a small nod. "It's a pleasure to meet you." He paused for a moment, a light bursting in his eyes. "You must be the bastard daughter of Miss Della Randall." He smirked at her reaction. "I can tell by your unusual violet eyes... most extraordinary."

"That particular detail of my past isn't discussed in polite society." Miss Randall bristled.

"I'm not currently considered a member in good standing." Franklin strolled around them, his lips stretched into a taut sneer. "You would be residing with the Pierces, yes?"

"I am," Miss Randall replied, her eyes tracking Franklin's leisurely progress as he circled them. "However, my residence is no concern of yours."

"I'm simply making conversation." Franklin shrugged, aiming the pistol at her heart. "Under the current circumstances, I'm afraid we will not be able to cultivate our relationship any further this evening. It seems a shame to dispose of someone as striking as you; however, I cannot allow any witnesses. I shall endeavor to make your demise as quick as possible." Franklin paused and grinned, his eyes traveling the length of Sam.

"Conversely, Miss Hastings, I have no intention of giving you one bit of reprieve. I'm disappointed you managed to cover my handiwork beneath your mask. Nevertheless, once I'm finished with you, no one will recognize you, not even your own brother."

Sam shivered under his sinister gaze, icicles sliding down her spine. The penny knife- hidden in her bodice pressed its cold metal frame against her skin. A knife would hardly defend Miss Randall and herself against a gun, but any weapon was better than none. Would she be able to retrieve it before Franklin could react?

An odd crunching sound reached her ears, distant but advancing quickly. Miss Randall squeezed her hand once, a signal she heard the sound as well. Someone approached from behind them. Sam prayed Franklin wouldn't realize the significance of the noise.

The crunching sound grew louder, and it was more than one set of feet. Was it Edward and Lord Westwood? Could they have found her this quickly? Her breath caught in her throat as a quartet burst through the archway, boisterous and intoxicated.

"Robert!" Miss Randall said, relief in her voice.

Franklin cursed and disappeared behind the fountain with a hiss. Neither Mr. Shirely nor his friends noticed his departure.

"Charlotte," Mr. Shirely slurred. He sidled up to her and looped an arm around her waist, hauling her against him. "How delightful to discover you this evening. I was under the impression you weren't attending our little party."

"Robert, I would never miss an opportunity to attend the annual masque. I must say, your timing is superb." Miss Randall smiled winningly at him. "I hope you and these lovely gentlemen can escort Miss Hastings and me out of this maze as we are completely lost."

Mr. Shirely leaned toward Miss Randall, a sneer stretching across his lips. He tapped the side of his head. "Women aren't capable of logical thought. It is no wonder you can't determine the correct path. We would be pleased to lead you to safety."

"Robert, you are a dear." Miss Randall wrapped her arm around his waist, widening her smile. "Miss Hastings and I would be lost without you."

He grinned stupidly in her radiance, then glanced over at Sam, his eyes narrowing to slits. "Miss Hastings." He acknowledged her darkly. "I have a grievance to settle with your fiancé's brother."

"Then, I suggest you take the matter up with Mr. Reid as I have no contribution to your concern nor any control over his actions," Sam replied, taking a small step sideways. *This current situation could quickly escalate into something far worse than Franklin's pistol.* She shivered under Mr. Shirely's leering smile. He flung a heavy arm over her shoulders, pulling Sam closer until her head knocked against his greasy hair.

"I believe you do," he murmured. His friends closed around Sam with menacing grins.

Miss Randall calmly placed a warning hand on Mr. Shirely's chest, sliding it upward so she could grasp his chin, then yanked it toward her, speaking as one would to a child.

"Robert, this is not the proper setting where your complaint can be resolved."

He pouted, permitting Miss Randall to cajole him into submission. Dropping his arm from Sam's shoulders, he allowed her to move away from him and the overwhelming smell of alcohol. His friends, taking their cue from him, loosened their semi-circle surrounding Sam and Miss Randall.

"Now, dear cousin," Miss Randall said, her sweet tone barely a whisper. "I believe you offered to rescue two ladies in need. Are you a man of your word?"

"I am," he replied, his mouth pulled into a frown.

"Excellent." Miss Randall released her grip on his chin. "Shall we proceed? Gentlemen?"

One of the men hovering on Sam's right offered his arm with a bow. "Miss Hastings, it would be my pleasure to escort you through the maze."

Sam hesitantly accepted his arm with a tiny curtsy. "Thank you for your generous assistance, Sir."

"Mr. James Bloomhaven." He gestured to himself.

"Mr. Bloomhaven, may I offer my congratulations for

your sister's upcoming wedding?" Sam said as they passed under the archway leading back into the maze. Behind them, Robert's two spare friends straggled, their quiet conversation a concoction of rumbles and grunts.

Mr. Shirely, overhearing Sam's comment, snorted. "If it were up to me, Mr. Henry Martin wouldn't live to see his wedding day."

"Would you leave Miss Bloomhaven and her child without a husband and a father?" Miss Randall asked incredulously.

"I made the exact same point," Mr. Bloomhaven muttered.

"We did take an opportunity to share our disapproval of his actions." Growling, Mr. Shirely punched his hand, grinding his fist into his palm.

"Robert!" Miss Randall said, her jaw dropping. "You promised me you would refrain from violence."

"I promised I would prevent James from exacting his vengeance," Mr. Shirely replied with a grin. "James had no part of the beating, nor was he aware of our actions until after they occurred."

"Nor were you supposed to discuss that matter with anyone," a sickly-sweet voice announced from their left. Miss Shirely emerged from the shadows, her pale pink gown sparkling in the nearby light from a lantern. The matching pink mask rested on the blond curls framing her delicate face.

"Good evening, Alice," Miss Randall said coldly, adding the barest of nods.

"Charlotte." Miss Shirely's hate-filled gaze slid from her brother's face to her cousin's. "I was informed you didn't plan to attend this evening."

"An apparent falsehood."

Miss Shirely raised her eyebrows but said nothing. Her critical gaze slid over Sam, then returned to Mr. Shirely.

"I'm also surprised to discover Miss Hastings in your company. I was unaware the two of you were acquainted."

"We were escorting Miss Randall and Miss Hastings to the maze egress," Mr. Bloomhaven explained. "The ladies were trapped in the center of the labyrinth when we discovered them."

"Rescuing damsels in distress? That is very noble of you." Miss Shirely laughed, and her taunting eyes locked on Robert.

"Shelve your acerbic tongue, Alice. You will never catch a husband with that attitude." Miss Randall spoke quietly, but her words shimmered through the air and slapped Miss Shirely across her face. Miss Shirely's venomous glare shifted to Miss Randall again, who smiled sweetly and leaned closer. "I know about the failed engagement, Alice."

Miss Shirely seethed, her angry eyes twitching uncontrollably. Mr. Shirely snorted and turned from his irate sister, offering Miss Randall a wide grin.

"That is why you're my favorite cousin."

"Thank you, Robert." Miss Randall curtsied. "You're too kind."

"If you continue straight along this path, you will find the exit." He indicated the walkway to his right with a flick of his hand. "We will take our leave of you. Thank you for an enjoyable interlude." He bowed formally, as did Mr. Bloomhaven and their two unnamed friends. Turning, they disappeared into the maze again, their boisterous voices lost in the evening's festivities.

"Miss Hastings, shall we?" Miss Randall offered her arm, and the two ladies strolled down the path without a backward glance at Miss Shirely, who remained rooted, her hands clenched into fists.

As they neared the outlet, Sam grabbed Miss Randall's arm, her fingers creasing Miss Randall's black gloves. "Stop! Franklin is still in the maze. I must warn my brother."

Miss Randall took a deep breath as she stared at Sam. Her gaze traveled to the garden and the guests beyond the rose archway, then back to Sam.

"I suppose we should follow the other pathway. We are bound to find your brother and the rest of his party."

"Thank you, Miss Randall." A grateful sigh escaped Sam's lips.

"Should we bring some sort of weapon?" Miss Randall asked, glancing at their surroundings.

Sam yanked Franklin's penny knife from her bodice. Shock answered Sam's sheepish grin, Miss Randall paling significantly.

"Interestingly,"—Sam unfolded the knife—"not one member of my family would find that action surprising."

Miss Randall offered a weak smile in return.

"You're under no obligation to accompany me."

"I can't allow you to venture back into the labyrinth alone," Miss Randall replied, holding out her hand. Accepting the knife, she slashed it through the air with a grin, the blade flashing menacingly. "I do hope we meet Alice again."

CHAPTER 19

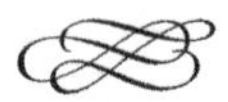

"Thomas, I, too, am beginning to doubt your abilities." Edward's exasperation reverberated off the leaves of yet another dead end. "This is the second time we've needed to backtrack. At this rate, Samantha will have had time for tea."

Thomas shrugged and flung Edward an easy smile. "We could employ Benjamin's method and simply climb over the top of the hedge."

Benjamin rolled his eyes, knocking into Thomas' chest as he passed him. "Yours is not the company I wish to keep this evening."

Edward whipped around and glared at Benjamin through narrowed eyes. Taking one step closer, he punched Benjamin's shoulder with as much force as he possibly could, then walked toward his wife, who waited with Miss Clemens at the head of the trail.

Miss Hastings' words echoed in Benjamin's head. 'Must you antagonize him?' *Yes, he must.* Benjamin grinned to himself, massaging his shoulder, and fell into step with

Thomas. A quiet chuckle carried across the space between them.

"Did you deserve that?" Thomas asked.

"Without question." *And so much more...*

As they neared the original pathway, Edward's angry voice reached their ears.

"I have already given you my answer, Mr. Lockhearst."

"I don't agree with your response," Mr. Lockhearst snarled.

Benjamin sighed, his eyes rising to the stars overhead, and shook his head. *Another delay.*

"Mr. Lockhearst, your opinion doesn't change my decision. Samantha has chosen to marry Lord Westwood."

"And I'm given to believe she is satisfied with that choice." Benjamin joined Edward with a growl, flanking Edward's right side.

"Lord Westwood." Mr. Lockhearst greeted him with a cold nod. "I have a grievance to settle with you."

"That seems to be a common theme this evening," Thomas muttered, earning a nervous giggle from Miss Clemens. Gliding backward, Thomas edged closer to the ladies, positioning himself directly between Mr. Lockhearst and Miss Clemens.

Mr. Lockhearst reached into his coat pocket and extracted a pistol. With a sneer, he pointed it directly at Benjamin's chest. "I demand satisfaction."

"Even if you dispatch Lord Westwood, I will maintain my rejection of your proposal," Edward replied, subtly twitching aside his coat to reveal the gun hidden against his hip.

Scowling, Mr. Lockhearst tightened his grip on the weapon. "Then I suppose I must offer your sister my regrets for the unexpected loss of her fiancé."

"Mr. Lockhearst!" Miss Clemens spoke, her typically meek voice colored with shock. Every head whipped in her direction, Thomas' mouth dangling open in surprise. Lifting her skirt, she stepped around him and approached Mr. Lockhearst. She curtsied to him.

"Would you truly commit a cold-blooded execution in the presence of ladies, Mr. Lockhearst?" She tilted her head and gazed at him with wide chocolate eyes. "I considered you to be a refined gentleman. Was I mistaken in my assessment of your character?"

Mr. Lockhearst paused, frozen in shock. He studied Miss Clemens as if noticing her existence for the first time. "I don't think I've ever heard you speak, Miss Clemens."

Flushing, Miss Clemens glanced down, her gloved fingers twisting together. "I rarely have anything of import to say."

"I doubt that." Thomas' compliment caused Miss Clemens to blush again. She glanced up at Thomas, peeking at him over her shoulder. He winked.

"Miss Clemens, do you not think me capable of murder?" Mr. Lockhearst asked, his eyebrow arched so high, it disappeared into his hair.

Returning her attention to him, she appraised him for some moments, then slowly shook her head. "I do not, Mr. Lockhearst," she replied, pointedly glaring at the pistol still trained on Benjamin.

"Interesting," Mr. Lockhearst murmured. He lowered the gun, tucking it back into his coat, and puffed his chest—inflated by Miss Clemens' estimation of his character. He flashed a winning smile at her, similar to the kind he favored on Miss Shirely during the croquet game. "Miss Clemens," he said, softening his gruff tone. "I recently heard gossip inferring you were engaged to Mr. Shirely. Is there any merit in that rumor?"

"There is none, Mr. Lockhearst," Miss Clemens replied firmly, holding his gaze.

"Indeed." He responded with a wider smile. "And do you possess a sizable dowry?" he asked through his toothy grin.

"I do not," Miss Clemens replied, casting her eyes toward her shoes.

"Such a pity." Mr. Lockhearst clucked. He turned his attention back to Benjamin, his voice thick with arrogance. "We will find a way to settle this matter that does not involve your death as Miss Clemens seems to think me incapable of such atrocities." He glowed, his eyes flicking over her. "I loathe changing her good opinion." Nodding to Mrs. Hastings and Miss Clemens, Mr. Lockhearst disappeared down the pathway.

Benjamin glanced at Edward with a grimace and shook his head.

Edward clapped Benjamin on his shoulder. "I suppose you're a better fiancé than Mr. Lockhearst, even with your less-than-desirable history."

"Aunt Abigail is providing you with a generous dowry. She specifically discussed the sum with Benjamin and me. Are you aware of the amount?" Thomas addressed Miss Clemens with a questioning look.

"I am," Miss Clemens replied with a deft nod. "However, I find Mr. Lockhearst's beastly personality abhorrent and not at all suited to my temperament. Nor do I wish to be attached to any man who is solely interested in my dowry."

Thomas hooted with laughter. "Miss Hastings is quickly becoming a terrible influence on you, Miss Clemens. I do hope it continues." Miss Clemens blushed again, subtly shifting closer to Thomas.

Benjamin wondered how her growing infatuation continued to elude Thomas. Surely, Thomas' observant nature would afford him the ability to recognize adoration. Then again, Benjamin only realized Miss Clemens' affection for Thomas after Miss Hastings drew his attention to the new development during the Leveret ball.

Samantha. He could hear her laughter floating through the bushes. Benjamin closed his eyes and imagined her wandering among the hedges. His mind roamed down maze pathways searching for her, checking every hidden alcove. He found her alone, glowing in blue, and his body ached to follow his mind. Honeysuckle floated in the evening air.

Benjamin's hungry eyes snapped open. "One of us should return to the start of the maze and follow Miss Hastings' path. It might get us to the center faster."

"Miss Clemens, for someone with little social standing and an exceptionally plain countenance, I'm impressed you managed to capture the attention of two different gentlemen this evening. It's a pity you could not keep it." Venom poured from the shadows.

Thomas' head flew up at the insult. He took a protective step toward Miss Clemens but found himself restrained by Edward, who shook his head subtly.

"Mr. Shirely is not a gentleman," Mrs. Hastings replied evenly as she greeted the newcomer with a curt bob. "Good evening, Miss Shirely."

"Mrs. Hastings," Miss Shirely purred. "It is a pleasure to see you again."

"Likewise, Miss Shirely," Mrs. Hastings replied, her voice tightening. She acknowledged the two ladies hovering near Alice's shoulder. "Misses Leveret."

"Mrs. Hastings," they chorused and curtsied, their identical plum costumes moving in unison.

Miss Shirely turned away from Mrs. Hastings with a sneer. "Miss Clemens, it's polite to bow to your betters."

"I shall endeavor to remember your instruction when I meet them," Miss Clemens replied, holding Miss Shirely's frosty gaze.

She arched an eyebrow, stunned by Miss Clemens' retort. "Miss Hastings' influence has not enhanced your character."

"On the contrary, I find Miss Clemens' attitude greatly improved," Mrs. Hastings replied, sliding her arm around Miss Clemens' waist.

"That is your opinion." Miss Shirely sniffed and smoothed her shimmering dress. "Husbands prefer their wives to act demure."

"I'm surprised to learn you know what qualities a good wife should possess, Miss Shirely. How many seasons have passed without a proposal?" Mrs. Hastings asked, offering Miss Clemens a subtle wink.

Bristling, Miss Shirely shot Mrs. Hastings a withering glare. "I appreciate your concern regarding my future. However, I am entertaining numerous prospects."

"That is excellent news, Miss Shirely," Mrs. Hastings replied, tilting her head. "I look forward to receiving your announcement."

Benjamin turned away, covering his snicker with a cough. *Perhaps Miss Hastings inherited her sharp tongue from her sister-in-law.*

Miss Shirely growled, returning her spiteful attention to Miss Clemens. "You will regret your rejection of my brother's offer."

"I sincerely doubt I will." Miss Clemens raised her chin.

"Miss Clemens, it's unfortunate your new acquaintances have neglected to inform you of the ramifications of crossing me and my family," Miss Shirely said, taking a step closer and stabbing her finger at Miss Clemens. "I shall ensure no man makes an attempt to gain your favor for the rest of your seasons."

"There are worse things than spinsterhood."

"I can think of nothing more delightful," Thomas said, stepping forward, pushing through Edward's restraining arm.

Miss Shirely's gaze jumped to Thomas, then slid to Edward and Benjamin, a deep blush spreading over her face. *Had she forgotten they were standing there?* She greeted them with a dazzling smile and a deep curtsy.

"Gentlemen, how delightful to see you at this festive occasion," she simpered, clasping her hands in front of her. "I do hope you are enjoying the evening."

"Miss Shirely," each man replied, offering a cold, short bow.

"I had the pleasure of conversing with your fiancée earlier," Miss Shirely said, peeking at Benjamin through her eyelashes.

"Did you?" Benjamin asked in a low tone, increasingly grateful for not extending a proposal to Miss Shirely. *Aunt Abigail's estimation of her character was correct.*

"I did. She and Miss Randall were hopelessly lost, stuck in the center of the maze." Miss Shirely painted a concerned look across her face. The effort appeared excruciating as she struggled to maintain her compassionate attitude.

"Damn," Thomas muttered, glancing at the walkway to his left. "How long ago did you leave Miss Hastings' company?"

"Not ten minutes ago, Mr. Reid." Miss Shirely regarded Thomas peculiarly. "My brother," she emphasized the word as if refuting Mrs. Hastings' low opinion of Mr. Shirely, "rescued both Miss Hastings and Miss Randall and escorted them safely to the opening of the labyrinth."

"I must thank him for his assistance," Edward replied with a frown. His gaze slid to Benjamin. Neither of them wanted to be in Mr. Shirely's debt.

"Considering Mr. Shirely's current state, I'm surprised he possessed the capacity to aid anyone." Thomas' comment earned a scowl from Miss Shirely.

"Miss Randall can be very persuasive." She shot Thomas a

meaningful glance, but Thomas looked away, refusing to acknowledge her implied insult.

With a sniff, Miss Shirely turned to her silent companions. "Ladies, I find this conversation tedious. Let us seek out some remarkable company."

Miss Shirely and the Leveret sisters turned and headed deeper into the maze, the ugly purple hue of the Leverets' dresses disappearing into the shadows. Miss Shirely's nasal tone carried for the next few minutes, proclaiming malicious abuses regarding Miss Clemens' character.

"I suppose I should be honored Miss Shirely spends so much of her time thinking about me," Miss Clemens said softly.

Thomas snorted.

"Perhaps we should return to the maze entrance," Edward said, echoing Benjamin's earlier thought. "Sammie may be waiting for us."

"Or she may tire of waiting for you and decide to search the maze." Miss Hastings rounded the corner opposite where Miss Shirely vanished. Miss Randall's ghostly form followed silently, grasping an unfolded knife tightly in her hand, her white knuckles glowing against the darkness of the labyrinth.

"Samantha." The word held every bit of Benjamin's pent-up longing, the smoldering fire inside him threatening to explode into an inferno.

She ran into his embrace, knocking Edward aside in her rush. Benjamin wrapped his arms firmly around her. Leaning into his chest, she nuzzled Benjamin's neck with a happy sigh as a tremble rolled down her back.

Edward growled, stepping toward them, but his progress was stopped by Mrs. Hastings, who put a gentle hand on her husband's arm, shaking her head. He glared at Benjamin and back at his wife, his eyes bulging. She shook her head again, arching an eyebrow. Sighing, his shoulders rolled forward, and he nodded with a grimace.

Apparently, Edward's interference had been a topic of recent conversation between the two of them. He must remember to thank Mrs. Hastings for her assistance.

"I have missed your company." Benjamin pressed his lips into the warmth of Miss Hastings' skin. His shoulder earned a blow from Edward, who had broken free of his wife. He snarled at Benjamin. Benjamin smirked.

Miss Hastings twisted in Benjamin's arms, glaring at her brother. "Stop acting ridiculous! Miss Randall and I encountered Franklin at the center of the maze. He threatened to murder both of us. Right there." She grabbed Edward's sleeve, hissing, "Edward, he had a pistol."

Miss Clemens gasped, her skin paling. She fainted in a graceless heap on the sharp gravel path. Miss Randall, her eyes rolling madly, followed, collapsing atop of Miss Clemens, the penny knife slipping from her fingers. It tumbled, blade first and stuck into the ground, millimeters from Miss Clemens' head.

"Thomas, which young lady would you prefer to assist this evening?" Benjamin asked with a half-hidden grin as he studied the two unconscious women. "They both seem quite taken with your rescuing abilities."

Miss Hastings struck Benjamin in the same place as her brother. He rubbed the tingling spot on his arm and grinned at her. "Is this additional lack of manners something else inappropriate in which Edward instructed you?"

"It is," Miss Hastings replied as she knelt next to the ladies' immobile forms. Benjamin crouched across from her, capturing her gaze with his hungry eyes.

"Do you think a husband should be aware of all his wife's capabilities prior to the wedding?"

"No." She shook her head adamantly. "It would ruin the surprise."

Benjamin glared over his shoulder at Edward. "You're not going to warn me of her talents either, are you?"

Edward smiled and shook his head. "No, I am not."

"Gentlemen." Mrs. Hastings inserted herself between Edward and Benjamin and knelt. "Given the current state of Miss Randall and Miss Clemens, I propose we postpone this discussion of Samantha's inappropriate education."

Thomas snickered and stooped beside Miss Hastings, fanning Miss Clemens and Miss Randall with his mask, his gaze flicking toward Benjamin.

"I wish to revise my earlier statement regarding Miss Hastings' dreadful influence over Miss Clemens."

"You believe Miss Clemens is a terrible influence over Miss Hastings?" Benjamin asked incredulously.

"Not at all. I believe Edward is the cause of both ladies' unsuitable behavior."

Miss Hastings burst out laughing.

Miss Randall moaned, drawing Thomas' attention. He and Mrs. Hastings helped her sit forward, moving her off Miss Clemens' supine figure, who groaned in kind.

"What happened?" Miss Clemens asked. She looked around and flushed, embarrassed by her prone position, struggling into a sitting position.

Miss Randall, lifted to her feet by Thomas, stood unsteadily and brushed the dirt from her gown. Still off-balance, she stumbled and toppled forward. Thomas easily caught her, wrapping his arms around her petite waist. She smiled gratefully, her violet eyes sparkling in the light cast from a nearby lantern. Momentarily losing his ability to speak, Thomas stared, enraptured. Edward glanced at Benjamin, amusement in his eyes.

"Thomas," Benjamin called, crouched beside Miss Clemens.

In a dreamlike movement—fluid and unhurried—Thomas raised his head and regarded Benjamin with a curious expression. "Yes?"

"Would you care to assist me?" Benjamin indicated Miss Clemens, who remained seated on the pebbly pathway.

"Certainly." Thomas reluctantly passed Miss Randall to Mrs. Hastings, who wrapped a supportive arm around her shoulders.

Miss Clemens stubbornly climbed to her feet without assistance, pushing away Benjamin's and Thomas' arms. Benjamin wondered if her sudden solitary attitude was driven by the foolish smile pasted across Thomas' face.

"Edward, Lord Westwood, Mr. Reid, I suspect you want to search the maze after Samantha's shocking announcement. However, I have no desire to patiently wait while you complete that happy task. Considering the depraved behavior Mr. Morris previously exhibited, I believe it best to return to the country estate. Samantha? Miss Clemens? Would you care to accompany me?"

"I would," Miss Clemens replied, her tone flat.

"Actually..."

"Samantha, my invitation to you was not a question," Mrs. Hastings said as Edward and Benjamin nodded in concurrence.

Miss Hastings opened her mouth to protest, but Benjamin placed a single finger over her lips, the caress eliciting a small tremor that traveled the length of her body. The diamond necklace shimmered in response. She blushed, holding his gaze.

"Are you planning to argue with me?" he asked.

"I am," she replied. Edward snorted.

Benjamin ran his fingertip along the diamonds

surrounding Miss Hastings' delicate throat. She shivered again and bit her lip. Benjamin grinned and leaned closer, his warm breath brushing lightly over the most sensitive part of her ear.

"I bet that I can change your mind. Would you like me to try?" he whispered against her skin.

"No, I would not." Edward ripped his sister away from Benjamin and pushed her toward his wife.

"You will have a difficult time locating anyone in this maze," Miss Randall said dreamily. She leaned against Thomas, who had reclaimed her from Mrs. Hastings.

"Miss Randall is correct," Miss Clemens added in an unnerving monotone. "We didn't manage to reach the center of the labyrinth. How will you find someone who is trying to remain hidden?"

Edward grumbled his agreement and ran a hand through his hair. He turned to Miss Randall. "Miss Randall, as Mr. Morris has threatened your life this evening, would you prefer an escort to your home?"

"I'm extremely grateful for your offer, Mr. Hastings." Relief washed across Miss Randall's face. "Aunt Hattie would never loan me the coach so I could depart the masque early. I'm sorry to be such a burden."

"It's no trouble at all," Thomas said with a broad grin. "I would be delighted to accompany you on the journey."

"Mr. Reid, you cannot attend Miss Randall alone," Mrs. Hastings said, lowering her voice. "Think of her reputation."

"I will travel with you." Miss Hastings volunteered as the group retraced their steps toward the maze's entry. Edward scowled at her.

"Then, I will accompany you as well." Benjamin's arm brushed against hers. Heat flickered between them, sparks threatening to combust with each step.

"I must tell Aunt Hattie. However, ambushing her in such

large numbers may cause a scene." Miss Randall glanced at Miss Hastings. "Perhaps we can inform her of my departure."

"That's an excellent idea, Miss Randall." Mrs. Hastings nodded. "Lord Westwood and Mr. Reid will meet you at their carriage."

Edward's objections overruled, he accepted defeat. "Sammie, please—"

"Be cautious," Miss Hastings said, imitating her brother's intonation. Edward glared at her in irritation, then without warning, he embraced her roughly. Just as swiftly, he released her and turned to his wife, offering his elbow.

"My dear." Mrs. Hastings entwined her arm through his as they proceeded through the maze arch toward the line of carriages decorating the expansive drive. Miss Clemens trailed behind them silently, almost invisible.

Benjamin stepped behind Miss Hastings, encircling her waist with his arms, and dropped a light kiss on the top of her head. Biting her lip, she glanced up at him, her eyes indicating Miss Clemens' shrinking form. Benjamin shrugged, having no recommendation how to heal a broken heart.

"Miss Hastings, shall we?" Miss Randall called, gesturing for Miss Hastings to follow her. Benjamin released his grip on Miss Hastings, losing sight of her among the crowd of masks. He prayed one of them was not Franklin Morris.

CHAPTER 20

Miss Randall and Sam scoured the garden for Mrs. Pierce over the next ten minutes. After passing the refreshment table a third time, Miss Randall stopped, her face scrunched with worry. "Where could she have gone?"

"Perhaps your aunt decided to try her hand at solving the maze," Sam said. *Exploring the labyrinth again, especially with Franklin still loose, seemed extremely risky. Was it worth tempting fate twice in one evening?*

"No," Miss Randall replied, quickly dismissing Sam's idea. "Aunt Hattie never ventures into the labyrinth."

"Why?" Sam asked, following Miss Randall as she wove through the throng.

"She's afraid of small, enclosed spaces. More than five minutes in the maze would be torturous," Miss Randall said in a distracted voice, her gaze searching the grounds.

"Did you notice your uncle?"

Miss Randall paused mid-step, turning to Sam with a peculiar expression. "No. Actually, I have not seen either of them all evening."

"Did you not arrive with them?" Sam frowned.

A flicker of pain slid through Miss Randall's eyes.

"My current residence is a little cottage on the edge of Uncle Horace's estate. It has been my living situation for some time. Unbeknownst to Aunt Hattie, Uncle Horace sent the carriage to my door an hour prior to their departure so I wouldn't need to walk."

"That was extremely kind of him," Sam said, unsure how to respond to Miss Randall's admission.

"I rarely have contact with anyone in the family except Uncle Horace." Her mouth pulled into a smile. "He writes to me weekly."

"Do you get lonely?" Sam lowered her voice, leaning toward Miss Randall.

"I find the solitude refreshing, although there are moments when I miss conversing with Uncle Horace." Miss Randall's gaze slid across the masked faces of the group next to them. "He possesses a fabulous sense of humor."

"I regret causing you to depart the masque early. It deprives you of societal contact."

"I find your company much more amusing. Leaving this party early is no great loss. The Shirelys are dreadful hosts." Miss Randall leaned in. "I planned to give my excuses long before our accidental meeting."

"Miss Randall, your opinion of your family, a family who took you in as a penniless orphan, should not be shared with outsiders." Mrs. Shirely pulsated behind them, her irate eyes twitching.

"Aunt Lillian." Miss Randall acknowledged the family matriarch with a tiny curtsy.

"Perhaps your lack of manners and education is truly to blame for this show of ungratefulness." Mrs. Shirely scowled.

Miss Randall narrowed her eyes. "Thank you for your

honest criticism, Aunt Lillian. My faults can only be attributed to the disinterest Aunt Hattie—and the entire family—subjected me to during my childhood. Please accept my apologies for Aunt Hattie's inability to raise proper children."

A purple hue exploded on Mrs. Shirely's face as she ground her teeth, struggling to maintain her composure.

Was she irate because of Miss Randall's allusion to Mrs. Pierce's barren condition or her improper instruction of Miss Randall? Perhaps a bit of both. How often did Miss Randall jab barbs into this particularly egregious wound?

Mrs. Shirely glared at Miss Randall, a silent argument occurring between them, malice glowing on Mrs. Shirely's face.

"Charlotte, I expect you to conduct yourself properly while in public, including refraining from denouncing the family who financially supported you."

"I didn't choose to be part of this cruel family," Miss Randall said, her hushed voice strained with rage.

"Your mother made that decision for you." Mrs. Shirely's mouth set furiously. "Selfish woman."

"Della," Miss Randall enunciated acerbically. "Her name was Della, and she was your sister."

"She," Mrs. Shirely hissed, "was careless. She left me to clean up her mess, yet again."

"Just like Aunt Hattie," Miss Randall replied and tilted her head.

Mrs. Shirely struggled not to physically attack Miss Randall.

"Hattie possessed enough sense not to ruin our family name."

"Is that how you see me, a constant blemish on your good name?" Miss Randall shot back.

"Your birth cost me a husband," Mrs. Shirely growled, millimeters from Miss Randall's face.

"I think you survived the scandal adequately, Aunt Lillian." Miss Randall smirked and gestured about at the house and expansive grounds.

"Your disrespectful attitude can only be attributed to your mysterious inheritance, no doubt. I wonder how you would act if I confiscated those funds."

"You have no control over my affairs." Miss Randall smiled sweetly. "And you never will again."

"Miss Randall, you are no longer a welcome guest. I must ask you to leave immediately." Mrs. Shirely jerked her head toward the drive.

"With pleasure." Miss Randall curtsied. "Please inform Aunt Hattie of my departure."

"Inform her yourself," Mrs. Shirely snapped. "She declined my invitation."

"When did she do that?" Perplexed, Miss Randall stared at her aunt, her mouth dropping in shock.

"I received her refusal late this evening. She claimed Horace's gout was intolerable, and they would not attend this evening's soiree. Such terrible manners." Mrs. Shirely sniffed. "It is a wonder you're not a complete heathen."

"Not unlike your son," Miss Randall replied with an arched eyebrow, her voice dangerously soft.

"Good evening, Miss Randall." Mrs. Shirely's eyes popped from her head. She turned her burning ire on Sam. "You will not repeat one word of this discussion, or I will personally have you cast out of society."

"Be careful who you threaten, Aunt Lillian," Miss Randall said and gestured to Sam with a graceful flow of her arm. "Your rough tones will offend Lord Westwood's future wife."

"I'm well aware of your engagement, Miss Hastings." Mrs. Shirely glowered at Sam. "However, I very much doubt you will fulfill that marital obligation. Lord Westwood's continued interest can only be accredited to your scandalous behavior."

"Mrs. Shirely, when I am your better, I shall remember your unfounded accusations," Sam replied softly.

"If. The word you want to use is *if* you are my better," Mrs. Shirely sneered in an equally quiet tone. "Engagements have been broken off before."

"You have experience with that, do you not, Aunt Lillian, as does your daughter?" Miss Randall leaned forward, eyes flashing, her head nearly bumped Mrs. Shirely's.

"Charlotte, I heard you were unable to attend this evening." All three ladies swiveled in the direction of the booming voice. Mr. Shirely lumbered toward them with a large smile, unaware of the heated exchange he interrupted.

"How could I miss your annual masque, Uncle Alexander?" Miss Randall raised on her toes to plant a chaste kiss on her uncle's bearded cheek. "The maze is my favorite attraction."

"Unfortunately, Charlotte must retire early," Mrs. Shirely said with feigned disappointment, forcing a smile to cross her thin lips. Sam hoped the action was as painful as it looked.

"That is a shame, Charlotte. We rarely see you." Mr. Shirely flung a jovial arm around his niece's shoulders and hugged her roughly. He noticed Sam and licked his lips appreciatively as his beady gaze unhurriedly traveled the length of her gown. Turning to Miss Randall with a broad smile, he indicated Sam with a jerk of his head. "Charlotte, before you take your leave, you must introduce me to your lovely companion."

"Uncle Alexander, I would like to introduce you to Miss Samantha Hastings." Miss Randall obliged unenthusiastically, still trapped under her uncle's heavy arm. She finally managed to extricate herself from his indelicately familiar grasp.

"Miss Hastings." Mr. Shirely lifted Sam's hand to his

mouth and slobbered on her silk glove. "It's an immense pleasure to meet you. I must say, you look ravishing this evening."

"Mr. Shirely." Sam curtsied, retracting her hand with a shudder of revulsion, the scent of alcohol overwhelming her senses. Mrs. Shirely's shrewd eyes narrowed maliciously.

"Hastings," Mr. Shirely muttered to himself. He retrieved a folded handkerchief from his breast pocket and mopped the top of his balding head absently. "Why have I heard the name?"

"My brother, Mr. Edward Hastings, just arrived home from a long trip," Sam said, distracted by the numerous beads of sweat popping out across the top of Mr. Shirely's crimson brow.

"A long trip?" Mrs. Shirely cut in with a snort. "He returned from the grave."

"Ah, yes. I remember. Frightened nearly a half dozen ladies into a dead faint." Mr. Shirely chuckled, amused by his joke.

"She's also the future wife of Lord Westwood," Miss Randall said, glaring at her aunt.

"Well, you have done well for yourself, Miss Hastings, a fine catch, I hear. Perhaps you can give my daughter some advice as she seems to be lacking husband snaring capabilities."

Mrs. Shirely's purple hue blackened, and her mouth pressed so tightly, half her face disappeared into a thin line. "My dear," she ground out, "we cannot keep these ladies from their departure. Charlotte is anxious to return home due to Horace's ailing condition."

"Of course," Mr. Shirely replied. "Miss Hastings, it was wonderful to meet you." He lifted her hand again for a second kiss. Sam grimaced, grateful for Wilhelmina's insistence on gloves.

"Charlotte, please convey my sympathies to Horace. Gout is extremely painful." He smiled winningly at Miss Randall and lifted her arm, drooling on her glove as well. His wife extracted Miss Randall's hand from his grip, aiming to steer him and his silly grin into the crowd of guests.

"Miss Hastings, may I request one more moment of your evening?" Mr. Shirely, a mountain of stubborn blubber, ignored his wife's fruitless attempts to propel him forward. "You and your extremely fortunate fiancé must join us for dinner within the next few weeks. I'm told he is an astute businessman. I would like his insight on a proposition I am mulling over."

"I doubt someone as successful as you would need my judgment regarding any financial situation. However, we would be honored to accept your invitation, Mr. Shirely." Lord Westwood's deep voice rumbled from behind her, causing a slew of shivers to dance over Sam's skin. Without turning, she leaned back. His strong arms wrapped about her waist, and a happy sigh escaped from her lips.

"We," Mr. Reid emphasized the word, "decided your tardiness might be grounds for concern." His easy grin floated over Lord Westwood's shoulder. Subtly, he moved between Sam and Miss Randall, creating a small space for himself.

Mr. Shirely gulped quickly, and his flabby face paled. "I believe I may have ingested too much drink this evening, Lord Westwood, as now I see two of you."

"They are twins, my dear. That is Lord Westwood's brother, Mr. Reid." Mrs. Shirely patted his arm reassuringly. Sam caught her fleeting eye roll.

"Ah, I see now." Mr. Shirely extended his hand to shake both Lord Westwood's and Mr. Reid's hands. "Gentlemen, I apologize for my blunder. I'm rarely current on today's social connections. I leave all those details to my fine wife." He simpered at Mrs. Shirely. She swallowed a spiteful remark, her countenance resembling a person who bit into sour fruit.

Sam wondered how the unfortunate couple had agreed upon their union. *Which splendid quality of Mrs. Shirely ensnared Mr. Shirely—perhaps it was her overwhelming beauty?* Mr. Shirely's loutish social skills would run off any well-bred lady. Sam concluded either he possessed an enormous fortune—which by the size of the estate seemed viable—or Mrs. Shirely had no other options. Possibly both theories worked in conjunction to form this tragic display of matrimony.

"Mr. Reid," Mr. Shirely said, "it would be a privilege if you would join us as well. We would be honored if you accompanied Charlotte. She spends far too much time alone in her cottage."

Mrs. Shirely's restrictive grip tightened on her husband's arm. "Alexander, we do not discuss Charlotte's current living arrangements at parties," she seethed, forcing a syrupy pitch into her hiss.

"Nonsense. Hattie's dislike of Charlotte is common knowledge," Mr. Shirely replied blithely as his wife fought to curb her exasperation. He gazed at her with surprise, realizing his error.

"Gentlemen, ladies, please excuse my forthright comment. Lillian finds it a great task to keep me proper." He flushed with embarrassment, the pink hue a complementary shade to his wife's mauve face.

Sam offered him a kind smile. "I suffer from the same affliction Mr. Shirely."

"You do?" Relief passed through his eyes. "When?"

"Just this very evening," Sam replied kindly.

"What inappropriate thing did you do today?" Lord Westwood murmured in her ear, sending a second round of tremors cascading down her spine. Unconsciously, she arched her neck toward his wicked mouth, and he smiled against her skin.

"I made a wager with Mr. Reid," Sam said, fighting the telling flush creeping through her skin.

"Did you win?" Mr. Shirely asked curiously, ignoring his wife's renewed efforts to drag him away.

"She did," Mr. Reid said, nodding at Sam.

"How delightful." Mr. Shirely grinned, lifting Sam's hand for a third kiss. Turning to his wife, he finally noticed her attempts to steer him out of the conversation.

"Of course," he said. "We are keeping Charlotte from Horace. Lord Westwood, Mr. Reid, it was a pleasure to speak with you this evening." Mr. Shirely bobbed his head politely as his wife dragged him roughly through the guests.

"Is your uncle ill?" Mr. Reid asked as they walked toward the coach.

"Aunt Lillian informed us neither Uncle Horace nor Aunt Hattie attended the masque." Miss Randall glanced at him, worry in her eyes. "It's unusual for Uncle Horace not to notify me of his absence. I would like to check on him before returning to my cottage. May we stop by the main house first?"

"Certainly," Mr. Reid said. He offered his arm, assisting Miss Randall into the waiting coach.

"I think Thomas is smitten," Lord Westwood murmured as Thomas climbed in after her.

"That is a pity." Sam clucked her tongue. "Just last night, Miss Clemens confessed her attraction for your brother. It's quite apparent he doesn't harbor the same affection."

"Thomas is an unusual gentleman. His taste may surprise you." Lord Westwood chuckled to himself, showing no remorse for his brother's impending troubles. His thumb discreetly rubbed tiny circles on the exposed skin of Sam's upper arm. "I imagine Thomas is due for a long season."

"I believe you are correct." Sam's eyes half-closed as delightful tingles rippled through her body.

"Have you been sleeping in my bed?" Lord Westwood's voice rumbled.

Heat crawled into her cheeks, and she opened her eyes. Biting her lip, she shook her head, staring into his blazing emerald eyes.

His wicked voice swirled around her. "Tonight, you will."

CHAPTER 21

"How long have you lived in the cottage?" Miss Hastings' question floated through the semi-darkness of the carriage. Miss Randall's dazzling eyes glinted, hardening as she turned toward Miss Hastings. *A strange reaction to Miss Hastings' query.*

Thomas twisted toward Miss Randall, curiosity burning in his face. It was lucky their mother didn't witness Thomas' burgeoning interest, or her meddling would increase tenfold. Benjamin snickered. *Thomas would be married before the season was through... or he would be dead.*

A chilling feeling washed over Benjamin as his gaze slid across the faces in the coach, the weight of his responsibility pressing down on him. If he failed, someone he loved would die. He glanced at Miss Hastings, his throat tightening. He'd give his last breath to protect her from her cousin. The edge in Miss Randall's voice pulled him from his thoughts.

"Shortly after I received my inheritance, I relocated to the cottage," Miss Randall said, a sneer fleetingly gracing her lips. It disappeared so quickly, Benjamin wasn't certain he'd seen it.

"Once I possessed financial freedom, I no longer needed to adhere to Aunt Hattie's restrictive condemnation."

"Are you nervous being on your own?" Thomas asked, moving forward to the edge of the bench.

"I'm not alone, Mr. Reid." Miss Randall sparkled in his direction. "The daughter of the Pierce's housekeeper looks after the cottage, and it's a short stroll to the main house, should I desire company. However, I appreciate your concern regarding my well-being."

"Miss Randall, I fear you're unaware of the peril you have placed yourself in by conversing with Miss Hastings this evening," Benjamin said, redirecting the conversation.

"I regret we involved you in this dangerous matter, an unforeseen consequence of our plan." Miss Hastings extended her gloved arm across the aisle and clasped Miss Randall's hand. "I'm shocked Franklin's depravity drove him to exact his revenge at the masque."

"Apart from the confrontation in the labyrinth, I have never interacted with Mr. Morris." Miss Randall glanced at Miss Hastings, confusion on her face. "I assume he was merely intoxicated, not one bit serious about his threat. I see no reason why he should pursue his fanciful intimidation or even remember it. Your precautions are foolish, Miss Hastings. Moreover, Aunt Hattie always spoke highly of Mr. Morris, and I have heard only praise regarding his character."

"Her opinion of him is skewed," Miss Hastings replied and retracted her arm, earning a glower from Miss Randall for the contradiction.

"Aunt Hattie is an excellent judge of character," Miss Randall said, raising her chin. The air crackled.

"Is her estimation of Miss Hastings accurate?" Benjamin asked quietly, his eyes locked on Miss Randall.

"No," she said, drawing out the word. "Aunt Hattie was incorrect in her assessment of Miss Hastings."

"Then is it possible she is also wrong concerning Mr. Morris?" he pressed.

Miss Randall's violet eyes twitched—a miniscule reaction—as she considered Benjamin's argument.

"He and Miss Hastings spent quite a bit of time together this season. I presumed there was mutual affection between the two. What could he have done to fall so far in your esteem?"

"Aside from tonight's chilling example of his true nature?" Benjamin's acidic voice reverberated in the cabin.

How could this silly woman blindly ignore her own encounter with death? Even Miss Clemens, in her innocence, understood the seriousness of Franklin's threat.

Miss Randall tilted her head thoughtfully, her mouth twisted into a delicate frown. "Yes, with the exception of his lack of etiquette this evening."

"Franklin murdered my father." Miss Hastings' hand curled into a fist. "That was not due to improper manners."

"He also nearly succeeded in stealing you from me," Benjamin growled. He snaked his arms around Miss Hastings, dragging her flush against his side. She trembled and laid her head against his shoulder, allowing him to lightly trail his lips across her forehead. The rumble in his throat was soothed by the light scent of honeysuckle as it danced through the carriage, intimately caressing his face.

"Perhaps you should show Miss Randall what atrocities Mr. Morris is capable of committing," Thomas said, an obvious attempt to deflate the tension building in the carriage.

Miss Hastings scooted forward on her bench—Benjamin's arm remaining loosely wrapped around her waist—and removed her gloves one finger at a time. She slid the silky material down her arms until the bruising on her pale skin glowed in the coach's lantern light. Her hands gently slid behind her head and tugged at the string holding the mask over her eyes.

The muted light skimmed across her battered face when she fixed her gaze on Miss Randall.

"Oh!" Miss Randall gasped, gawking at the contusions. She leaned across the aisle to inspect Miss Hastings' injuries. "Is Mr. Morris responsible?"

"He is."

"How did you survive this vicious attack?" Miss Randall asked in awe, raising her hand to touch Miss Hastings' cheek. Miss Hastings flinched.

Miss Randall paused, fingers outstretched, glancing up as if asking for permission. Miss Hastings nodded, watching Miss Randall warily as she gently pressed one finger on the largest bruise, which gleamed in various shades of purple.

Wincing, Miss Hastings drew away with a sharp intake of air, folding herself into Benjamin. Miss Randall followed, her hand inching toward Miss Hastings. Benjamin glared at her until she dropped her arm. Leaning forward in his seat, Benjamin adjusted his body until it blocked Miss Hastings from Miss Randall's probing fingers.

"Those are the wounds you can see." He snarled. *The worst ones, the ones hidden beneath her clothing, no one else had witnessed.* Benjamin shuddered, his hands clenching. *He would kill Morris.*

Thomas extended a restraining hand, placing it on Benjamin's chest. After a deep breath, Benjamin relaxed against the coach, wrapping his arms around Miss Hastings again, the red haze gathered in the corners of his vision ebbing.

"Morris is a viable threat," Thomas said, his body hovering on the edge of his bench. "The attack at the masque is evidence of his desperation."

"I'm certain I will be perfectly safe," Miss Randall scoffed and waved her hand. "Mr. Morris has no complaint with me." She looked around the faces of the coach for reassurance—none came.

"Franklin slaughtered my father in a house filled with people. He tried to execute both of us tonight during a party and would have succeeded if not for the interference of Mr. Shirely. Franklin would have no qualms attacking a woman who resides alone with only a housemaid for protection," Miss Hastings exploded, her body tensed with aggravation as she flew forward on the bench. Benjamin's arm stiffened around her waist, restraining her to his side.

"Did Mr. Shirely truly rescue you from Mr. Morris?" Thomas asked incredulously, his exaggerated expression causing Miss Hastings to laugh aloud.

"He did," Miss Hastings said as she melted into Benjamin again. "Mr. Shirely was quite the gentleman."

"More so than I?" Benjamin murmured, his lips millimeters from her intoxicating skin.

"I thought we established you were not a gentleman," she replied, her passion-filled gaze flicking to him.

Desire coursed through Benjamin's veins, hunger unfurling in his stomach. He longed to nuzzle Miss Hastings' soft skin and inhale the honeysuckle aroma which followed her every movement, to continue the moment begun earlier this evening before Franklin—once again—attempted to separate him from her. The tingles running through his limbs served to remind him of the decadent seduction waiting once he found a moment of privacy.

"As I have previously explained, Miss Hastings, gentlemen have their limits, and you continually try mine, especially in coaches."

A delightful blush circulated through Miss Hastings' face, racing toward her bodice. She glanced away, discreetly fanning her pink skin. Attempting to hide the grin gracing his mouth, Benjamin also looked away, swiveling his head toward Thomas.

"I suppose we must offer our gratitude for his magnanimous deed," Thomas grumbled, unaware of the intimate conversation between Benjamin and Miss Hastings. He crossed his arms in irritation and pouted, his lower lip pushed out dramatically. Miss Hastings laughed.

"We can do so when we dine with them," Benjamin replied, his fingers drawing absentminded patterns along the velvety skin of Miss Hastings' wrist. She shivered under his caress.

"Am I to understand that you are not a supporter of Robert's good character?" Miss Randall asked, her face blank.

Thomas locked eyes with Benjamin, who shook his head subtly. Thomas ignored his signal. "I have yet to see any of Mr. Shirely's positive attributes."

Benjamin groaned and lifted his eyes to the roof of the coach.

"What would you call his rescue of two ladies this evening?" Miss Randall asked in an oddly calm tone.

"A fortuitous accident," Thomas replied, his tone dark. "I don't think his original intention was to lead both of you to safety."

"They weren't," Miss Hastings muttered, her low comment catching Benjamin's attention.

"Should I arrange a private audience with Mr. Shirely?" he whispered in her ear.

"That isn't necessary," she replied and raised her voice, speaking clearly. "Miss Randall handled the predicament with grace."

Miss Randall blushed. "Miss Hastings, your flattery is unfounded."

"Not at all, Miss Randall. Had I discovered Mr. Shirely on my own, the situation may have ended differently." A tiny shudder rippled through her. Had his leg not been pressed against her, he wouldn't have felt the tremor. His fingers folded into a fist, his knuckles cracking loudly.

"Do you still wish to dine with the Shirely's?" Thomas glared pointedly at Benjamin's hand.

"Regardless of Mr. Shirely's true designs this evening, the result of his intervention protected both Miss Hastings and Miss Randall." He forced the words through clenched teeth.

"Are we to overlook his attack on Miss Clemens?" Thomas' anger rolled through the cabin.

"What attack?" Miss Randall asked, her face paling. Her head whipped toward Thomas.

"No." Benjamin ignored Miss Randall's question. "However, at this moment, we need as many supporters as possible. An alliance with the Shirely family would prove most beneficial in capturing Mr. Morris. I'm certain Edward and Mrs. Hastings would agree with me."

"Unless they're assisting him," Thomas muttered.

"What attack?" Miss Randall repeated loudly. Her hand closed around Thomas' upper arm.

"Your cousin cornered Miss Clemens in an alley with the intent of taking liberties with her person." Thomas' fiery tone surprised Benjamin. *Perhaps Miss Clemens' broken heart could hope...*

"When Miss Clemens protested by slapping him, the esteemed Mr. Shirely raised his hand in retribution," Thomas growled, leaning toward Miss Randall.

"That's dreadful." Miss Randall paled further. She removed her hand, tucked it in her lap, and bowed her head, her lower lip trembling. "How did she escape his rage?"

"I intervened."

"You gave Robert that black eye?" Miss Randall asked, her soft voice cracking as she peeked up at him.

"I did." Thomas' smile was cold.

"Robert needed a beating," she said, exhaling a shaky breath. "If you receive another opportunity, would you strike him once for me? Jeramiah was my favorite cousin."

"Did he kill Jeramiah?" Miss Hastings gasped, pulling out of Benjamin's embrace.

Miss Randall twisted toward Miss Hastings, her eyes rounding. "I never thought him capable."

"Until the matter with Morris is resolved, we will need to investigate our neighbors," Benjamin said, drawing Miss Hastings back on the bench. "That includes dining with the Shirely's."

"Does that mean I must act pleasant toward Miss Shirely?" Miss Hastings grumbled, curling into his chest.

Benjamin laughed, lifting her chin. "Polite is all I ask of you... both of you." He glared at Thomas, who cursed under his breath.

"It's not a difficult task Mr. Reid." Miss Randall patted Thomas' arm. "I have been pretending to be civil for years, and I would much rather that Alice was run over by a coach."

Thomas choked on his laughter. "You must give me some advice, Miss Randall."

She glanced around the carriage as if fearful her aunt would hear her divulge her secret, then nodded and moved closer to Thomas.

"As a child, whenever I acted inappropriately or embarrassed Aunt Hattie, she would beat me with a cane and lock me in an empty maid's chamber for days with no food. I practiced in front of the mirror, fabricating expressions that concealed my true thoughts. Once I perfected my face, the punishments stopped."

"Why did you stay?" Miss Hastings asked, her horrified tone conveying the same thought plaguing Benjamin.

"I had no other family, no one to assist me." Miss Randall offered a sad smile. "I never knew my father, who abandoned me before birth, and my mother passed away during childbirth. No one returned to claim me. I never learned my father's name."

"As much as you detest the family you are connected to, it would be prudent if you surround yourself with people you trust until Morris is arrested," Benjamin said, the arm wrapped around Miss Hastings constricted, pulling her hip flush with his.

As long as he could touch her, could hold her, he knew she was safe.

"Are you suggesting I move back into the main house with Aunt Hattie and Uncle Horace?" Miss Randall's flabbergasted tone was laced with the anger of her painful admission.

"It would be wise." Benjamin's heart squeezed with sympathy. Miss Randall, subjected to years of abuse, had risen above her tormentors, and now, he was sending her back to them... for protection.

"Franklin specifically discussed your family and your current residence. He knows where to find you." Miss Hastings leaned forward, dragging Benjamin with her, and grasped Miss Randall's hand.

"I fail to understand why Mr. Morris would turn his sadistic attention on someone as slight as myself." Miss Randall's lip trembled, the realization of how dangerous Franklin Morris truly was crashing down on her. Her shoulders slumped.

"You were a witness to his murderous intentions. He will eventually come for you." Miss Hastings' grim words hung in the carriage.

Miss Randall gulped, her violet eyes lightening to lavender. "But Mr. Morris has no qualms with me." Her high-pitched voice bordered on hysteria.

"Desperate men tend to be extremely dangerous and unpredictable," Benjamin said, knowing his words would terrify her.

Miss Randall's breath came in short gasps. "What does he want?"

"He's looking for this." Miss Hastings indicated the elegant necklace adorning her throat.

"Your jewelry?" Miss Randall raised her eyebrows.

"He's seeking to claim the entire ancestral collection." Miss Hastings indicated the comb in her hair. "The pieces are exceptionally valuable."

"His motivation is greed? Why not give him the equivalence in money?" Miss Randall asked, her hopeful gaze bouncing around the coach. Her proposal was met with silence.

Miss Hastings responded after a moment, her voice shuddering as she spoke.

"Franklin has a long-standing grievance against my father and my family. Even with the jewelry—or monetary equivalent as you generously recommend *we* pay—his anger would not be sated."

"You need to warn your aunt and uncle as well," Thomas said, his features in half-shadow.

Miss Randall spun to face him. "They won't believe me."

"You must convince them." Thomas covered her free hand with his and squeezed. "Their lives are in jeopardy."

CHAPTER 22

"Perhaps you could accompany me to speak with them, Mr. Reid," Miss Randall said, her face nearly chalk-white. She looked as though she was about to faint. "While you are not on Aunt Hattie's list of esteemed colleagues, Uncle Horace has enough reason to listen to your concerns despite Hattie's prejudices. He will see the danger of the situation."

Mr. Reid turned toward his brother with an evil grin. "All this unpleasantness could have been avoided if you simply married Miss Shirely." He moved out of arm's reach of Lord Westwood, whose annoyance crackled dangerously.

Miss Randall glanced at both men in surprise. "When Aunt Hattie revealed Alice was to marry the most eligible bachelor this season, I had no idea she was referring to you, Lord Westwood."

Snickering, Mr. Reid clamped his hand over his mouth, gesturing to Lord Westwood to answer the question.

"It was a brief consideration on my part." Tightening his grip around Sam's waist, he leaned closer and whispered, "However, I find my current fiancée much more suitable."

"As do I," Mr. Reid said, winking at Sam. Then, sighing dramatically, he turned to Miss Randall. "I suppose, since my brother is unwilling to assist me, I will champion your cause and endure the critical eyes of your aunt."

"Thank you." Miss Randall beamed. For the second time that evening, she patted Mr. Reid's arm. He radiated under her singular attention. Lord Westwood tapped his fingers against Sam's arm, and she nodded once in acknowledgment, her face scrunched into a worried frown. *How could sweet Miss Clemens compete with someone as striking as Miss Randall?*

"We can speak with Miss Clemens together if you like," he murmured out of the side of his mouth.

Sam trembled when his warm breath brushed against her sensitive skin. "I will talk with her alone, which will save her embarrassment."

The coach pulled into the drive leading toward the main house. Leaping from the coach, Mr. Reid spun and offered his arm to Miss Randall, bowing with a grand gesture. She placed her quaking hand in his and climbed from the carriage. His hand firmly gripping hers, Mr. Reid escorted Miss Randall to the door.

She raised her hand and rapped twice. No one appeared. She glanced at Mr. Reid, a tiny line appearing in her forehead. He shrugged. Rapping a second time, Miss Randall pounded on the door with a closed fist.

"Do you have a key?" Mr. Reid's voice carried across the drive.

"No," Miss Randall sourly replied. "I'm not allowed."

Mr. Reid reached around Miss Randall and attempted the knob. The door—unlocked—swung open slowly to reveal the inky cavern of the foyer. Miss Randall and Mr. Reid disappeared into the blackness. A minute later, Miss Randall's blood-curdling shriek echoed into the night.

Scrambling from the carriage, Lord Westwood and Sam

raced to the open door. Hurtling inside, Lord Westwood grabbed Sam, forcing her to remain behind his body. He stopped in the entranceway, and Sam slipped out of his grip, darted around him, and tripped over Miss Randall's sprawled form. Miss Randall screamed again.

A small circle of light approached from upstairs, highlighting the rug over which Miss Randall tripped. "What are you doing here? Miss Randall, your aunt will have my head if she catches you in the house!"

Miss Randall, staring up from the floor, greeted the surly housekeeper with a defiant frown. "Good evening, Mrs. Larson. I came to visit Uncle Horace. Aunt Lillian stated his poor health prevented both my aunt and him from attending this evening's soiree, and I was concerned for him."

Mrs. Larson continued her slow, heavy-footed descent, stopping once she reached the tips of Miss Randall's shoes. The lamp Mrs. Larson carried cast gruesome shadows across the entranceway.

"Mrs. Shirely is incorrect. They left for the masque several hours prior to your unannounced visit. They are not expected to return until well after midnight."

"They never arrived at Aunt Lillian's house," Miss Randall said as she climbed to her feet, delicately smoothing the wrinkles from her skirt. She kicked the wrinkled rug back into place and studied Mrs. Larson carefully. "Did you see them leave?"

Opening her mouth to reply, Mrs. Larson paused and exhaled slowly. "Well, no. I was feeding the chickens when I heard the coach wheels on the drive. I assumed they departed for your aunt's estate."

Miss Randall whipped around to face Mr. Reid, her hands clutched to her chest. "Do you think they are in danger?"

"We cannot know yet," Mr. Reid replied, his tone hesitant. "They could have broken a carriage wheel on the road."

"We would have seen them," Sam said as she rose from the floor with Lord Westwood's assistance. She glowered at Mr. Reid. "Do not put false hope into Miss Randall's head."

Lord Westwood nodded in agreement. "If they never arrived at the masque, it's likely Mr. Morris called upon Mr. and Mrs. Pierce before they departed."

"You stated your uncle sent the carriage for you." Sam looked to Miss Randall for confirmation, and she nodded. "Was there anyone else here when you left?"

"I didn't see anyone."

Mr. Reid stroked his chin as his gaze slid between his brother and Miss Randall. "Perhaps the missive came from Franklin instead."

"Aunt Lillian knows Hattie's hand." Miss Randall shook her head. "If the letter was falsified, who forged it with such great aptitude?"

"It's possible your aunt did write the letter. Morris can be extremely convincing." Lord Westwood replied, his tone hinted at something dark.

"Where would he take them?" Miss Randall flew at him, her hands closing around his coat, desperation flowed from her body.

"I don't know." He gently pried her fingers from his jacket.

"Mrs. Larson, have you seen anything or anyone suspicious tonight?" Mr. Reid asked, his voice almost pleading.

"No," she replied quickly, then paused, her mouth working furiously as she considered the evening's events. "They may have traveled past Miss Randall's cottage. I remember hearing a horse whinny."

"We need to investigate your cottage," Mr. Reid said and shepherded Miss Randall through the entranceway, murmuring reassurances.

Sam and Lord Westwood followed languidly. Taking the

opportunity to slip his arm around Sam's waist, his fingers edged downward and tightened momentarily on her hip before he loosened her again, then descended the veranda steps. Sam slid past him, pressing her body against his, looking up at the exact moment of contact, and bit her lip.

"I intend on sleeping in your bed tonight, Lord Westwood," she whispered, sashaying toward the coach.

"I do as well." Catching her hand, he roughly pulled her against his mouth, kissing her unrelentingly until Sam pulled away, panting. Her stomach clenched. Chuckling softly, he released her to stagger toward the waiting carriage. Mr. Reid's impatient face appeared around the back coach wheel, his mouth pursed as Sam approached, drunkenly weaving around him.

"We have pressing matters which need attending, dear brother," Mr. Reid said, his gaze flicking to Lord Westwood.

"Mrs. Larson," Lord Westwood called from the steps. She popped her head out the open door. "For your own personal safety, I would recommend locking up the house until we can locate Mr. and Mrs. Pierce."

Mrs. Larson gulped. "My Lord, my daughter works in the cottage."

"We will ensure her safety as well, Mrs. Larson," Lord Westwood replied with a curt nod. "Would you prefer her to return to the main house?"

"No, thank you, my Lord." Mrs. Larson shook her head. "Her place is assisting Miss Randall. I can't remove her from her job." She vanished into the house and slammed the door with a definitive click of the lock.

Lord Westwood rounded the back of the carriage and climbed into the coach, finding Sam seated next to Miss Randall, her arm wrapped tightly around Miss Randall's shaking shoulders. Sam shrugged, offering him a silent apology.

Flashing a sour grin, Mr. Reid patted the empty bench seat next to him. Lord Westwood grimaced and dropped into the seat. The carriage lurked forward, rolling rapidly toward the cottage on the edge of the property.

"Whoa," Mr. Davis commanded the horses from the driver's seat. The coach slowed, stopping directly in front of a dirt path leading to a small cottage. A petite garden, illuminated by candlelight from the parlor, sat to the right of the pathway, neat rows of vegetables lining the patch, blooming in various states of growth.

"I wish you to remain in the coach until we ensure Morris is not here," Lord Westwood murmured in Sam's ear. She nodded a quick bob, giving his hand a squeeze. He climbed from the coach, Mr. Reid following him. Sam hugged Miss Randall, whose tremors increased with each passing minute.

A tiny girl, barely fourteen years old, burst from the front door, holding a lantern. Wisps of brown hair, loose from her bun, fell in strings around her pale face, accentuating her large brown eyes. She rushed past Lord Westwood and Mr. Reid, knocking them aside in her desperate attempt to get to the carriage.

"Miss Randall!" the little mouse-girl squeaked.

"Miss Larson!" Miss Randall extended her hand gracefully —which Mr. Reid jumped to her side to claim—and stepped fluidly onto the path leading to the cottage doorway. She embraced the girl. "I'm so pleased to see you."

"Miss Randall, I have been extremely concerned," Miss Larson replied, twisting her hands in the apron which hung from her waist. "I thought he took you, too." She locked her arms around Miss Randall's waist, sobbing uncontrollably.

"As you can see, I am perfectly safe," Miss Randall said, leaning back. She framed the young girl's face with her hands, wiping away the tears. "What did you mean by *he took you too*?"

"A masked man came by the cottage earlier this evening in Mr. Pierce's carriage. He wanted me to inform you he called." Miss Larson glanced at the ground.

"Who was the man?" Lord Westwood interrupted, helping Sam step from the coach. He wrapped his arm around her waist, discreetly dropping a kiss on her head.

"I don't know his name, my Lord." Turning her wide eyes toward him, Miss Larson shook her head so hard, Sam feared it would fall from her slight shoulders. "I didn't think to ask."

"It's of little importance, Miss Larson," Miss Randall said kindly, capturing the young girl's attention again. "Please continue your story."

"The man rapped on the door loudly. I heard him curse to himself before he knocked again. Once I opened the door—only a bit—he demanded I grant him access to the cottage. I informed him you were away, and no visitors were allowed entrance unless the mistress of the house was present. He flew into a terrible rage, screaming blasphemies and throwing your favorite bench into the garden." She indicated a faded, wooden bench, overturned and sullenly neglected in the center of the garden.

"How terrifying," Miss Randall said and placed her arm over the girl's slight shoulders, "It is well you didn't usher him into the cottage." Miss Randall's head inclined slightly as she squinted into the semi-darkness at the garden. "Were any of the turnips damaged?"

"A few," Miss Larson replied, turning her gaze to the garden. She sniffed once. "I didn't inspect them closely. I was afraid to leave the safety of the cottage, nor do I have the strength to lift the bench."

"I can assist you," Mr. Reid said, puffing out his chest.

Poor Miss Clemens, her unrequited interest in Mr. Reid can only end badly. Sam laid her head on Lord Westwood's shoulder, watching Mr. Reid thread his way through the garden rows, nimbly dancing on his toes to avoid crushing more vegetables.

"Was there anyone else in the carriage?" Lord Westwood asked, drawing Miss Larson back to the discussion.

"Yes, my Lord," Miss Larson replied with a curtsy. "Mr. and Mrs. Pierce, dressed in their masks and costumes, watched the entire episode."

"Did they say anything?" Mr. Reid grunted as he hefted the bench from the garden bed. Righting it, he placed the bench under the parlor window.

"No, sir." Miss Larson curtsied a second time. "I hoped they would intervene, but neither of them moved, just sat like statues."

"After throwing the bench, did the man leave?" Lord Westwood asked, his gaze gliding over the shadows stretching around the cottage. *Was Morris watching them?*

"He requested a bottle of wine. I looked to Mr. Pierce for confirmation. He gestured his consent, so I gave the man one from the cellar. I hope you are not angry with me, Miss Randall." The words tumbled out in a rush, smushed together into a garbled mess by Miss Larson's terror.

"If Uncle Horace indicated his agreement, I have no qualms with you giving them some refreshment." Miss Randall offered her a faint smile. "Do you think the man will return?"

"He didn't say. He only stated I should inform you of his visit."

Miss Randall glanced at Mr. Reid, her violet eyes filled with fear. "What should I do?"

"Stay with us," Mr. Reid said, jerking his hand toward the coach. "There are plenty of rooms at the country estate, and Mother adores houseguests."

"That would be delightful," Sam said with an encouraging nod.

"You may bring Miss Larson with you," Lord Westwood added, gesturing toward the driver's bench. "Mr. Davis wouldn't mind the company."

The scowl on Mr. Davis' face revealed the opposite, but he kept his mouth shut and merely nodded.

"I will collect my things." Curtsying again, Miss Larson scuttled into the house.

"It will take me some time to gather a traveling trunk," Miss Randall said, her gaze on the cottage. "Miss Hastings, would you be willing to assist me?"

"Certainly," Sam replied, peeling Lord Westwood's arm from around her waist. He lifted her hand, pressing a searing kiss on her palm. Shivers skated up her arm. His eyes glowed.

"Do not tarry. We need to keep moving. Morris can't be too far behind us. By now, he knows we left the masque with Miss Randall and discovered her aunt and uncle missing."

CHAPTER 23

"How are we going to fasten the lid?" Miss Randall asked, hysteria bubbling in her voice as she hastily ripped dresses from her armoire and tossed them into a nearby traveling trunk. The trunk, covered in a faded hide, was barely visible beneath a growing mound of clothing. "What if Mr. Morris returns for me, and I'm still packing?"

"Lord Westwood and Mr. Reid will ensure our safety," Sam replied, her tight tone belying her confidence. *What if he returned? Would Lord Westwood and his brother overcome Franklin and his accomplice?*

"I just need one more dress," Miss Randall said, diving back into the armoire.

"Do you only have the one trunk?" Sam asked warily as she tucked the haphazardly thrown frocks into the studded chest. The final dress, flung without aim, landed atop of Sam's head.

"Unfortunately." Miss Randall spun with a grimace, her gaze landing on the trunk. She giggled when she saw the location of the last frock she threw. "My apologies, Miss Hastings, it appears I'm attempting to clothe you as I pack."

Sam laughed and pulled the gown from her head. Handing it to Miss Randall, Sam rose from her kneeling position while Miss Randall dropped the dress onto the pile.

"That should be the last item." Miss Randall pantomime closing the trunk.

Sam flipped the lid over—a five-centimeter gap remained between the lip and the trunk edge. She placed her hands on the top and pushed it down. Studded letters, embellished on the lid, flashed in the lamplight. She glanced up at Miss Randall.

"Who is D. R.?"

"My mother, Della Randall," Miss Randall replied, a hitch in her voice. She glided forward and traced the letters lovingly. "I rarely travel, so I have no need for luggage. However, Uncle Horace secretly gave this to me when I relocated to the cottage. He thought I should have something my mother owned." Her glowing eyes flicked up, pleading. "I swore I wouldn't reveal my possession of the trunk to Aunt Hattie."

"Would she not see the trunk when she called on you?" Sam shoved, but the lid didn't close.

"Aunt Hattie would never deign to visit me." Miss Randall's eyes narrowed. "She hates this cottage." Leaning forward, she slammed her hands on the lid, placing all her weight on the trunk, but the lid still refused to catch the lock.

"Why? I realize the cottage is petite, but it holds a quaint charm." Sam leaned forward, adding her full weight to the stubborn lid.

"I agree." Miss Randall forced a smile and glanced up, blowing out an exasperated breath, ruffling the dark hair framing her face. "Aunt Hattie once told me her recollections of this cottage are horrifying. She never speaks of them."

"What happened?" Sam whispered.

"I don't know." Miss Randall shrugged, an indication even Mrs. Pierce was capable of secrecy. "She sequestered in this cottage for several weeks during my infancy. Aunt Hattie abhors anything associated with those memories, including me. I have my suspicions, though."

A light tapping echoed in the bedchamber. Miss Randall shrieked and shrank away from the sound. Sam's heart hammered wildly as it jumped into her throat—a sickening lump of terror.

Franklin wouldn't knock.

The door edged open gradually, and Miss Larson peeked her head into the room. Her hair, smoothed into an acceptable hairdo, was pinned beneath a white cap. She clasped a worn carpetbag tightly in her trembling fingers, which vibrated in a dingy blur as she slipped into the room. The lantern she carried also shook uncontrollably.

"My apologies, Miss Randall, I didn't mean to startle you," Miss Larson said with a curtsy.

"Have you gathered all your personal belongings?" Miss Randall asked, grunting as she attempted to push the chest lid closed again.

"I have." Miss Larson paused, her eyes cast downward. "Miss Randall, I hope you aren't too disappointed in my service."

"Certainly not. You did admirably well for your first position. I understand this new development is alarming. I encourage you to return to your mother's protection. Once this nonsense is resolved, I would be pleased if you resumed your post."

"I would be honored, Miss Randall, if you would allow me to continue my service." Miss Larson bowed low. "I would just like to tell my mother goodbye before we leave."

"Would you like an escort to accompany you to the main house?" Sam asked softly, not wanting to frighten the girl further.

"No, thank you, Miss Hastings." Miss Larson shook her

head, speaking to Sam's shoes. "I'm perfectly capable of walking the short distance between the cottage and the Pierce residence."

Abandoning her effort to force the trunk closed, Miss Randall rushed to Miss Larson, flinging her arms around the younger girl. "Please allow Mr. Reid to convey you to your mother."

"If those are your wishes," Miss Larson replied, standing motionless in Miss Randall's embrace.

"They are," Miss Randall said, a hard edge in her voice as she released Miss Larson.

Miss Larson curtsied once again, then disappeared into the hallway darkness, her lantern light extinguished immediately. Miss Randall leaned into the corridor to ensure Miss Larson complied with her demand to request Mr. Reid's accompaniment to the main house, then turned back to the room and blew out a deep breath, her hands resting on her hips as she glided gracefully toward the partially open chest. She tilted her head to the right and left as she contemplated the brimming crate.

"What do you propose we do about my trunk?"

Sam glared at the stubborn chest. "You could sit on the lid," she said, gently pushing down on the top.

"That may work." Miss Randall giggled, glancing around the room as though they would be caught in their improper activity. "However, I believe we should try it together. Our combined weight would be most effective."

Both ladies sank onto the lid simultaneously. The lid groaned and touched the top of the trunk but did not close completely. Sam slid off the lid, poking excess material back into the chest, chewing her lip absently as she worked around the edge.

"Perhaps we could jump on to it," Sam said, lifting her gaze.

"From the bed?" Miss Randall asked, a gleam in her eye. Her gaze flicked from the bed to the temperamental lid, which she remained seated atop.

"Hopefully, we won't break the trunk lid." Sam trailed her fingers over the corner.

"It's fairly sturdy." Miss Randall rose with a grin, the closure springing away from the lock. She climbed onto the bed and positioned her feet at the edge. Gesturing to Sam, Miss Randall held out her hand to pull Sam up beside her. Grasping Sam's hand, she nodded once.

They jumped, landing deftly on the lid, their hands still linked. The lid moaned and clicked closed. Miss Randall leapt off the chest, slid the key into the lock, and wrenched it to the side.

"I think that will hold." Miss Randall walked around the three visible sides of the trunk, and nothing protruded from inside.

Sam hopped down from the lid. "I very much doubt we will have enough strength to move your trunk."

"Once Mr. Reid returns, he and your fiancé should be able to carry the chest," Miss Randall said airily, waving her hand. "Since we have some time before Mr. Reid arrives, I would like to ensure the cottage is properly closed up."

Sam trailed Miss Randall through the cottage's small rooms, following the light emitted from her lantern. Beginning in the kitchen, Miss Randall methodically secured each window and door—including the well-stocked pantry door—as she moved through the miniscule living.

Four rooms in total—one kitchen, two bedchambers, and one parlor that doubled as a dining area. The parlor window, through which Sam could see Lord Westwood pacing anxiously outside, must have been Miss Randall's favorite view. An armchair, the most decadent object in the room, resided next to the window, angled toward the garden.

Over the fireplace rested a mantelshelf, decorated with tiny animal figurines intermingled with various novels and expensive dishware. Sam wandered over to the chimneypiece, reading the faded titles with curiosity. Her fingers trailed lovingly over the binding, marveling at their well-preserved state. She moved aside an elephant figurine to look closely at one title, pulling the book from the shelf.

"Have you read Miss Jewsbury's novels?" Miss Randall asked as she sidled closer to read over Sam's shoulder.

"I haven't, but I'm intrigued by female authors." Sam craned her neck to read the spines of the other books on the mantelpiece. "How many has she written?"

"Three, thus far," Miss Randall said, pulling the book from the shelf. "However, 'The Half Sisters' is by far my favorite. Would you like to borrow it?"

"I would, thank you." Sam accepted the book, leafing through the worn pages.

"Ladies, are you ready to depart?" Lord Westwood entered the parlor, startling both women. Sam yelped, dropping the book, and it bounced once, then landed on her shoe. Sam leaned over and plucked the novel from the floor, wiping the cover carefully before turning to Lord Westwood.

He raised his eyebrows silently, questioning the new addition in her hand. Sam grinned sheepishly and shrugged.

"The library at Westwood Estate is well stocked, Miss Hastings, as you already know. There is no need to pillage books from someone who possesses so few."

"I doubt this particular book is in your library, Lord Westwood," Miss Randall replied with a wink to Sam.

Mr. Reid bounded into the room. "Miss Larson is safely returned and seated atop the coach next to Mr. Davis. The main house is shuttered tightly, and Mrs. Larson will not allow any person outside the family into the home. Shall we be on our way?"

"There is one small matter left unattended," Miss Randall said, her eyes sliding to Sam, who covered her laugh with the book.

"Which is?" Lord Westwood asked, raising an eyebrow.

"My trunk."

"That is easily remedied," Mr. Reid replied gallantly, bowing low.

"Easy is not the word I would associate with Miss Randall's trunk." Sam snorted.

"Which word would you attribute?" Lord Westwood's intrigued voice swirled around her.

"Heavy."

"However, it's not too heavy for two strong gentlemen such as yourselves." Miss Randall smiled, her eyes glittering brightly.

"I can manage." Mr. Reid's chest puffed with his claim. He grabbed the lantern and dashed to the bedchamber. Several grunts, followed by a few well-chosen curse words, echoing down thc hallway.

Lord Westwood stood patiently in the parlor, an amused expression tickling his lips. Another profanity flew down the corridor. "There are ladies present," he called, a smirk in his voice.

"Then perhaps you would like to assist me with this happy task," Mr. Reid's muffled voice replied.

"How much does the trunk weigh?" Lord Westwood glanced at Sam and Miss Randall. Both ladies shrugged, exchanging a grin.

"We had to jump on the lid to secure it," Sam said before bursting into giggles with Miss Randall.

"I wish I could have witnessed that particular endeavor." Lord Westwood laughed. He bowed to both ladies and disappeared down the hallway to assist his brother. Snatches of a muted conversation drifted into the parlor.

"Shall we, Miss Hastings?" Miss Randall bowed ridiculously and linked her arm through Sam's, dragging her toward the exit. Pausing, Miss Randall placed her hand against the door frame and took a deep breath. She glanced at Sam as a tear slithered down her flushed cheek. "I fear I shall be away a long time." Her voice cracked.

Sam patted her hand. "Do not think about what you are leaving, but what you are heading toward."

"A crowded country estate?" Miss Randall glanced at the small garden. "I do love my serenity."

"A change of scenery." Sam gave her hand a comforting squeeze.

Miss Randall returned a tight smile. "It will be nice not to dine alone," she said, her voice falsely bright.

"I felt the exact sentiment when Wilhelmina asked me to move to the townhouse," Sam replied, understanding Miss Randall's misery.

Miss Randall turned away from her cottage. "How long did you feel that way?"

Sam licked her lips. "I still do."

"At least I will have you to keep me company." Miss Randall nodded to Miss Larson and climbed into the carriage, claiming the forward-facing bench, indicating the cushion to her left.

"Miss Clemens is also staying at the manor with her aunt. I find her quite agreeable," Sam said as she flopped less gracefully on the seat next to Miss Randall.

"I'm concerned for my aunt and uncle," Miss Randall burst out, smacking her palm on her leg. A tear streaked down her cheek. "What will I do without them? They are all I know."

"Until we receive news, let us hold a positive outlook on the fate of your aunt and uncle." She didn't want to confirm Miss Randall's worst fear. Past history showed Franklin incapable of mercy. The possibility of survival was not in Mr. and Mrs. Pierce's favor.

"If something horrible did happen to them,"—Sam covered Miss Randall's hand with hers—"you can take comfort knowing you already have financial freedom afforded by your benefactor."

"True," Miss Randall replied, her voice small. "However, I will be alone, and I will lose my home. The land belongs to Uncle Horace. As a woman—an illegitimate woman at that—everything will pass to my cousin, Mr. Peter Pierce."

"I haven't met Mr. Pierce. Is he a kind gentleman?" Sam racked her memories, but Wilhelmina had never mentioned Mr. Peter Pierce.

Miss Randall shrugged. "I know very little about him except for the fact he remains unmarried."

"Perhaps he will allow you to continue to live in the cottage."

"No," Miss Randall said with a sad shake of her head. "Aunt Hattie revealed to me one evening, after several glasses of libation, that Peter's mother, Mrs. Jane Pierce, is quite volatile. Peter kept her out of society due to her unstable condition—one of the reasons he can't find a wife. He will want the cottage to keep her hidden from prying visitors."

"I will ensure you are not turned out into the cold, Miss Randall," Sam said emphatically. Even if that meant she became a permanent resident at the Westwood townhouse.

"Aunt Hattie most definitely underestimated your character, Miss Hastings." Miss Randall smiled, her eyes shining with tears.

"That occurs fairly often." Sam sighed.

Lord Westwood and Mr. Reid appeared in the doorway, the troublesome trunk balanced between them and hefted it onto the back of the coach with a collective groan. Twin grimaces appeared when the brothers realized they would be sharing a bench once again instead of seated next to a lady.

Jostling his brother aside, Lord Westwood climbed up first, claiming the bench directly across from Sam, winking audaciously at her. She blushed. Mr. Reid followed closely, slamming the coach door closed with more force than necessary. Huffing, he grumbled for a minute, then flashed an enchanting smile at Miss Randall.

"No trouble at all, Miss Randall," he said as Mr. Davis snapped a whip, and the carriage rocked forward.

None of the inhabitants noticed the shadowy figure hiding in the foliage to the right of the cottage. Franklin stepped from the darkness, his mouth stretching into a sneer.

"Soon, Samantha, we'll be together soon, and this time, Lord Westwood won't be able to protect you."

CHAPTER 24

The idle prattle from Thomas and Miss Randall droned into a constant buzz, like insects on a hot summer's afternoon. Benjamin's mind drifted as he watched Miss Hastings. She folded her body against the coach wall, pressing into the side as if trying to separate herself from the intimacy between Thomas and Miss Randall. Benjamin longed to wrap Miss Hastings in his arms and kiss her senseless.

Discreetly, he slid his leg forward until his boot skimmed along the side of Miss Hastings' shoe. She glanced up at the contact, a gasp sticking in her throat. Flushing, she shifted her eyes sideways and furtively checked Miss Randall's profile, confirming her ignorance of Benjamin's wayward foot.

Miss Randall kept her gaze locked on Thomas, smiling as he joked about switching places with Benjamin during their youth.

"Did anyone ever figure out your ruse?" she asked.

"Our mother." Thomas' laugh seemed odd, given their precarious situation, but he realized Thomas was attempting to distract Miss Randall from her worry. "She knew our true identity despite all our efforts."

"How?"

"Family secret, Miss Randall." Thomas winked.

Miss Randall studied Thomas intently, leaning forward to compare his features with Benjamin, who eyed her scrutiny warily in the semi-darkness of the cabin.

"I cannot discern a difference," she said, scooting back on her bench. "I suppose it must be your personalities which reveal the truth."

Benjamin flicked his attention back to Miss Hastings. His foot, happily caressing her instep, stroked its subtle seduction during Miss Randall's inspection. Miss Hastings rouged, her delectable skin glowing pink. Biting her lower lip, she trembled and held his hungry stare. Benjamin shifted, and his pants uncomfortably stretched as he imagined the innumerable activities he wanted to perform to prolong Miss Hastings' blush.

"Miss Hastings, are you feeling alright?" Miss Randall asked, placing her hand on Miss Hastings' forehead. Benjamin retracted his leg with a smirk.

"I'm fine, Miss Randall." Dropping her gaze to the floor, Miss Hastings inhaled and exhaled slowly, forcing the color from her cheeks. "Thank you for your concern. I'm a little warm from the enclosure of the coach."

Thomas snorted, turning to stare at Benjamin with raised eyebrows, and Benjamin elbowed him.

"Miss Hastings, I had no idea you were affected by heat. Would you prefer to exchange seats with me?" Miss Randall's worried tone caused Thomas to choke. Benjamin thumped him roughly on the back. Thomas glared up at him with watering eyes.

"Thank you for your kindness, Miss Randall. However, the journey is nearly finished. I shall manage the last few minutes." Miss Hastings avoided Thomas' and Benjamin's stares—one amused, the other ablaze.

Miss Randall's arrival at the country estate was a quiet affair. Owing to the late hour, only Edward remained awake. He paced the veranda, impatience coloring his steps. The carriage halted in a cloud of dust, which barely settled before Edward wrenched the coach door from its hinges.

The irritated diatribe lodged in his throat as he caught sight of Miss Randall, seated nervously next to his sister. Edward cocked his head at Benjamin, who subtly shook his head.

"Miss Randall, what a pleasure to see you again so soon," Edward said warmly, extending his hand. "You must be exhausted from this night's trying events. I suppose I should wake Lady Westwood to find an available chamber in which you can reside before I have a small discussion with your chaperones."

"There is no need to wake the house. Miss Hastings can show Miss Randall to the chamber next to Miss Clemens' room," Thomas said, stretching his long legs as he climbed from the coach. "It's currently unoccupied."

"Thank you all for your generosity." Miss Randall spun around, acknowledging each man. "I apologize for causing so much trouble."

"None of this is your fault, Miss Randall," Thomas said, helping Miss Larson down from the driver's bench. "We will have your trunk brought upstairs as soon as our business is concluded."

"Instead of waiting for your chest to be delivered, I have a nightdress you can borrow," Miss Hastings said as she followed Benjamin from the coach, his firm grip on her hand. "I'm certain you would much rather rest than wait half the night for your clothing."

"I would, thank you, Miss Hastings," Miss Randall replied, exhaustion evident on her delicate features.

"Edward," Miss Hastings inclined her head in his direction. "I hope that plan is acceptable."

"It is." Edward's voice held the same weariness coursing through Benjamin's body. "Your trunk will be brought to your room tomorrow morning, Miss Randall. Have a pleasant evening."

"Goodnight, gentlemen," Miss Hastings and Miss Randall chorused. The ladies turned and trudged toward the house.

"Miss Larson," Miss Randall's musical voice echoed across the drive, "you may reside in my chamber tonight. I know you must be terrified." Miss Larson nodded once and clutched her traveling bag to her chest, silently trailing after her mistress.

"Sammie." Edward's voice chased his sister's retreating form. "I expect you to sleep in your chamber tonight, no more late-night library explorations."

Miss Hastings paused, and Benjamin could make out her grin in the flickering candlelight.

"I have a prior agreement with Lord Westwood concerning my sleeping arrangements."

"Which is?" Edward asked, annoyance creeping into his voice.

"Something that will be enforced this evening," Benjamin replied, his gaze on Miss Hastings.

"I will strike you again, Benjamin," Edward warned with a withering glare.

"I have no doubt. However, until that happy occasion, shall we continue our discussion in my study?" He smiled and gestured toward the house.

Edward growled, snapping his jaw. Miss Hastings took advantage of Edward's distraction and disappeared inside, yanking Miss Randall along by her arm.

"What is wrong with your chamber? Is it haunted?" Miss

Randall's faint voice asked as Miss Larson shut the front door. Benjamin grinned, wondering how Miss Hastings would respond.

"Thomas Reid!"

The words echoed through the chilly air. A fury, approaching on foot, repeated the same yell again in a heavy brogue. Stomping through the grass, a ring of light appeared, a will-o-wisp rapidly flying across the meadow.

"Alana, come back. Now is not the occasion for your absurdity. Stop, Alana!" Aidan's voice hissed from the shadows.

"No, I will not wait a moment longer," Alana replied. "Thomas has successfully avoided me for eight years, and I intend on ending that ridiculousness tonight."

Thomas paled. "Benjamin, I..." His eyes darted to the stamping carriage horses, impatiently tugging at their harnesses.

Benjamin nodded once. Deftly, Thomas freed the closest horse and vaulted onto its back. Wrapping his hand tightly in the horse's mane, he nudged its flanks. The horse reared on its hind legs, landed nimbly, and bolted with Thomas atop. He encouraged the horse into a full gallop, and within seconds, he'd vanished in the darkness.

A moment later, Alana appeared, her blue eyes blazing. "Where is he, Benjamin?" she said, planting her fists on her hips, her unbound hair flying in all directions. "I know you are not he."

"Good evening, Alana," Benjamin replied smoothly. His eyes flickered over to Aidan, who was huffing next to Alana.

"I couldn't stop her." He panted, leaning forward on his knees to catch his breath.

"Don't apologize for me, Aidan." Alana flashed, blue fire in her eyes.

"Alana!" She jumped, startled by Benjamin's ire, and

turned to him, still ablaze. "A warning next time, Mrs. Dubois, if you please. We have experienced a tiresome evening, and your appearance only complicates matters."

"Did you find him?" Aidan's question floated quietly from his crouched position.

"No." Benjamin grimaced. "We underestimated Morris. He assaulted Miss Hastings and Miss Randall at the masque several hours ago."

"That is daring." Aidan rose with a groan.

"Or desperate," Benjamin replied, and Aidan nodded his agreement.

"Alana, what can we do for you at this hour?" Edward addressed the spitfire quietly as she paced behind Aidan.

"I would like to speak with Thomas," she replied, her tone softening considerably.

"As you can see, Thomas isn't here." Benjamin gestured between Edward and himself.

"Have I missed him again?" She blew out an exasperated sigh, ruffling her auburn hair.

"You have."

"I don't know what to do. He refuses to see me, returns my letters. I'm driven mad by his indifference." A note of hysteria colored her statement.

Benjamin glared coldly at her, clamping his jaw tightly. He wrestled with his desire to exact vengeance for Thomas, to shred Alana into a pool of tears. She shrank under his scrutiny, acutely aware of Benjamin's internal struggle. He managed to hold his tongue—a near-impossible task—only undertaken for Thomas' kind heart as he would deplore any mistreatment of Alana, even in his own anguish.

"You must speak with Mr. Reid on that private matter," he said through clenched teeth.

"Benjamin," Alana said, her eyes begging for forgiveness, for pity. "I never meant to hurt him. We were both so young."

He refused to reply, biting his tongue until the taste of blood filled his mouth. Benjamin turned to Aidan and acknowledged him with a bow. "Aidan, I don't envy your troubles."

"That particular feeling is mutual." Aidan wrapped an arm around Alana's slumped shoulders.

Inclining his head, Benjamin conceded Aidan's statement.

"Come, Alana," he murmured, "we must find Da before he shoots at another coach."

"Missing again?" Benjamin asked, his gaze hopping over the tree line behind Aidan.

"Hunting marauders. He raced out the kitchen door nearly an hour ago. We still cannot find him." Aidan sighed as a rifle blast echoed in the distance.

Alana allowed her brother to drag her from the estate. She glanced over her shoulder, her pleading gaze finding Benjamin. He turned his back on her and trudged toward the veranda, trailed closely by Edward.

"Is Thomas returning any time soon?" Edward asked, climbing up the steps.

"No," Benjamin replied, his throat tightening on the word. Thomas might not return for several weeks.

"Should we be concerned about him?"

Pausing on the veranda, Benjamin turned his dark gaze on Edward.

"Definitely."

"I would still like to discuss the sudden arrival of Miss Randall this evening," Edward said, glancing backward at the darkness.

"Certainly." Benjamin sighed, plodding toward the door. There was only one place he wished to be—in bed with his arms around Miss Hastings. "We can proceed without Thomas."

"How long will he be absent?" Edward's eyes reflected the concern in Benjamin's face.

"It depends on the horse."

Reaching the study door, Benjamin ushered Edward inside and pulled the door behind him, ensuring their conversation was muted from the rest of the household. He gestured to one of the available armchairs, and Edward gratefully sank into its plush cushion.

"Some refreshment?" Benjamin gestured to a crystal decanter on the edge of his desk—unobtrusively left by Mr. Davis.

Edward shook his head, closing his eyes with a heavy sigh. As Benjamin lifted the decanter off the silver tray to pour himself a drink, a handwritten note dropped from the base of the carafe. One word was scrawled on the slip of paper —London.

Quickly Benjamin secreted the missive in his coat pocket. His gaze lifted to Edward, who had pressed his fingertips against his eyes, a low moan rumbling in his chest. Taking residence in the opposite chair, Benjamin took a long swallow of brandy from his half-full snifter and waited patiently for Edward to gather his mind.

"How long does Miss Randall intend to visit?" Edward dropped his hand. His eyes, circled by fatigue, held an unasked question.

"Indefinitely," Benjamin replied, chasing the statement with another sip.

"Is her sudden desire for country living due to the incident in the maze with Franklin this evening?"

"It's one of the reasons." Benjamin thought of Miss Hastings, waiting warm and snuggled in his bed, and wondered how much of this necessary conversation could be postponed until later that morning.

"Have you spoken with her aunt and uncle regarding her

current whereabouts?" That question was his wife's influence. Edward seemed to be extending his role of eldest brother.

"I haven't had the opportunity." Benjamin drained his glass. "They are missing."

Edward raised an eyebrow, assessing Benjamin's somber mood. "Do you think they are still alive?"

"Morris called upon Mr. and Mrs. Pierce earlier this evening. He chose to make a second stop at Miss Randall's cottage, but she was not at home, having already left for the masque. He left explicit instructions for the housemaid to inform Miss Randall thus." No, he didn't think Morris had left them alive but didn't need to speak those words aloud for Edward to know his mind.

"I assume the ladies' maid was the slight girl who followed Miss Randall into the house." When Benjamin nodded, Edward added, "I would like to question her as well."

"I doubt you will learn much more than we did," Benjamin replied, rising and setting his glass on the desk.

A deep sigh escaped Edward as his hand gripped his forehead, massaging the wrinkle that had etched itself across his face.

"The hour is much too late to think clearly," he said, peering at Benjamin through his fingers. "I suppose your explanation for your disappearance over the past few days is also a convoluted tale?"

Benjamin half-smiled, nodding. "It is."

"I propose we discuss these matters tomorrow. I can't reason properly at this hour."

A dull thump from the ceiling caught Benjamin's attention, and he grinned. Miss Hastings was out of bed and moving through the upstairs hallway. He wondered if Edward would realize the meaning of the sound.

After a moment, a discernible squeak echoed through the silent house. Edward's head snapped up, and he caught

Benjamin's fleeting grin. Edward's eyes flew to the closed door, suspicion radiating from him. He pressed a finger against his lips and slipped across the study.

"Samantha, so help me if you are in that hallway..." Edward ripped open the door, and shadows greeted him. Edward stuck his head into the corridor, glancing left and right.

"Are you satisfied?" Benjamin asked, leaning against the edge of his desk, his arms crossed in amusement.

"Hardly," Edward replied from the doorway with a surly glare. "You may jest about my protective nature—yes, I know what Samantha says about me—but you haven't known her as long as I have. She attracts,"—Edward paused, his eyes roving over Benjamin's countenance—"trouble."

"What are you saying, Edward?" Benjamin growled. He crossed the room in two giant steps, his eyes narrowed.

Turning fully toward Benjamin's approaching ire, Edward opened his mouth to speak but hesitated, his gaze sliding over Benjamin's tense body.

"I have known you many years. I know all your faults, your weaknesses, and your scandals. I know—like Thomas—you detest the confines of marriage."

"I'm still waiting for your point Edward," Benjamin said, his voice dangerously quiet.

"Sammie needs someone to watch over her, to guide her in the proper direction. She is young, impulsive, and headstrong —a challenge in all respects. She's also extremely naïve." Edward paused, debating his next words. "Are you certain you're the best man for her, Benjamin?"

"I have risked my life and my family's lives for your sister—the woman I love," Benjamin replied, his hands closing into half-fists. "What are you questioning? My devotion or my ability to provide for Samantha?"

Edward forcibly bit his tongue and approached Benjamin

slowly, his blue eyes burning intensely as he roughly gripped Benjamin's shoulder.

"You are my closest friend, a brother in all respects, but you have no idea what this household was like when you vanished on your wild adventure. The screams..." Edward shuddered, his mind on the past. "I realize you had reason, but I can't bear Sammie's agony a second time. If you cause one more ounce of pain, I will personally make her a widow."

"Understood," Benjamin replied, twisting out of Edward's grasp. "Is there anything else you wish to discuss?"

"You were never my choice for a suitor." Edward glared at Benjamin.

"Your objections were previously noted," Benjamin growled, his face dark. "You revealed them many years ago."

"My basis for protest has not changed."

"Ephraim recanted his doubt."

Edward's mouth dropped open. "How did you know?"

Benjamin smirked. "He wrote me—before he passed—and stated he misjudged the relationship between Miss Hastings and me, that his decision was based solely on your testimony."

Edward glanced toward the ceiling. "I found her journal. She confessed her attraction for you—an entire page inscribed with *Lady Samantha Westwood*. I didn't know what to do. It was only a matter of time before I needed to intervene. She's extremely persistent—once she set her mind on you, I would have been unable to dissuade it. Yes, I told Ephraim my concerns. He played the role of enforcer as I could not. I could never say no to Samantha. How could I after all the tragedy she endured?"

"Instead, you hid behind your great-uncle." Benjamin's accusation vibrated off the walls of the study.

"He was a much better guardian. I made a mess of Sammie's education. She will never fit into society." Edward's hand slashed toward the direction of his sister's—Benjamin's—chamber. "The least I could do was to protect her from scoundrels like you."

"Your opinion of me was wanting. Your sister was a twelve-year-old. I would never seduce a child," Benjamin spat, livid at the allegation.

"No, but what about a fifteen-year-old? Three years is a long time for Samantha to nurture an attachment."

"You seem stuck on the idea that I can't control myself."

"Can you?"

Benjamin glared at him.

"She changed you. I noticed a difference in your attitude."

"How so?" Benjamin snarled.

"Two years of correspondence? Two years Benjamin! The man who refused to commit to any woman wrote to my sister for two years." Edward threw his hands in the air, pacing away from the door.

"She needed someone to listen to her." Benjamin lowered his voice.

"She should have talked to me." Edward spun around, his eyes flashing, and Benjamin was struck with the thought that Edward had ended their correspondence because he was jealous.

"Edward, think back to that particular period. You were in a dark place. Those months after her accident—you blamed yourself. I used to carry you home in the early morning hours, incoherent, bloodied, and broken. How many times did you wake up on the floor in your own vomit?"

"There is not much I remember from that portion of my past." Edward's shoulders bowed as his gaze dropped to the floor. "When I came to my senses..."

"When you met your lovely wife..." Benjamin smiled.

Edward nodded and lifted his head. "I realized your influence over Samantha was greater than I originally believed."

"I did nothing to coerce Miss Hastings. What influence did I possess?"

"She started wearing dresses."

Benjamin snorted. "That was the basis for your over-reaction?"

"Yes. I noticed other minute changes as well. However, when I read her journal, I knew it was time to separate you."

"Without speaking to me about your concerns?" Benjamin yelled, slamming his hand on the back of the nearest armchair. "We were friends. You should have come to me."

"You were an unsuitable companion. No discussion was warranted." Edward crossed his arms over his chest.

"I'm a different man,"—Benjamin gestured between them—"as are you. That particular moniker no longer applies to either of us."

"I should have left her in the country," Edward grumbled and shook his head. "She would be far less trouble."

"She would be dead," Benjamin said. Edward flinched, then grimaced, accepting Benjamin's argument. Benjamin placed his hand on Edward's shoulder. "Do you still object to my influence?"

"A part of me will always resist the idea of the two of you together," Edward admitted, unfolding his arms.

"Would you prefer I end the engagement and break her heart?"

Edward's eyes burst from his head. "I don't care what it costs you, Benjamin. You will make her happy."

"I already do." Benjamin grinned wickedly.

"Good night." Edward stalked from the room. He moved to slam the study door, but Benjamin blocked it with his boot. Growling, Edward stomped down the corridor and paused next to the library door, his fingertips resting on the doorknob.

Benjamin ventured into the corridor, observing Edward's

internal debate with delight. Quickly, Edward shoved open the library door. He glanced back at Benjamin, his irritation seeping slowly into the floor. "She listened for once."

"Have a pleasant evening, Edward." Benjamin turned toward his study.

"Working late tonight?" Edward asked civilly, a glaring attempt to smooth over the quarrel he initiated.

"I have some urgent business which requires my attention, unless you prefer I spend the evening ensuring your sister remains in her chamber?" Benjamin cocked his head and smiled.

Edward choked and purpled. Spinning around, he marched upstairs.

Benjamin listened for the slam of Edward's chamber door. Slipping down the corridor into the library, Benjamin gently pushed the door until it caught the latch. Padding to the center of the room, he cleared his throat, his eyes searching the room.

"Come out, Miss Hastings."

CHAPTER 25

An exasperated grumble emanated from one of the far curtains. Sam peeked out from behind the cloth and frowned at him.

"How did you know I was in here?"

Lord Westwood pursed his lips, striding to the window. His fingers closed around the drape and yanked it aside.

"I believe the agreement was you would be sleeping in your bedchamber this evening."

"I'm not dressed for bed," she said, gesturing to her clothing.

"That is true," he replied, his face bursting into a giant grin, and he slipped his arms around her waist, drawing her close and brushing his lips across her mouth.

She leaned back, her body humming from his touch. "Was it necessary to antagonize my brother?"

Lord Westwood shook his head and laughed. "How much of the conversation did you hear?"

"Everything," Sam replied, then added, "once Edward opened the door."

"I see." Lord Westwood leaned forward, his eyebrows

raised in an exaggerated fashion, and whispered. "A full page of Lady Samantha Westwood?"

She blushed, the heat crawling through her face, and stared at her shoes. "Journals are supposed to be private."

"Are you still angry with me for not writing you back?"

"No." Her head rose to meet his gaze. "I forgive you. Edward, however, has some retribution due."

"As your fiancé, I do hope you allow me the pleasure of witnessing that punishment." Lord Westwood grinned.

She mirrored his smile. "As my fiancé, I would expect you at my side."

"That is where I intend to remain. However, I'd like to know what has you so agitated this evening that you snuck into the library."

Sam lifted the heavy curtain and gestured him forward. She allowed him to slip under before dropping the drape again, creating a cubby between the window and the drape. "On a clear night, you can see all the way to the main road."

"Did you see anything interesting this evening?"

"Mr. Reid." She pointed at the gate at the end of the drive. "I've seen him twice tonight."

"Have you spent much of your time in this niche?"

Turning her attention to the window, Sam's breath fogged the nearest pane, edging outward to the surrounding glass. "I have lingered here a fair amount of time over the past few days."

Lord Westwood wrapped his arms around her, the warmth of his chest seeping into her back. "You are never to wait for me at this window again," he murmured softly in her ear, his lips dancing lightly across her skin.

"Why?" She twisted in his arms to stare at him.

"I swore never to leave your side." His eyes burned intensely.

"Never?" Sam asked, her voice hitched. "You wish to remain beside me every moment of every day?"

"Hardly." Lord Westwood rolled his eyes. "I meant, I would not leave the same location. If I go to London, you go with me."

"You are taking me to London?" Sam squealed, vibrating happily in his arms.

Nuzzling his face against her hair, Lord Westwood inhaled deeply, then bumped his forehead against hers.

"I must go to London straightaway for some urgent business, and I cannot bear to be separated from you once again."

Sam flushed and glanced down. Lord Westwood tipped her chin until her blue eyes met his burning green eyes. Holding her gaze, he bent slowly, allowing the flames building between them to smolder, then pressed his lips to her mouth. Accepting his invitation, Sam wrapped her arms around his neck, twining her fingers in his hair.

She pulled him closer, causing his lips to curve against hers. He deepened the kiss, his tongue dipping into her mouth, and she moaned, every nerve in her body catching fire. Panting and dizzy, Sam pulled away, knocking the back of her head on the cold window glass, and took several deep breaths as the heat faded from her cheeks. Her eyes lifted to his, and she scowled.

"Why are you not as affected as I when you kiss me?"

"I am," he replied, his voice thick. "I possess a bit more self-control than you."

"Hmph." Sam folded her arms.

"Miss Hastings." Lord Westwood cupped Sam's chin and stroked his thumb over her lower lip, sending a delightful tingling sensation across the sensitive skin. "Do you suppose I might convince you to retire to your chamber for the remainder of this evening?"

"Lord Westwood, I'm in disagreement with your suggestion. As I'm not yet tired, I see no reason to go to sleep."

"Who said you would be sleeping?" Lord Westwood rumbled. He pressed his body against her, his arousal digging into her stomach. "I very much would like to show you how greatly you affect me."

The library door creaked open. Someone silently slipped into the room, pacing a lazy circle past the fireplace and drifting near the curtains which hid Sam and Lord Westwood. After completing a lap, the visitor settled into an armchair nearest the crackling fire.

Sam's eyes rounded in fear. "Edward?" she mouthed.

Lord Westwood shrugged and glanced toward the ceiling, his mouth working. Light flashed in his eyes, changing them to a glowing, brilliant green. He grinned and placed one finger across Sam's lips.

Dropping his blistering gaze to his hand, Lord Westwood traced his fingertip along the seam of her mouth. Shivers cascading down Sam's back, she bit her lip in anticipation, leaning against his body. Slowly shaking his head, Lord Westwood grinned and gently separated himself from her. She pouted.

Grasping Sam's hand, he edged along the wall opposite the fireplace and the intruding late-night guest. Noiselessly, he pulled her from behind the curtain, scooting sideways along the bookshelf. They paused—exposed—when the interloper leaned over to leaf through a book discarded on a nearby table. The hand flicked two pages before lifting the book from the table.

Without warning, Lord Westwood grabbed Sam and yanked her backward into a shelf. She lost her balance, yelping in distress, her cry immediately muffled by his large hand.

"Shh," he hissed, his warm breath caressing the nape of her neck.

Sam gulped and nodded. Glancing around, she realized they stood in a space behind the bookshelf—a tunnel. The library disappeared as the wall panel slid closed. A crack of light, visible underneath the panel base, dimly lit the tunnel end.

"Where are we?" Sam whispered.

Lord Westwood smiled and held up his hand, indicating she remain quiet. He interwove his fingers with hers, tugging. As they moved away from the library, the path sloped sharply. Darkness reached out to greet them, swallowing the light and plunging them into pitch black. Fearful, Sam curled into Lord Westwood, grabbing his arm with her free hand. He chuckled in the dark.

"Thomas and I always forgot to replace the oil in the lanterns. Eventually, we both learned to walk through the tunnel blindly."

"Where are we?"

"Somewhere underneath the courtyard," Lord Westwood replied, his voice wrapping around her like a comforting blanket.

"When did you discover this passageway?" She glanced behind them, unable to see anything in the darkness.

"Thomas and I built it." His proud boast echoed down the tunnel.

"Incredible." Reaching out her hand, she trailed her fingers on the wall of packed dirt. "How long did it take?"

"One extremely long, hot summer." She chuckled at his grim response. "Mother complained we kept disappearing for hours and trudging in after nightfall, covered in dirt."

"I do hope I will be able to view it at some point in the future."

"I will try to remember a lantern for our next escape." Lord Westwood laughed. "This passage leads to a trapdoor in the stables. You should be able to see light through the floor-boards soon."

As he spoke, a tiny light appeared in the distance, growing larger as they approached the end of the passageway. In the dimness, Sam discerned Lord Westwood's outline—a solid mass moving determinedly toward the light, mumbling to himself.

"Are you counting?"

"I am," he replied, bobbing his head in rhythm with his feet.

"How many steps does it take to walk the entire tunnel?"

"522."

They walked in silence for a moment, and Sam's mind flashed back to the night Lord Westwood appeared in the library. She spun, her eyes flashing, and ripped her hand from his grasp. He looked back at her in confusion.

"You lied! You did visit me."

"I did." He grinned sheepishly.

"I thought you were a dream."

"That particular date is exceptionally difficult for Thomas." Lord Westwood sighed. "I returned to offer him my support as I do every year on that anniversary."

"It seems an odd thing to memorialize, a broken engagement."

"It's not a joyous occasion..." Lord Westwood's voice trailed off as he regarded her in surprise. "How did you come to learn of Thomas' misfortune?"

Sam glanced at her fingers, twisted in front of her, and wandered several steps away. Lord Westwood caught her arm and turned her around to face him. The semi-darkness cast shadows across his somber face. Sam bit her lip.

"Was it Aunt Abigail?" he asked, his voice dangerously soft.

Sam flushed and nodded once, dropping her gaze to her

fingers again. Lord Westwood's quiet tone unnerved her. She shivered as he approached, his anger rolling in waves.

"Who else was privy to this information?"

"Lady Westwood, Wilhelmina, Miss Clemens, and the dressmaker." Sam dutifully repeated the names, her gaze locked on her trembling hands. Lord Westwood—near enough to touch—tipped her face, staring into her eyes. He studied her, appraising her answer.

"Mrs. Hastings and my mother were previously aware of the situation," Lord Westwood said, his eyes narrowing. "I don't know much about the dressmaker, except that she has worked for my mother on numerous occasions, and I have heard no rumors from her mouth. Miss Clemens is my only concern. Does she enjoy gossip?"

"Not in the slightest." Sam vehemently shook her head. "Miss Clemens prefers to blend into the fringes."

Lord Westwood raised his eyebrow. "If you trust her judgment, then I shall not address the matter with her."

"Did you intend to visit me as well?" Sam asked, a painful twinge shooting through her heart.

"No. I knew leaving you a second time might prove too difficult. However, Thomas mentioned the screaming, said it was horrific. I merely wanted to check on your well-being." He muttered the last to himself as if distracted by the memory of the evening. His head snapped toward Sam, glowing green eyes glaring in irritation. "When I discovered you missing from your chamber, I panicked. Thomas suggested I investigate the library."

"Why didn't you stay?" She tucked a loose strand of hair behind her ear and turned away, walking toward the tunnel's end.

"Thomas didn't explain the magnitude of your troubles." Lord Westwood walked to her side. "He knew if I were made aware, I would end my search for Mr. Morris."

"You would have stayed?" Her teeth worried her lip.

He focused his burning gaze on Sam and pulled her into his arms, eliminating the chaste distance between them. Sam's heart thudded in her chest, expanding in its cavity until she could hardly catch her breath. She leaned into him unintentionally, a flower reaching toward the sun.

"If you had asked, I would have. I wanted to. I wanted to gather you in my arms and carry you to bed myself. Do you not understand, I can't survive without you? Bereft of your love, I would find myself roaming the meadows with your dear Uncle Aengus—eternally chasing your sweet voice."

Sam glanced away, pressing the pads of her fingers against the sides of her eyes. *Do not cry.* Turning her face from Benjamin's intimate proximity, she pulled out of his arms and shuffled a few paces out of reach.

"You still left," she whispered with her back to him.

"We were close to capturing Morris. Once we trapped him, I would never need to leave you again." He materialized beside her, wrapping his strong arms around her shoulders. She shivered in response, whipping around to meet his fiery gaze.

Crushing her body to him, he trailed a blazing line of kisses on her jaw. She trembled, arching her back. His lips moved down her throat to her collarbone. Breathless, she wrapped her arms around his neck. He lifted her easily and urgently pressed her against the tunnel wall—dirt crumbling around them.

"Perhaps this isn't the best location to prove my continued interest in your charms," Lord Westwood said as bits of dirt rained onto his coat. He slid her slowly down the length of his torso, and she shuddered again. A wicked smile crossed his mouth. "However, we are only a few meters from the stables if you would care to continue this discussion above ground."

He indicated the path—which concluded abruptly—

blocked by a ladder, ending just below the floorboards. Lord Westwood nimbly climbed the ladder, lifting the edge of a floorboard directly above his head with his right hand. It groaned and rose slowly, revealing an empty stable. Pieces of hay drifted down like snow, tangling in Sam's unbound hair. Accepting his hand, she followed him up the ladder.

Brushing hay from her skirt, she stepped into the center of the pen.

"In which horse's stall are we?"

"Phantom," Lord Westwood replied, his lips twitching. He lowered the trapdoor and kicked hay over the top.

Sam glanced around the empty stall. Tack, draped with cobwebs, decorated the wooden walls. Stalks of hay, scattered absently about the floor, intermixed with a half-full feed trough near the corner of the stable. Sam arched an eyebrow.

"Phantom?"

"Thomas names all the horses," Lord Westwood said, the corner of his mouth lifted again—a private joke.

"Even the invisible ones?" Sam asked, returning his smile.

"Yes." He grinned. "What gave it away?"

"None of the hay is trampled."

Lord Westwood laughed and unhitched the gate. Leading Sam into the main walkway between stalls, he closed the gate. The nameplate flashed, *Phantom* engraved in flowery script on the gold tag.

"Your brother has an amusing sense of humor," Sam said, earning a snicker from Lord Westwood.

He grasped her hand lightly, stroking his thumb thoughtfully across the sensitive skin on her wrist, and led her down the row of stalls. A horse whinnied in front of them, tethered to a black carriage. Mr. Davis' head bobbed around the horse, forcefully fastening straps.

"Mr. Davis." Lord Westwood greeted his manservant with

a nod. "My schedule has been moved forward several hours. When can we be ready to depart?"

"In a half-hour, as long as the mare doesn't give me any trouble," Mr. Davis replied, continuing his task.

"You said you wouldn't leave me." Sam's accusation flew, an icy lump settling in her stomach.

"We are leaving together," Lord Westwood corrected her, touching his forehead to hers. "I have business in London. Have you forgotten already?"

"I didn't realize you meant we were leaving tonight." Sam gasped, a small bubble of panic catching in her throat. "What will Wilhelmina say? What will Edward say? Who would be our chaperone?" Her voice raised an octave.

Lord Westwood allowed his gaze to leisurely travel the length of Sam as she babbled. Smiling, he extended his hand.

"Miss Hastings, when did you become so proper?"

Sam's jaw dropped.

She thought of Franklin, the endless social events, and her last week of loneliness. She thought of Lord Westwood, his blazing green eyes and wicked mouth, her fiancé, her future husband. Staring at his offered palm, she placed her hand in his.

"We should write Edward a letter."

Lord Westwood lifted her hand to his mouth, dropping a light kiss on her fingers.

"An excellent idea, Miss Hastings, we can do so once we've reached our destination. Would you care to take a walk around the grounds while Mr. Davis completes his task?"

"Is it prudent to wander about at this hour?" she asked, her gaze sliding across the shadows stretching into the stables.

"Certainly." Lord Westwood winked. "Mr. Flannery is patrolling with a rifle."

Sam laughed.

"Mr. Davis, will you meet us at the main road when you

have finished harnessing the horses?" he addressed the dark head on the opposite side of the sleek mare.

"Yes, my Lord," Mr. Davis's muffled voice replied.

Pausing again, Sam glanced at Lord Westwood. "Did you pack me any clothing?"

"We can purchase anything you need in London."

"How long have you been planning this escape?" Sam asked, her mouth twitching.

"Not long." Lord Westwood winked. "About six days."

"Thank you for rescuing me, my Lord." Sam curtsied playfully.

"My Lady." He bowed and pulled her into the darkness. Sam laughed as they ran across the courtyard.

Only one resident witnessed their harried departure, Miss Clemens, watching from the library window. She gently placed her hand against the glass, an unseen farewell gesture to her friend.

"Good luck, Miss Hastings," she whispered, her breath fogging the glass.

CHAPTER 26

March 14, 1853

M*r. Hastings* (Dearest Edward),

I have kidnapped your sister. I do not apologize, nor do I ask forgiveness for this admission. As you stated earlier this evening, I am never to leave your sister's side again, and I have no intention of doing so.

(Please do not hit him, Edward.)

An unexpected business situation arose, which requires my immediate presence and therefore, your sister's as well. I anticipate this can be resolved within a fortnight; however, I cannot guarantee that date. Please ease Mrs. Hastings' mind by informing her we will return in time for the second engagement party.

(Please do not hit him, Edward.)

As no one is aware of our location or departure, we should be safe to wander about freely. If you need to contact us, you may send a letter by way of my townhouse. Mr. Davis will forward the correspondence to us.

(Please do not hit him, Edward.)

This is a much-needed rest for Miss Hastings, considering the ordeal she recently experienced at the hands of her cousin, Mr. Franklin Morris. I accept full responsibility for this irrational escapade and will accept whatever castigation you deem necessary upon our return.

Sincerely,

Benjamin, Lord Westwood and his fiancée, Miss Samantha Hastings

~

"I REALLY THINK he may kill you this time." Samantha folded her hand through Benjamin's. She laid on her back, in the center of the bed, staring up at the ceiling of their rented rooms.

Tingles raced through Benjamin's fingers. He glanced up from the letter, lifting her hand to his mouth.

"That is a risk I am willing to take."

"To be a widow before I am a wife." Samantha shook her head and rolled over, extracting her hand from his. She propped herself up on her elbows, her eyes perusing the letter.

"We are rectifying that situation today." He wrapped an arm over her and pulled her close, his mouth claiming her lips with a brutal kiss.

She pushed him away, her eyes narrowing. "What do you mean?"

"You and I are getting married. As much as I enjoy seducing my fiancée, it's important she maintains a respectable reputation. Therefore, should anything occur due to this escapade,"—he wiggled his eyebrows—"you would already be secretly married, and the scandal will vanish."

"It won't *completely* vanish," Samantha muttered, her lips thinning.

"True." He inclined his head in acceptance. "But it would

be far less destructive to your reputation." Benjamin slid off the bed, dropping onto his knees. He took her hand, clasping it between both of his. "Samantha Hastings, will you do me the incredible honor of becoming my wife?"

"Yes, I will... Lord Westwood." Her mouth twitched. She'd used his title on purpose.

"There will be no more of that," he said, rising.

"What?" She fluttered her eyelashes at him.

"Lord." He lifted her to her knees, and his mouth captured hers, his tongue sliding past her lips, teasing her tongue. Her hands skated up his shirt, yanking the material upward. Benjamin grabbed her wrists, stilling her wandering fingers, and a groan rumbled in his throat. "We are going to be late, Samantha."

"Then, I suggest you do not tarry removing my clothing."

Desire flared, raging through his body. "I'm shocked by your scandalous words. Is your fiancé aware of your impropriety?"

She smiled, her face lighting with happiness. "He insists upon it."

It had been a while since he'd seen true joy on her face. If there was breath in his lungs, Morris would never take that from her again.

Laughing, Benjamin released her wrists and plucked the missive from the bed. He folded it, set it on a small desk, and sealed the letter, speaking to her over his shoulder, "As I said, we have an appointment."

"I had hoped to distract you." Samantha crawled from the bed and crossed the floor. Wrapping her arms around his waist, she buried her face in his back.

"I find you extremely distracting." He spun around and pressed his lips to her mouth.

His body hardened, responding to her soft curves, and a myriad of excuses why they could postpone the wedding for another day scampered through his mind. The idea of spending the day with Samantha writhing beneath him as she called out his name was extremely tempting, but protecting her included preventing the gossiping ladies of the ton from using his reputation against her, and that meant marriage.

He broke the kiss, drawing in a ragged breath, then leveled his gaze and arranged his features into a stern frown, trying to recall the expression Edward used whenever he dealt with his sister.

She burst into giggles. "You look like Edward."

"That was my intention."

The humor draining from her face, she chewed on her lower lip.

"Benjamin, what if something happens to Edward while we are away?"

"I have instructed Mr. Davis to contact us with any important correspondence."

"Do you trust him?" Samantha tilted her head.

"Mr. Davis has been in my employ for a long time. He has never done anything to jeopardize his post."

"I heard he used to work for the Shirelys." Samantha leaned around Benjamin and lifted the sealed letter from the desk, turning it over in her hands. "Did Mr. Davis mention the reason he no longer worked with them?"

"No, merely that he was grateful for his current position." Benjamin's forehead creased. Had he underestimated Mr. Davis? The man had been nothing but loyal in his service. Was it all a façade? His eyes flicked over Samantha, fear pooling into his stomach. "What have you heard?"

"Mr. Davis worked for the Shirely family at the time young Jeremiah died. He left shortly after the boy's passing." Samantha twisted her fingers together as she revealed the secret. "I think the two things are related."

Benjamin exhaled. Samantha's information wasn't new to

him. Mr. Davis had hinted at the same thing, but Benjamin hadn't pried.

"The only thing your story proves is that Mr. Davis is a valuable servant who understands the importance of secrecy, even after his service has completed. That one fact should put your mind at ease."

She nodded.

"Besides,"—he grinned, his arms winding around her waist—"someone has to witness our union."

A rap echoed in the room. Samantha twisted in Benjamin's arms, trembling. Releasing her, he strode to the door, placing his hands flat against the surface.

"Who is it?"

"It's Mr. Davis. I have come to collect you and your guest." Without instruction, Mr. Davis didn't acknowledge Benjamin's title or name.

Benjamin unlatched the door and pulled it open, ushering Mr. Davis into the room. Once Benjamin closed the door, Mr. Davis moved in front of Samantha and bowed low.

"My Lady."

"That is not my title, Mr. Davis."

"Ah,"—he tapped the side of his nose—"it will be soon."

"Is everything prepared?" Benjamin asked after locking the door. He crossed the room, his arm finding Samantha's waist again.

"Yes, my Lord." Mr. Davis' gaze flicked down but returned to Benjamin's face. He swore Mr. Davis smirked, but the emotion vanished as quickly as it appeared. "Miss Hastings, may I say how delighted I am that you will become mistress of the house. If there is ever anything you need, do not hesitate to ask me."

"Thank you, Mr. Davis." Samantha curtsied without pulling free of Benjamin's embrace.

"It would be my honor to witness your marriage." Mr.

Davis glanced up at Benjamin. "The coach is waiting, my Lord."

"We will meet you downstairs in a few minutes, Mr. Davis," Benjamin replied, dismissing him.

Mr. Davis bowed and exited. Benjamin followed him to the door and twisted the key once again.

"Do you intend to lock me in every room we visit?" Samantha arched an eyebrow.

"Only the ones in which I seduce you," he rumbled, returning to her side. "And since we now have several minutes, I believe you requested I disrobe you."

"Lord Westwood!" Samantha gasped, her hand flying to her mouth in mock outrage. "You are truly wicked!"

He laughed, wrapping her in his arms. His mouth skimmed along her jaw as he murmured, "I am the *World's Most Wicked Rake.*"

"Prove it to me," Samantha said with a moan, sliding her hands under his shirt.

"I shall, Miss Hastings," he replied, passion raging through his body. "I shall."

EPILOGUE

Franklin,

As of late last evening, or early this morning, I'm not sure which, Miss Hastings vanished. Lord Westwood has also disappeared. I'm inclined to believe they are together but can give you no direction which way they headed. Mr. Hastings is extremely aggravated by their sudden departure. However, there seems to be no urgency to recover Miss Hastings from her present hidden location. I will advise you upon her return. Have patience. In the meantime, please don't have all the fun without me. I plan to visit within the next few days, and I would prefer you keep your guest alive.

FRANKLIN CRUMBLED the note in his hand. He growled at the fireplace, hurling the crumpled ball into its hungry flames. They flared, happily lapping the edges of the parchment. Samantha's disappearance irked him, a move outside of his control. He ground his teeth in frustration. *How long could she stay away?* A lengthy absence from society would give the gleeful gossips much to whisper about. *She could be gone no longer than a month. Anything beyond that time period would be difficult to explain.* He would wait and use the time to heal. Absently, he rubbed his right shoulder. The wound ached. Samantha would suffer for her impudence… for shooting him. Snarling, he grasped a poker and stabbed the charred letter violently until it crumbled to ash.

A small grin tugged at the corner of his mouth. At least he still had a guest to occupy his days. She would wake any moment. Humming, Franklin rubbed his hands together, warming them in front of the crackling fire before he shrugged on a heavy coat. He had waited a long time to punish Hattie. With a smile, he left the cottage and headed toward the stables.

Unlatching the door, Franklin slipped into the stables, his gaze finding a horseless carriage. Its two occupants remained immobile—one drugged, one dead.

Hattie moaned twice, groggy and incoherent. It wasn't the first time she had been witnessed in this catatonic state; however, this was the first time her unconsciousness was caused without her consent. Her eyelids fluttered, and she groaned again. Gradually, she opened her eyes and gazed around at her surroundings. She blinked several times, trying to clear the cobwebs from her mind. Still seated in her gilded carriage—two empty goblets at her feet—she tried to puzzle out the night's events, a worried crease in her brow. Her mouth worked furiously as her gaze rested on a supine wine bottle, teetering precariously on the edge of the bench across from her.

Intelligence was not one of Hattie's charming attributes—although one could argue Hattie possessed no positive qualities whatsoever. Indeed, even without the mental challenges she faced, the amount of opium Hattie had ingested in her glass of wine would ensure her memory remained a hazy outline of events.

A spark in her eyes indicated the moment her mind

processed a recollection. She gasped and twisted to her left, checking on her husband, who she remembered began the evening with her. At first, she assumed he was merely intoxicated, passed out with his limbs sprawled in an ungentlemanly position. She shook him once, then a second time, less gently than the first, fury crossing her face. Reaching her hand back to slap his swollen face, she realized her wrists were bound. Pale terror washed through her cheeks, visible in the carriage shadows. A loud cry, wounded and fearful, echoed through the tiny barn.

She struggled to stand and bumped the top of her head against the carriage roof. Finding her feet immovable, Hattie bent over with a grunt. In the dimness, she squinted at her shoes, running her fingers over the rope binding her ankles to the carriage floor. A shriek of anguish escaped her colorless lips. Wobbling, Hattie lost her balance and toppled backward, landing inelegantly on the bench cushion, a cloud of hay dust puffing into the air.

Hattie sneezed once, and her lashed hands flew to her face to stop the barrage of sneezes that followed. Twisting in her seat, her gaze fell on a pile of hay bales, neatly stacked in the corner. Her eyes narrowed in annoyance, and she sneezed again, rubbing her nose on the back of her hand.

"Hattie." Franklin acknowledged her with a grotesque grin as he stepped into a pool of light. "It's a pleasure to see you again. Are you enjoying your evening?"

"Franklin." She gasped, startled by his voice, her eyes flying around the barn, seeking him. "Help me."

"What of your dear husband? Should I assist him, too, or solely you?"

She glanced sideways at Horace, peaceful in his deadly repose, and returned her gaze with a snarl. "What did you do?"

Franklin slowly shook his head, clucking in response. "My question first, Hattie. Where are your manners?"

"No." She accompanied the word with a withering scowl. "I'm not having a pleasant evening. I woke to find myself tied up in my carriage and abandoned in a filthy barn, filled with bales of hay." She growled the final word, fighting a sneeze that tickled her nose.

Cocking his head to the side, Franklin studied Hattie with morbid curiosity, his mouth stretched wide, black eyes glittering with malice. She deflated under his hard scrutiny, shrinking back against the bench carefully so she didn't brush against her deceased husband.

"The most egregious act I have committed this evening was hiding your body in a barn," he said, tapping the tips of his fingers together. He rocked on the balls of his feet, hovering between light and shadow. "Extraordinary. Have you no feeling for your husband? Do you not wish to know how his demise came to be? What of your poor, orphaned niece? Do you not care about her fate either?"

"Wretched girl," Hattie burst out, stomping her foot on the carriage floor. "If this whole predicament is due to a grievance you have with Charlotte, I suggest you kidnap her. Carry out whatever disgusting atrocity you wish on her person. We will ignore this terrible travesty which has befallen my poor Horace."

Franklin raised an eyebrow in surprise. *Hattie didn't know the family secret—the truth behind Charlotte's lineage.* Lillian held her promise and her tongue. Perhaps she earned a reprieve for her son—Mr. Robert Shirely and his friends were due a horrendous punishment for interfering with Franklin's second attempt to take Samantha's life. Even so, Lillian's cooperation didn't earn Mr. Shirely's friends a reprieve.

How many more chances would he find to exact his revenge upon Samantha, especially with the return of her overzealous fiancé, Lord Westwood?

The recovery of the Hastings jewelry was truly becoming a

chore. He should have smothered Samantha the night of her parents' final party when he had the opportunity. Little imp. Franklin knew she was trouble from the moment he discovered her crouched behind a pot on the stairwell.

After the party concluded, he crept back into the townhouse, a silent silhouette of rage. He couldn't press the pillow over Samantha's sweet face, so much was her resemblance to her mother, Rebecca. Franklin remembered gazing down at the mass of auburn curls spread behind Samantha's head like a halo and found himself imagining Rebecca descending the stairs on his arm instead of Matthew's. He watched Samantha sleep a few minutes, wondering how different she would appear if she was his child. Hopefully, Samantha would retain all the wonderful qualities of her mother's beauty and grace. His chest throbbed unexpectedly.

Rebecca's abrupt demise unnerved him. *Why did she relinquish her life?* He asked the question repeatedly over the past ten years, and each time he arrived at the same conclusion. There was no answer—until Samantha's callous remark. *Was it possible Rebecca truly loved Matthew? Could one die of a broken heart?* He certainly did not. He survived Rebecca's rejection, transforming into something more powerful, something greater.

Rebecca. After all this time, her name still drew a sigh from his lips. All the other ladies were simply distractions, dalliances to fill the emptiness. Not one of them compared to Rebecca—including the woman currently seated in front of him, knotting her fingers nervously in her lap.

"It is very kind of you to offer someone else to suffer in your stead. However, I believe Miss Randall would much rather remain in her new living arrangements." Franklin smirked, flashing his teeth.

"What living arrangements?" Hattie asked, confused.

"Miss Randall is currently residing at the Westwood Estate.

Given the distraught nature of her highly excitable maid, Lord Westwood and Mr. Reid whisked Miss Randall away from her cottage as soon as they learned of your disappearance."

"I don't understand." The furrow in Hattie's forehead increased. "Why have you abducted me?"

Grinning, Franklin sauntered closer to the coach, resting his arm on the window frame. He leaned forward, conspiracy on his lips.

"Lillian knows our secret," he whispered, watching the color drain from Hattie's face a second time.

"No, it's not possible." Hattie swallowed and shook her head so violently, it looked as though she went into convulsions. "I never told anyone, not even Horace." She muttered a few more words and turned toward Horace as if questioning his confidentiality.

"Hattie," Franklin called softly, his satin voice seductively washed through the carriage. "I'm not finished speaking with you. Look at me."

Reluctantly Hattie twisted her body until she faced Franklin again, her eyes rising to his smoldering gaze. Humiliation beaded sweat across her forehead.

"How does Lillian know?" Hattie asked, her lower lip trembling.

"Someone had to pay the doctor," Franklin replied, his lip curled into a sneer.

Shock vibrated through Hattie's chest. "I thought you did. You told me you would take care of everything."

"And so I did." The sneer stretched tightly over Franklin's depraved mouth.

"I couldn't keep it," Hattie whined, her body trembling, a mountain of shivering blubber. "It would have ruined my engagement to Horace. Look what happened to Lillian after Della returned in that delicate state. Lillian's fiancé ended their engagement, 'a scandalous family,' he called us. We would have been destitute without Horace's money."

Franklin spat in disgust. He ripped open the carriage door and leapt into the coach, growling. Slamming the door closed behind him, he flung the wine bottle at the wall behind Hattie. It exploded, raining bits of glass and red drops of wine onto Hattie's hair. She flinched but remained seated on her cushion.

"Always thinking about money," he said with a cluck, his anger dissipating. Reclining on the bench across from Hattie, his mouth crooked into a half-smile. "You were not always so concerned about finances. I can remember a time when you only thought of passion."

"That was many years ago, Franklin." Hattie flushed and glanced at her hands. "I'm no longer that woman."

"Such a pity," Franklin said with a playful shake of his head.

"You would not have married me," Hattie said softly.

She was searching for reassurance, something to grasp onto to ease her fear. Franklin tilted his head and destroyed her hope, expelling the secret Lillian had withheld from her sister all these years.

"Certainly not. If I refused to marry Della, why would I marry you?"

"D-D-Della?" Hattie's face paled. "Why would you need to marry Della?"

Franklin leaned closer until his breath caressed Hattie's ghostly countenance.

"Don't be so conceited to believe you are the only Randall sister I seduced."

Hattie's mouth popped open like a fish gasping for air. "When?"

"Sometime before you informed me of your pregnancy,"

Franklin mocked, threading his fingers through Hattie's hands.

"And Charlotte?" Hattie swallowed.

"Miss Randall is the result of that union."

Hattie gasped, yanking her bound hands from Franklin's grasp.

"Please don't tell Charlotte. It would devastate her. She deserves a chance at happiness, not to be connected to someone as monstrous as you."

"Lillian stated those exact words to me when I revealed to her that I was Miss Randall's father. She refused my paternal claim, preferring to leave Miss Randall in your capable hands." Franklin snorted. "She paid me handsomely for my silence."

Stunned, Hattie remained motionless, unable to speak.

"I'm surprised by your concern for Miss Randall, Hattie. The rumors regarding your maternal character are not gracious. I believe Miss Randall has suffered numerous injustices by your hand. I fail to see how I could damage her character any further. I met Miss Randall at the Shirely masque last evening—an extraordinary young woman. Don't worry, Hattie, I didn't reveal her true lineage... yet." He tilted his head again, his calculating eyes assessing Hattie. Callously, he sneered, "Miss Randall is extremely beautiful, as was her mother. Thankfully, neither lady received your coloring."

Hattie's eyes exploded. "How dare you!" she snarled, her mouth barely able to form the words to express her indignation.

Franklin leaned forward, trailing one long, cold finger down Hattie's burning cheek. She shivered, vibrating with anger. Retracting his hand thoughtfully, Franklin smiled, his face distorted by half-shadows.

"We had some pleasurable nights together. Do you remember?" he cooed softly, drawing on years of inbred genteel manners. Hattie returned his smile faintly, her tongue silenced by his mesmerizing stare.

"I have always wondered." Franklin's fingers grasped her chin, pinching the flesh as he wrenched her head. "When you were forced to lie with your husband, how many times did you think of me, of what I could do to you?"

"Every time," Hattie replied after a moment of contemplation. "Horace didn't compare to your aptitude."

"Indeed?" Franklin grinned widely. "I'm extremely pleased with your answer."

Glancing at the deceased man to her left, Hattie sucked on her lower lip hesitantly. She returned her attention to Franklin. Attempting a winning smile, Hattie indicated Horace with a flick of her bound wrists as if she was inquiring about the weather.

"How did he die?"

"An overdose of opium, concealed in his wine," Franklin replied, his gaze sliding to the dead man. "While Horace did nothing directly to deserve my discontentment, he also did nothing to protect my daughter from your jealousy."

"You are planning to kill me as well?" Hattie asked, her voice indicating her realization of the danger she faced.

"Yes," he taunted, releasing her chin, "As well as your illegitimate niece."

"What has Charlotte done to you?"

"She interfered," Franklin snarled and narrowed his eyes. "If you expect me to show you the same leniency I showed your husband, you will be severely disappointed."

Hattie dropped to her knees, her brown eyes pleading with Franklin. She brought her lashed wrists to her chest as if praying before placing them gently on Franklin's leg. Biting her lip, she managed to appear contrite.

"Franklin, please, spare me. I will do anything you ask, give you anything you want," she begged, staring into his cold eyes.

Franklin paused, considering her statement, his eyes dragging slowly over the woman crouched on the floor between his legs.

"Anything?"

"Anything," Hattie repeated seductively, sliding her hands up his thigh.

Franklin glanced down at his leg in disgust and shook it free from Hattie's grasp. She stared in shock, her mouth popping open like a fish gasping for oxygen. Leaning forward, Franklin's lips stopped millimeters from Hattie's mouth.

"My dear," his voice lovingly caressed, "there is only one thing I want from you..."

Hattie swallowed, her breath catching as she waited to hear the one thing that would give her salvation.

He smiled.

"I want you dead."

The End...But not quite

Samantha and Benjamin may be safe, but they've left their friends and family to the mercy of an angry killer. If you thought the first two books in this series were thrilling, that's nothing compared to the trouble brewing for Daphne and Thomas in the next book in the Wiltshire Chronicles series. Grab your copy today of A Perfect Deception, or take a peek at the excerpt on the next page!

ABOUT THE AUTHOR

USA Today Bestselling Author Alyssa Drake has been creating stories since she could hold a crayon, preferring to construct her own bedtime tales instead of reading the titles in her bookshelves. A multi-genre author, Alyssa currently writes a blend of historical romance, paranormal romance, and romantic suspense. She adores strong heroines with quick wit, and often laughs aloud when imagining conversations between her characters.

She believes everyone is motivated by love of someone or something and is always curious to discover what's hidden beneath the first layer. When she's not whipping up chocolate treats in the kitchen, Alyssa can be found searching for fairy houses and mermaid eggs.

http://www.alyssadrakenovels.com

READ MORE FROM ALYSSA DRAKE

LOVENOTES NEWSLETTER
SUBSCRIBE NOW!

AVALISSE ROSS MYSTERIES
VIRTUALLY YOURS (book 1)
ETERNALLY YOURS (book 2)
FOR BETTER OR FOR CURSED: Mendsville Case Files

~

DAMSELS DEFEATING DISTRESS

FORTRESS OF DESIRE

SHELTER OF INNOCENCE

HARBOR OF SECRETS

~

PARANORMAL TALES FROM FIREFLY ISLAND

DEPARTED (free)

CURSED

SUMMONED

DAMNED

POSSESSED

HORRIFIED

HEXED

CONJURED

~

SPELLS FROM THE PAST

TIMELESS MAGIC (book 1)

~

TWISTED FAIRYTALES

HAIR, SHE BEARS

~

THE WILTSHIRE CHRONICLES

AN IMPERFECT BARGAIN (free)

A PERFECT PLAN (book 1)

AN IMPERFECT ENGAGEMENT (book 2)
A PERFECT DECEPTION (book 3)
AN IMPERFECT SCOUNDREL (book 4)
AN IMPERFECT INTRODUCTION
(Available in Wicked Christmas Nights boxed set)

~ Coming Soon ~
A PERFECT RECLUSE

A PERFECT DECEPTION (WILTSHIRE CHRONICLES, #3)

Disowned by her mother and suffering from unrequited love, a dismayed wallflower steps out of the shadows and into the path of a vindictive killer...

Through a chance introduction, Miss Daphne Clemens finds herself thrust into a dangerous situation, sequestered on a country estate with the one man she wants, but cannot have: Mr. Thomas Reid.

Following the abrupt termination of his engagement, Thomas expected to remain a bachelor forever, but Daphne's captivating presence reopens his heart to the possibility of love... until a body is discovered just outside the estate.

Thomas realizes someone in the household is working with Mr. Franklin Morris, feeding information to a killer intent on murdering every person in the chateau... including Daphne. All evidence points to a servant, but when the girl accused of the crime is found to be innocent, Thomas fears he may be too late to save Daphne's life.

Delve into A PERFECT DECEPTION and discover how the strength of true love can overcome a broken heart and the deviousness of unbridled jealousy.

EXCERPT

Slogging around the corner came Miss Clemens, her linen dress—sopping and indecently sheer—clinging to her body. A shapeless yellow bonnet drooped over her face, covering her eyes, the brim resting on her nose. Thomas wondered how she could see where she was going.

"Sudden rainstorm?" Thomas asked, leaning against the doorway with a grin. Miss Clemens trudged past him with as much dignity as she could muster, refusing to acknowledge his comment. Thomas crossed his arms over his bare chest, watching her progress in amusement, his mouth twitching. "It's impolite to ignore someone who is speaking to you, Miss Clemens."

Miss Clemens paused in her trek across the courtyard, glanced upward, and sighed, speaking to the sky. "I fell in the river."

"May I ask how you managed that incredible task so early in the day?"

"You may," she replied and turned toward him. Gasping, her hands flew to her mouth, and she spun around again, whirling toward the house. "Mr. Reid!"

Thomas glanced down, confused by her reaction, and realized he was improperly dressed. He ducked into the barn, collected his shirt, which had been hung this morning to prevent spoiling, from a nearby stable gate, and whipped it over his head. Once he was dressed, Thomas returned to the doorway, pleased to find Miss Clemens, her back still to the barn, waiting for him.

"I'm now properly attired," he said, resuming his position and crossing his arms again. "You may resume your story."

Rotating in a sluggish half-circle, Miss Clemens hesitantly peeked through her fingers at Thomas. She flushed but held his gaze. Swallowing nervously, she spoke, her soft voice only just reaching his ears. "It's quite simple. I merely lost my balance and fell into the river."

Thomas tilted his head. "That's all that occurred?"

"It has been alleged I am quite clumsy." Miss Clemens offered him a tight smile.

Thomas studied her silently. His eyes unconsciously traveled over the transparent dress, drinking in the feminine shapes highlighted underneath, each breath causing the material to tighten over her chest.

"Are you?" he murmured, surprised by the direction of his thoughts.

"Apparently, I am." She gestured to her saturated dress.

"Miss Clemens!" Mrs. Hastings bellowed from the veranda. She marched the length of the floor, muttering to herself. "Where is that girl? Samantha has been a terrible influence over her. They probably disappeared together this morning."

Miss Clemens' brown eyes rounded, pleading with Thomas.

"Please," she mouthed.

The mist in Thomas' brain cleared. He shook his head free of the wicked images racing through his mind. His arm snaked out, grabbing her elbow, yanking her into the barn. She followed easily, her momentum carrying her forward and causing her to crash into Thomas's chest. He wrapped his arms tightly around her as they toppled backward into the hay mound.

"Miss Clemens!" A hint of irritation accompanied Mrs. Hastings' call as she stomped across the veranda, marched down the steps, and headed toward the stables.

Placing his finger over Miss Clemens' lips, they froze, a hay-coated statue of entwined limbs, listening for Mrs. Hastings' shoes to scrape across the courtyard. An audible sigh indicated her surrender, and she retreated, entering the house, the door slamming with her discontentment.

Miss Clemens exhaled, her sweet breath tickling Thomas' lips, and a surprising tingle ran the length of his spine.

"Oh!" She pushed up and crawled off Thomas' body. "I have ruined your clothing, as well."

Sitting up, Thomas brushed the hay from his chest, inspecting his garments, and shrugged. "Don't worry, I shall simply remove my shirt and hang it up to dry."

"What about your pants?" Miss Clemens asked innocently.

"Miss Clemens, are you requesting I remove all my clothing?" Thomas wiggled his eyebrows, unable to resist teasing her.

Her jaw dropped, all color draining from her face. "N-n-no, Mr. Reid."

"I'm merely jesting.".

Rising, he helped her to her feet and led her to the rear of the stables, stopping at a tiny room. He opened the door, reached into the room, and extracted two heavy blankets. Shaking the first one open, he laid it over Miss Clemens' shoulders. She shivered, staring into his eyes. Pulling the ends together, he wrapped the blanket tightly across her dress.

"That will keep you warm...and decent."

"How indecent am I?" Miss Clemens blushed, glancing down at her dress.

Thomas grinned. "Quite."

The End

A PERFECT DECEPTION – When the accomplice is revealed, will Thomas be able to save Daphne before she succumbs to a perfect deception?

Made in the USA
Monee, IL
08 September 2025